ONLY EVER YOU

A
Titan Group
ROMANTIC SUSPENSE

AMY COLE

To family so wonderful you'd choose them as friends.
To friends and neighbors so dear you'd choose them as family.

This book is dedicated to the friends, family members, and even kind strangers who have helped me get to this point.

Those who showed up for Romance Fiction Night at Red Fern Booksellers early on in this journey, the local ladies inviting me to speak at book clubs and PEO's, everyone who came to my first ever launch party, those who purchased the first book, who gifted the first book, gave reviews, you name it. Liking my posts, reading the book as beta readers, sharing my social media updates, sending encouraging texts, every single moment of kindness and support along the way matters to me.

I see you! Each and every one of you and your kind actions helped me continue and here we are, the next book.

I hope you love Luke and Hazel.

Once a Marine, always a Marine.

Luke Stratton has avoided his feelings for Hazel Burke most of his adult life, protecting and supporting her from afar. As the leader of an elite team of Marine Raiders, he knew that keeping Hazel safe meant staying away. Luke kept his focus on his missions until he was forced to retire after an operation went devastatingly wrong.

Sometimes our darkest fears prevent us from living a whole life. Sometimes they come true.

When Hazel's sister's life is threatened, Luke is her first and only call. Little did she know, that call would spark old emotions, ignite new desires, and pull her into a perilous international plot. Luke may have left the Marines, but he didn't give up his life of danger and intrigue. When threats lurk behind every door, Luke and Hazel will have to decide whether love is greater than fear.

CONTENTS

PART ONE
SEPTEMBER

ONE

HAZEL

HAZEL HAD JUST BITTEN INTO THE MOST SUCCULENT TANDOORI Chicken, flavors bursting across her tongue and her taste buds weeping for joy when she saw her phone light up on the table next to her notepad.

Vi flashed across her screen and she hit the green accept button as she finished chewing. She was excited to see if her sister had gone through with her first blind date, which happened to be with the extremely handsome Brandon Mills, for a posh fundraiser in upstate New York. Her sister was very much not the swanky fundraiser in a ballgown blind date type of person, but she was trying to branch out and had been set up by her boss. Of course, like all smart women, they'd cyber stalked the blind date before Vi left on the train and he seemed normal, and crazy hot. There had been plenty of photos to check out on social media.

Her heart clenched slightly. She was the tiniest bit jealous of Vi and her party, of her courage to try something new. Here she was, stuck in DC, no love life to speak of and every day mirroring the same as the one before it. Distracted by that glum realization, she picked up her phone to press it to her ear. At least she had the Tandoori Chicken from Rasika, she consoled herself.

"Vi! How was your fancy pants party and your dashing date?" Hazel asked her sister.

"Oh Hazey, I'm okay, don't freak, but we were in a car wreck!" Violet launched into telling Hazel all about her wild night, barely pausing between her words.

What Violet described next sounded like a rapid-fire version of a rerun from *The Dukes of Hazzard*. Car chases, police escort back to the hotel. So many words that Hazel didn't even know what to ask about first. She was in shock and could only utter a, "Geez, Vi. Slow down, start over!"

Vi's voice lowered even more, barely above a whisper now. "Shit, Hazey. I think I'm in trouble. Look, I don't know what's happening, but the police are the only people I've talked to and my Spidey-sense is going off. Something is wrong here. Don't call . . . " Her sister's voice was muffled. " . . . police.I gotta go."

"Vi!" she protested. "Wait, what's happening?" Her questions came too late—the line was already dead. What did she mean something was wrong there? Had she said *not* to call the police? Why shouldn't she call the police? Seriously, who doesn't just call the police?

Rolling her eyes, she texted Vi in rapid fire succession.

Hazel: Vi

Hazel: VIOLET!

Still no answer, great. If Vi was truly in trouble, she had no idea how to help her in Saratoga Springs. Hazel forced herself to pump the brakes on her wild thoughts and think through her options. It could be nothing; she should just call the police. And yet, Vi had sounded scared, which she never was. She also said her Spidey-sense was going off, which Hazel believed in. Her big sister was a no nonsense kind of person, never dramatic and never an alarmist. She'd also said she had already talked to the police, and now something else was happening. Vi was a journalist in DC. She knew when to trust her gut on something. Hazel thought about who else she could call.

She could call her dad and ask him what to do, yet that would freak her parents out. She huffed out an irritated half laugh. Vi was the person she would have called if she wasn't the one being cryptic on the phone. Everyone knew you called your older sibling when things got crazy. A flash of an idea lit within her. She may not be able to call her older sister, yet she *could* call a guy who was like an older brother. He was a former Marine, having retired a handful of months ago, and had always been dependable.

Shit, she felt so helpless sitting there while who knows what was happening to her sister a handful of states away from her. Was she really contemplating calling him versus the police? She'd sound crazy to him.

She thought about that another beat and realized that phone call would definitely make her sound crazy, and she doubted that the Marines were typically called in for situations like this, yet maybe Luke would know what to do. He always knew what to do when they were growing up and her parents were always raving now about how successful he had been in the Marines. He had been the one she called when she'd needed help to move into her DC studio and he'd been there less than an hour later. Luke was reliable, always, even if their relationship these days was mostly via text, emails and sporadic family visits.

He'd always said that "if you wanted something done, you called a Marine." Inwardly shrugging, that's what she decided to do. She figured if he had led a special forces team, he could help Vi from six and a half hours away. Or he'd tell her to call the cops and stop being crazy.

Decision made, she fired off one more text to Vi before she dialed Luke.

HAZEL: VIOLET KAY BURKE. You better answer me right now or I am calling the calvary.

Still no answer, which caused her concern to grow. The Marines it is, she thought to herself. She tapped Luke's contact and waited for him to pick up.

"Hazel? Hey, how are you, how is . . . " Luke answered practically immediately.

"Luke, I think Violet is in trouble. I don't know how or why, but she said something about maybe not calling the police and I just don't know who else to call," she rushed into the phone, glad he answered.

"Tell me everything you know." His voice had gone hard, the lightness from his initial greeting gone instantly. He wasn't laughing at her so far, so she continued with the wild story Vi had relayed to her in the hushed whispers earlier.

She told him about Vi's call and how she wouldn't pick back up and how she didn't answer her texts. She told him about the fundraiser, her date and the location as fast as she could spit words out, a knot of tears creeping up her throat. She relayed what Vi told her about the car she was in with her blind date, being in an accident, the officer taking her back to her hotel while they took the date to the hospital for observation, and how she was cut off right after telling her that her Spidey-sense was tingly.

"So you didn't call the police?" he asked.

"I didn't, should I? She seemed almost like I shouldn't, but that can't be right, right?" She felt like a fool, but she persisted.

"I didn't know who to call, so I called you." She let those words hang there. Luke had always been with her and Vi growing up. She knew she could count on him and she'd rather overreact and have them tease her later than under-react and leave her sister in real danger. If she was in actual real danger.

"I'm glad you called me, Hazey. You did the right thing,"

Luke said. "Was she working on any specific story that you're aware of?" he asked.

"Not that I know of. Do you think that's what this is about?"

"I don't know yet, but I will. I have a team guy in Lake George right now, which is close to her. I'm going to hang up and call him now and I know we can trust him to help her until we know what we are dealing with, even if that is just to escort her to the police station," he said, his voice reassuring her.

"But, Hazey, one more thing. I don't know what's going on yet, but until we do, I'd feel better if you were covered by my team. Are you home now?"

"No, but I could head there now," she replied.

"No, for now, I need you to share your location with me and get to the most populated place you can get to as quickly as possible. At least until we understand what we are dealing with and why. If this is a politician making sure a story doesn't come out, you could be leveraged with Vi. K?" he asked.

She was deeply relieved that he knew what to do and was jumping in that she simply nodded and whispered a small, "I'm at Rasika. Thanks Luke," before hanging up. She stared at her phone for another heartbeat before his warning rang in her memory and she quickly tapped into her settings and shared her location with him. She wasn't completely sure that it mattered where she was, but at that moment, she didn't care. She would do anything he asked if it helped her sister. She guessed that if this was related to some story Vi was on, she had better be safe than sorry.

She shot one more text off to her sister.

Hazel: You gave me no choice.

She then texted Luke two more times in quick succession, her patience fried.

HAZEL: Did you talk to her?

HAZEL: Please tell me what is going on.

She set her phone back down on the table next to her discarded meal. She waved to her favorite waitress, Tam, for the bill as she worried her lip between her teeth, concern for Vi overwhelming her thoughts. Vi wasn't just her big sister, she was her best friend. They talked every single day and saw each other almost as often.

"You're done already? What happened? I thought you loved this course," Tam said when she got over to Hazel.

"I do, but I've had something come up. I'm sorry, I gotta go." Hazel's hand shook slightly as she quickly fished out her credit card.

"Of course. I hope everything is okay," Tam said as she took Hazel's card.

Hazel couldn't reply. She didn't know if everything was okay. There had been something in Vi's voice she'd never heard before. She had sounded terrified, and Vi never sounded terrified. Her older sister was a rock.

She glanced down at her phone, yet there was still no reply from Luke. She glanced back up as Tam was returning.

"Thanks, Tam, I appreciate it." She shot her a quick smile and gathered her things, throwing the strap of her purse over her shoulder.

"No problem, Hazel, let me know you're okay, will you? You're kind of freaking me out." Tam studied her, frown lines bracketing her normally smiling mouth.

"Yeah, yes, of course . . . " she said distractedly. Throwing what she hoped was a reassuring smile back at Tam, she added, "I'll be back in soon, don't worry about me. I'm fine, all good Tam," she assured her as she made her way out of the dimly lit restaurant.

She had barely cleared the heavy curtains leading to the glass entry doors when she felt her phone vibrate in her hand.

"Luke, thank God, is she okay?" Hazel spoke into the phone as she was jostled through the door when another party was coming in. She stepped from the busy din of the alcove, past everyone waiting to dine, and out onto the quiet sidewalk.

"Please tell me she's safe," Hazel continued before he could get a chance to respond.

"Hazel, did I not tell you to sit tight when we spoke?" he asked harshly. She instinctively clenched her jaw at his words, but before she could lay into him for that tone, he continued.

"Vi is in danger, but I'm not sure from whom. I've sent Max, one of my guys, to help her and he'll be there in under thirty minutes. Once he gets there, he'll keep her safe until we know what's happening. Now, why the fuck are you in motion?" He growled out the last bit.

She rolled her eyes and took a deep breath. He was being an ass, yet she hadn't listened to him and she hadn't even realized it.

"You're right." She held up her hand as if he could see her. "I just stepped out of Rasika. I was having dinner for a new article on them when Vi called. I'm freaked out, and I started moving before I remembered what you said. I'm sorry okay, I need to know what is happening for Vi and I know what you said. I'm just at Rasika. Well, right outside of Rasika, not like a dangerous area," she retorted.

She heard Luke's low voice on the other end of the line talking to someone else before he got back on the line with her. "Brian and Nate are on the way to you." His voice was rising, his anger palpable through the phone. "Stop walking by yourself on a God damned dark sidewalk when your sister has been abducted for God knows what and by God knows who. Step into that bookstore on the corner and go immediately to the romance section. Brian and Nate will meet you there. Do not engage with anyone. Do not go anywhere else," he said tersely.

Huh, she mused to herself, maybe she wasn't the alarmist in

this situation. Maybe it was him. That brought a brief smile to her face. For always being calm and collected, he sounded bothered now, which was fine because she was going to have herself a little freak out soon if Vi wasn't accounted for. And, he was potentially overreacting, but again, maybe not . . . and he'd clearly said Vi was, in fact, in real danger.

"Fine, I see it ahead of me and will be there." She clicked off the phone before he could yell at her anymore. Her focus was all over the place and the last thing she needed was to get into an argument over the phone with one of her oldest friends, particularly if he was right. She had called him after all and he was helping, even if she felt like she'd just handed off the actual problem.

She stepped into the brightly lit bookstore and headed to the romance section. She paced the aisle there as she watched the front doors for Brian and Nate. She'd met them once before, when she'd moved out of her dorm at Georgetown after graduation about a year ago and had texted Luke to see if he'd help move her heavier stuff. He'd shown up with Brian, Nate, and another guy on his team, Sebastian. They'd had her moved into her apartment in less than one hour and the guys had been awesome. She'd tried to buy them all dinner to thank them for the help, but Luke had insisted they had plans and shuffled them out of her door. He'd turned around as if maybe he could stay and she noticed a flare of excitement tighten her chest unexpectedly.

Although she knew his face like her own, she'd seen less of Luke those last four years, with his deployments and her class schedules. The last time she could remember them all spending any actual time alone had been almost six years ago.

Her parents had taken them all to Virginia Beach when Luke was home on leave the summer after her freshman year of college. It had been an incredible week filled with laughter, sunshine, and warm beach days.

She remembered how handsome he'd been and how shy she suddenly felt around him. He'd always been good-looking, but that weekend she suddenly saw him as a man, not the guy next door and pseudo-older brother. He was early into the Marines then, but wow, he had been bulking up in the muscle department. Muscles, dimples, and that burnished wavy hair. Most importantly though, Luke was Luke. He had waited for her when they were running in the surf with Violet, made sure she got to her room okay when she drank too much wine (that would be three whole glasses, two of which her parents hadn't seen them sneak) while they'd been playing cards with her parents out on the deck overlooking the ocean, and had told her all about his new life in the Marines. He'd shared stories of his team, showed her photos on his phone, told her silly anecdotes about faraway places.

He was genuinely happy that week, she could see it shining in his eyes and hear it in the way he spoke. After that, she hadn't seen him as much. College was crazy for her between working two jobs and juggling a dual major. It hadn't eased up for her until right before her junior year, when she'd won a scholarship her advisor found for both her and Violet. It was specifically for upperclassmen who also worked off campus and were majoring in a journalism field, which both of them were. It was for multi-family member students too, which had been a dream come true. Vi was only nineteen months older than she was, so it had been a huge financial burden for their family to have them both in college at the same time. She had been worried she'd have school loans forever until her advisor had sat her down in her office and given her that incredible news.

She didn't know what Luke's life had been like during that time. She knew he was deployed often and trained relentlessly. He rose up the ranks and took every training opportunity he could get to lead the special forces team he'd been on. He'd wanted to be a Raider since he'd enlisted, and they'd all been incredibly proud of him when he'd made it. She couldn't think of anyone more dedicated than Luke had been about his goals.

After shuffling the guys out of her apartment the night they'd come to help her move, she tried to take him to dinner to thank him, but he'd also had plans that evening and had run after his guys to catch up. If she did the math right, that must have been shortly before they deployed for that last mission they had. They'd seemed so untouchable that day, like a superhero squad of hotness.

She'd been so stunned by the flare of excitement in her belly at the prospect of time alone with Luke, she was off kilter and bummed when he also took off. Disappointment settled unexpectedly in her gut. Since then, she only saw him occasionally and on holidays with her folks, but never more than a couple of hours. She'd anticipated those brief interactions way too much after that night.

Her trip down memory lane came to a crashing halt when a hand gripped her elbow from behind. She swung around, her other fist in motion to deck whoever had touched her.

"Woah, easy killer, it's me, Brian. Luke sent us." He blocked her fist flying at his face and then stepped back. "Remember me? I'm sorry I scared you." Deep blue eyes met her own, and he raised his hands in the universal sign for "I'm not a threat." He'd grown more facial hair than what she remembered and he'd lost the Marine's buzz cut since they retired, but she knew the face.

"Oh, thank goodness, yes. I'm sorry. I guess I am overly keyed up. I'm sorry Brian. Any word on Vi?" she asked, lowering her own hands.

"Nothing yet, but Max was almost to her when we walked in here. He'll get her, try not to worry too much about her right now. Let's get you somewhere safe," Brian replied.

"Can't we go back to my apartment until we know what's going on?" she asked.

The guys exchanged glances with one another before Nate spoke up. "Luke said not to take you back there until we have a scope and know what we're dealing with. Not yet anyway," he added. "It might be overkill, but Luke doesn't want to take any chances."

"Damn, I could use a hot shower and some sweats." She sighed. "As long as Vi is safe though, I don't care what we do," she said.

"We'll take care of you Hazel, I promise. Hopefully, Max will have Violet soon and we can try to get you home for those big evening plans of yours," Brian said, as he smiled reassuringly at her. He had kind eyes and a steadiness about him, which she needed in that moment. Kind eyes, muscles for days, and a charming dimple visible above his scruff when he smiled at her. Of course, Brian and Nate were both handsome guys. It seemed like a prerequisite to be on Luke's team. Former team, she corrected herself internally. They were all retired now, but apparently these guys still followed orders. She made a mental note to ask more about that later.

Nate nodded his head, and she made to follow Brian. As she did so, they seemed to fall into step around her. She felt like a celebrity being ushered into Via Carota in the West Village with the way they were walking. Faces scanning the crowd, muscles all bunched up, serious eyes alert on everything. It was intense and would look comical if she hadn't found herself in the middle of it.

They took her to a swanky Georgetown condo less than ten minutes away. They parked under the building and took an elevator to the top floor. It was private and secure, with a quiet luxury vibe. Brian had scanned his handsome face into a security panel within the elevator and then typed in a code. Once at the top floor, the elevator opened up inside of an all brick foyer. It appeared both well-maintained and minimalist. There was another set of double doors, where Nate took care of getting them through the security protocols. Less than fifteen minutes later, Hazel found herself in a gorgeous, albeit sparsely decorated condo overlooking the city from the floor to ceiling windows, which she gravitated toward.

"No one outside can see inside of the windows Hazel, and if they could and decided to be stupid, the glass is also bullet-proof," Brian told her. "You're safe here. Please treat this as you would your own home. Want some water? Or a shot of tequila?" He grinned at her.

"Okay, wow, I hadn't considered that. Should I be worried that someone will shoot at them? At me? Do you know something I don't about Vi?" She turned away from her reflection in the glass and met his eyes.

"Not at all." Brian chuckled in a self-deprecating way. "Shit, I'm sorry, Hazel. That's just me not being able to turn off the active-duty side even though we're retired. Old habits die hard and all. We're all still shaken by that last mission, and my brain automatically goes to worst-case scenario now," he said softly. "Doc has me working on that, though."

His words pulled at something within her. She knew that something had gone wrong, and that they'd all retired, yet she didn't know the whole story and she felt awkward suddenly. Should she ask? She kind of wanted to hug him, but that might be too forward. Before she could decide what to say next, he spoke again.

"I'm sure Vi is okay. Max is one of the best guys I know and he either has her covered, or he's taken her to the police station and he will stay with her."

As if he had conjured the phone ringing with his words, Nate pulled his phone from his back pocket, looked up at both Hazel and Brian and said, "that's Luke." He pushed the speakerphone button and spoke for everyone to hear, "Luke, man, we're good here. How is Vi?"

"Hazel is safe?" Luke asked tersely.

"Yes, she's here now and all good," Nate said. "Hazel, tell Luke how great we are, please." He smirked in her direction, the tension from earlier gone.

"Luke, they're amazing, as always. How is Vi? Any word? What do you think is happening?" Hazel spoke up to be heard on the speakerphone in the cavernous space.

"Hey Hazelnut. You've got the best babysitters imaginable. I called to give you the good news that Max has Violet and they are working to exfil the hotel in Saratoga Springs safely. He'll check back in often, but for now, they need to focus on getting away clean," Luke told them. He then continued with the less than good news, but his tone had softened.

"But guys, we have a situation developing with the blind date Vi had earlier in the evening, who is also the guy who was driving earlier in the night when they were run off the road. He's in the hospital in the Springs now, but Tad's FBI contact can't confirm his status. They have a team close by who can connect with some help, and I'll follow up when I know more," Luke said.

The guys exchanged a tense glance among them as Luke said, "Nate, take me off speakerphone."

Hazel frowned at Nate and made a reach for his phone. Nate, clearly not wanting to upset her, handed her the phone.

"Nate?" Luke asked.

"No, Luke, it's me. What the hell is going on and why can't I hear what you intend to say next? These guys are awesome babysitters, but there is clearly more that they aren't telling me. What do you mean exfil? Where will they go? The cops? Spill," she said angrily.

"Hazelnut, there are powers at play here that I don't completely understand and until I do, I need you to sit your ass on my comfy couch and wait," he replied stonily.

She rolled her eyes hard and tried again, "Luke . . . "

She was cut off by his harsh, "Please."

She handed the phone back to Nate, muttering under her breath. How dare he not trust her with what he did know. She was the one who had called him in the first place!

She saw Nate smile apologetically at her, and then she turned away from him. She saw his reflection back in those gorgeous windows as she plopped down on the huge leather Chesterfield sofa in the room. She watched Nate watch her from the reflection, nodding at whatever Luke was telling him. At least she had hot babysitters, and Vi was with someone who could protect her. She harrumphed and crossed her arms over her chest. Damn, she felt like a toddler, a giant twenty-four-year-old toddler. She uncrossed her arms and tried to relax her frowning face. The leather under her palms was cool and smooth, and she tried to soothe herself by drawing the infinity sign with her fingertips.

"Copy," Nate said into his phone before pulling it away from his ear and putting it back in his pocket. "Let's get you that water," he said in her direction.

"Are you hungry? We could get you something to eat," Brian added.

"No thanks guys. Unless you're ready to tell me everything there is to know at this point, I don't need anything," she deadpanned.

Both men looked bashful at that reply and then they scattered. Brian returned shortly with some water and sat in the large club chair facing her. He clicked on the massive TV above the fireplace in the room and Sports Center sprang to life on the screen.

Hazel felt discombobulated. She just wanted more information on Violet and didn't think she'd be able to relax until she knew Violet and Max had made it away from the hotel Vi had been staying in. It sounded as if Max knew what he was doing and she trusted Luke to send someone who could save her sister, but she was too tense to watch TV and nothing she could think of would stop her mind from going to the worst-case scenario. She took a few deep breaths and replayed her last conversation with Luke in her head.

"Brian, Luke said this was his couch. Is he renting this apartment?" she asked.

"It is a place that all of us have called 'home' at one point or another. It's more for an investment portfolio than it is for making a home though," he said.

"Investment portfolio?" she asked him quizzically. She wondered what he was talking about. Obviously, whoever owned this apartment was doing well financially. The location alone was worth millions, and the condo itself was a stunner. She supposed that Luke and the guys must also be earning a decent salary to be able to afford the rent on a Georgetown condo this swanky.

Brian and Nate were exchanging glances again. What the hell was going on here?

"Um, hello? Why are you guys leaving me out of the conversations you keep having with your eyes and facial twitches?" she asked them both.

Brian laughed. "Nothing is happening. We both must be tense for information too. Sorry Hazel. Do you want me to get you a book or magazine or anything? I know Sports Center can get boring at this hour. Should I change it?" he rattled off.

"Hey, Hazel, you could also get some sweats and a shower here if you want. We could scrounge something up for you if that still sounds good. I know it wouldn't be your own clothes, but it's something," Nate added.

They were clearly not sharing information with her freely and she got the feeling it was because Luke was trying to protect her. From whom? From what? She wondered. It wasn't like she was going to drive up there by herself and start yelling out into the dark for Vi.

She knew she was young, but she could handle whatever was happening . . . she thought so anyway. She'd never had to wonder about what she could handle in that realm, though so probably best to go along for now and then have her reckoning with Luke. He was their commanding officer, and those habits died hard, even in retirement, apparently. Also, a shower did sound heavenly right then. She'd retreat now to advance faster later.

"Sure, a shower would be great, guys. Show me where to go and I'll be out of your hair."

She didn't miss the relieved flash Brian shot Nate before he stood up from the club chair and motioned for her to follow him. "Right this way, milady," he joked, likely thankful she was being amiable.

TWO

LUKE

Shit, this was not good news. Whatever Violet was embroiled in was getting bigger and more dangerous by the second. He'd received word that Brandon was dead in the hospital from an accident that he could have walked away from. One he *should* have walked away from.

In fact, he had been alert and talking to Vi before heading over to the hospital. This clusterfuck had gotten intensely more complicated because Tad's contact had told him that Brandon was, in fact, Brandon Mills. Speaker of the House Mills' son. Fuck. He ran his hands through his hair, glad he wasn't active duty any longer and could keep it long enough to do so. He did not like how this was shaping up. When he'd seen Hazel's name on his caller ID and heard the fear in her voice, he'd immediately feared the worst. It had taken everything he had not to try to get to her himself, but he knew he needed to get Vi's situation in check, as it was more urgent. He also knew that Brian and Nate could pick Hazel up.

He'd been the team lead of his Marine special forces unit and he had the contacts for the business he was building now. Vi needed speed, and he had that via those channels.

What Luke didn't know was who the target was supposed to be in said clusterfuck. Tad's FBI friend had given them the details of the fundraiser up on the site of the Battle of Saratoga Vi had attended, and all of them were snakes. The top politicians of DC, all dressed in their finery and parading around an old battle site for shit's sake, all to raise money for their next re-elections. Like any of them knew anything about actual war. Vi could have been digging into any one of them for a story for her job at her DC newspaper.

From what they knew at that moment, the date was dead, the car had been hit intentionally, and someone had tried to take Vi out almost as soon as the cop had dropped her off at the hotel. That told him that the cops were part of it, and that someone wanted her dead, or missing. Likely both. Or the cops weren't part of it, but he knew they couldn't keep her safe if whoever it was had already taken out the Speaker of the House's son. Tad was working with the police in the Springs, through his FBI contact, thankfully.

Max's intel so far was enough to know that whoever was after Vi was also good at being bad and well-funded. They'd have to be to orchestrate killing the Mills guy in the hospital. He swallowed back the fear that threatened to rise up again, sending up a quick prayer of thanks that Max had been up at Lake George. He'd take care of Violet, he had no doubt of that. Now, he needed to try to figure out the pieces to this puzzle and trust that Brian and Nate had Hazel covered well enough.

Hazel. The little girl next door who had become all woman. He had known her his entire life. Her hazel eyes-her namesake, and her coppery hair trailing down her freckled skin. That slightly crazy laugh she belted out. She had been like a little sister he'd loved to play and laugh with, scheming against their parents with Violet. They'd spent summer nights playing hide and seek with lightening bugs, swimming in the pond down the road from their little hometown in rural Virginia and the winters playing in the snow. Their families had been inseparable, their moms had been best friends. That is, until his sweet mom Candy had died. His gut clenched at the thought of his mom and he idly wondered if he'd ever be able to only focus on the good things, and not the ending of his family. How his dad had abandoned him on the heels of losing his mom.

He thought again of Hazel, all grown up now. All grown up indeed. He pushed thoughts of that summer week in Virginia Beach from his mind; he needed her to be safe so he could focus on untangling this mess. He didn't need to think about how she had fucking shimmered that summer night, stepping out of the waves.

The next item of business was creating some plans for Hazel and Violet's parents, to ensure their safety in whatever this was. He made some calls and got his old buddy Brody to cover them physically, but more importantly, he asked his IT expert, Mila, to create an online ruse for everyone in the Burke family. That false digital footprint would show that Mom and Dad Burke were in a secure assisted living community for memory care instead of the condo in Pensacola Beach they'd moved to. Brody would be there to cover them physically if the false digital footprint fell through. Next, Mila would create a digital wild goose chase for Hazel that showed she was abroad "finding herself." Mila lived for this type of work and was the most trustworthy contact he'd had in the CIA, which is why he'd begged her to come to work for him and Tad when they'd gotten the green light to start Titan Group from the President himself, just a few weeks ago. Thankfully, he had been successful in recruiting her. Although, Wills was more to thank for that than he himself was.

"Thanks, Mila, as always," he said to her as they finished wrapping up those profiles and false trails.

"Luke-a-licious, I am glad to be of service! I can't believe that I might finally get to meet these Burke sisters I've heard so much about. Yay me!" Mila squealed. She was always a ray of sunshine, which of course had stood out in the gray and dark suit world of the CIA. She was practically beaming with happiness now though, and he felt a smile break out on his own face at her nickname for him. He wasn't starting a typical business, and he wanted his team to all be themselves. Titan Group may be sanctioned and operate on behalf of the US government when a more deft or direct touch was needed, but he didn't operate as a normal boss would. He was damn lucky to have recruited someone of her caliber, so she could call him whatever she wanted, even when she was giving him a hard time.

He chuckled. "Luke-a-licious? What in the hell is that, Mila?"

"Oh you know, just my little nickname for my hunky friend with the melty eyes, those dimples, those muscles, the tousled, burnished wavy hair . . . oh my!" She laughed right back at him. "You know the women around Langley love it when you are there for work, right?" she asked as she rolled her eyes. "Frankly, I just love giving you a hard time, but you have to know that you break the hearts around there."

"Not interested," he said softly. He was only interested in one woman in his life and that was a Bad Idea.

"I better go, Mila, I need to work on contingency safe houses and logistics next. I'll call you back for the next steps. And, please let me know if you find anything on Brandon Mills. This is fuckery. I can feel it."

"You got it, Luke-a-licious. Chat with you later, tater." She disconnected the video call feed.

His next call was to another old friend from his active service days who owned a place in Little Compton, Rhode Island. The property was perfect, as that friend was also in special forces and did not get unwanted company. It certainly helped that Luke had been investing his hazard pay for him too, and the oceanfront home was fully paid for with Luke's prowess with numbers and markets.

Once those plans were hammered out, he texted Brian and

Nate while he waited to hear from Max that they were clear of the Springs.

> LUKE: Hazel good?

BRIAN: Yep, she's in the shower now, but she has lots of questions.

Luke snorted, yep . . . she always had questions. It was the journalism degree the Burke sisters had both sought, always damn curious.

NATE: Are you coming tonight?

> LUKE: Not with you, asswipe.

BRIAN: LOL

NATE: Eye roll emoji, wasn't an invitation

> LUKE: I'm staying down here tonight, covering logistics and shell games, but I'll be up if you need me. I don't know our scope yet, but I want to ensure I have plans in place before I give Hazey the ugly truth.

NATE: What is the ugly truth?

> LUKE: Someone either wants her sister dead because of something she did, or they want her dead because she knows something. I don't see an avenue where Vi isn't a target, and until we know who has her in their crosshairs, I don't want Hazel outside of the building. Can you buy me some more time to get details?

BRIAN: Ya man, all good, but I don't appreciate withholding information from Hazel. She's not stupid.

NATE: It feels like kicking a puppy when she calls me on something and I don't answer her directly. Her eyes get all hurt. Fuck, I do not enjoy doing that. I hate hurting such a beautiful, kind-hearted woman, Luke. She's not asking for anything unreasonable here, just for some details.

LUKE: I know that. I do, and she's the smartest woman I have ever met. I'll fill her in on stuff later. I just need her safe for now. Her curiosity could get her killed and until I know what's going on, I am not taking any chances. Also, keep your goddamn hands to yourself. Do not notice she is beautiful and do not think about her kind heart.

BRIAN: LOLOLOLOL

NATE: You seriously want me to not notice you sent us to cover the smoke show that is Hazel Burke, who happens to be in a steamy shower as we text? God, I might need to go check on her.

Luke almost cracked his phone, he was squeezing it so hard.

LUKE: Listen fucker, team brothers or not, I will end you. Keep your goddamned eyes and hands away from Hazel.

BRIAN: You make this too easy buddy.

NATE: LOLOLOLOL, you really do. Couldn't miss the chance to rile you up man, chill. I know the way the wind blows.

Luke snorted and tossed his phone onto the desk in front of him. Fuckers. He must really be stressed to have fallen into their cute little trap so easily.

He wasn't far from them at all logistically, only the floor below them. He owned the entire building, but the top floor was designed as living space while the floor he was on was for work. He had his investment business and was in the midst of launching Titan Group, a new private security company of sorts who could partner with the upper echelons of government on contracts where discretion was paramount. His SIC or second in command, Tad, from their active duty days, came from a family who had been doing that for years and with their contacts, skill sets, ethics and desire to serve, albeit in a less bureaucratic environment, it made that the perfect fit as the next step for his team.

The reality was, he didn't have to work. None of them did. He had more money than he could spend in several lifetimes now, as did every guy on his team. He'd had a head for numbers and his team had trusted him with their "hazard pay," during deployments. He'd used the small trust his mom's life insurance had paid out and leveraged it with the hazard pay, progressing in stocks first, then real estate. He'd exceeded his own wildest dreams, and once you did well for long enough, your interest started to do well for your portfolio too. He could afford to never worry about anything again, but he just wasn't that guy, and neither were his brothers in arms.

The guys were all getting restless, even though they were all still grieving. Their last mission had been FUBAR from the beginning, with two of their fourteen person team out. The intel had been bad, they'd lost four guys, including Max's actual brother Alex. Max had gone berserk and had gone in after him, and they'd almost lost him too. Thank God for Seb. He'd pulled Max's ass out of that hovel while practically still on fire. Luke had been their pilot for that mission, their regular pilot sicker than a dog back at their base from food poisoning. Tad, being his SIC, had led that mission, something Luke was still talking to the military-issued shrink about specifically. He couldn't shake the feeling of having let them all down. Thank God for therapy though. The team doctors knew their shit and without them, he didn't think he or his guys would have lasted as long as they did on the Raiders. It was an intense way to live, and he made it

mandatory for his guys. He also didn't make anything mandatory that he didn't also do himself. He'd never be some asshole
hypocrite.

Losing those guys had meant losing part of himself. Alex had
been their youngest, and he knew Max was still devastated,
obviously. What he'd learned about grief in his life was that it
was fluid. You moved through the stages, but never sequentially,
and never on a timeline. Grief could slap you in the face and
bring you to your knees when you least expected it to, keeping a
wound fresh and bleeding, tender.

That's why Max had been up in Lake George with his black
lab, Blitz. He was taking time away from the city. That guy
needed to be in nature to move through his grief, which Luke
also understood. Of course, even though they all supported him
in that, that didn't mean they weren't teasing him about his leaf-
peeping, busting his balls about maybe trying some fresh cider
while there. Man, thank God Max had been there though. Bile
rose hotly in his throat thinking about Vi out there on her own
with these guys after her. He pushed those thoughts away and
started working on his PACE planning and comms. It had been
drilled into them from throughout the military, Primary, Alternate, Contingency and Emergency. Planning was what Luke did,
and he was damn good at it.

He tapped his phone to call Max, estimating that they should
be back in Lake George by then.

"Max, exfil good?" he asked.

"Not clean, took fire, but okay now. We had to ditch my truck
in a neighborhood in the Springs and take a Jeep, but we're back
in Lake George at my motel. We shouldn't stay here too long,
just in case."

"Agreed, and on it. I should have things finalized in the next
hour. How is Vi?"

"She's good. Solid. Incredibly beautiful and handling everything like a warrior queen in some historical romance," Max

said, his deep voice barely audible. "I put her in a hot shower to calm down and help with the adrenaline crash."

"Good. Ya, the Burke sisters are good in any situation. Tell me what you know. What do you mean that the exfil wasn't clean exactly?" Luke asked.

"They had the place well-guarded, and they caught us trying to sneak back to my truck. I had a hell of a time losing them and honestly, I must still be off my game because Violet had to save my ass to get us both out. I don't know why she didn't just leave me there to cover her, but she refused. And of course, Blitz had both of our asses."

Luke smiled at the thought of Max's black lab, Blitz. Blitz had been trained by the best, of course he would be right in the action to help his human.

Max continued, "Vi either truly doesn't know what's happening, or she's hiding something and I don't think that of her. Like I said, she's been incredible under literal fire and I trust that she doesn't know why they were after her. If they were even after her and not the date."

"Well, the date is dead, and the timing of that overlaps with them trying to find her in that hotel, which tells me that she is either the original target, or she is the target now. Otherwise, they would have just killed him and then left her alone, thinking it was all an accident," Luke said.

"Right. She said they were run off the road first and she just assumed it was a drunk driver. She would have continued to think that if some assholes hadn't been waiting for her in her room," Max replied.

"A loose end," Luke mused.

"Not on my watch, brother. I'll get us out of here, keep me posted," Max promised.

"Copy, brother," Luke said as he hung up.

He leaned back in his chair and stretched his back. He needed another hour or two to get them to a solid place and then he needed rest. He thought about Hazel upstairs in his shower. He wondered what they were giving her to wear. He closed his eyes and pictured her as she was that week in Virginia Beach six years ago. Her hair in a French braid down her back, freckles breaking across her pert nose and fair cheeks. Those hazel eyes, always light with happiness and curiosity. He thought about that black bikini she had strutted onto the beach wearing, her pert breasts bouncing along as she jogged out to join them in the water. Full hips with those little swimsuit strings tied at the sides. She had grown up when he'd been away.

God, he was hard already thinking about her in that damn suit. That had been the moment he *saw* her. Gone was his gangly little sister-like neighbor that he used to get into all kinds of trouble with. In her place was a woman he wanted to get in all kinds of trouble with, trouble of the naked and sweaty variety.

Those thoughts weren't helping his raging hard-on. It was always like this when he thought about her now. Her incredible creamy skin, with the sun giving her just the slightest wash of golden hue. He remembered her glancing back at him from the line of waves breaking against the sand, a smile splitting her gorgeous face. He could hear her laughing as she turned back to the water and splashed in deeper. My God, he remembered the little black bikini bottoms that had gathered down the middle of her ass. Her laughter was farther away and still, he couldn't stop staring after her. The sun had been setting, the Golden Hour upon them. Vi and her parents had been back at the beach house they'd rented.

It was in that moment that he knew without a shadow of a doubt that she was his person. What to do about it was the unknown for him. Hell, he was new in the special forces program, committed to Uncle Sam. He knew he was no good for her, but fuck, that smile, that laughter. That was his perfect moment in life. If everyone gets one, he'd go to his grave knowing that was his. He breathed out a knot of deep sadness, knowing he couldn't have more of those perfect moments with her. Not when he could never be whole himself.

Now, it was better to keep a bit of distance, so he didn't embarrass himself. He was a grown goddamned man, a combat veteran, a commanding officer, a billionaire . . . and he could not keep his dick in check around that woman.

He shook his head and took a deep breath, rubbing his hands across his eyes. He needed to buckle down and focus on planning right now, or Vi and Max wouldn't be safe, which meant that neither would Hazel. Later, when he was in his own shower, he'd let himself think of Hazel again in the ways he always did.

He looped Tad on the exfil at the hotel in the Springs so he could manage that headache with the alphabet soup guys and the police, then he checked in on the Little Compton house and then followed up with Mila and Wills, another member of his team was a straight genius, for security there. They worked a few more hours, setting up Max as an owner in that system and sending the feeds to his phone after checking back in with directions.

Once he knew they'd made it to the coast safely, he allowed himself to fall onto the couch in the meeting space they all used. He dreamed of Hazel, her copper waves brushing against his chest and her eyes warm on his own. Skin soft beneath his fingertips.

THREE

HAZEL

THESE BOYS WERE DEFINITELY STILL HOLDING OUT ON HER, BUT THAT was okay. She could bide her time until she thought of a plan to shake the updates from them . She felt niggle of conscious about that thinking, but she was an adult and it was time Luke realized that and shared what the hell was happening with her.

They'd left some joggers and a sweatshirt for her in the bedroom she'd been shown to by Nate. It had a gorgeous steam shower in the large, marble bathroom inside of it, the one redeeming quality about the situation she'd found herself in last night. The space was clean and had men's items in the shower. She'd smell like one of the guys now, but that was what had been available, and she didn't mind. It smelled amazing, and she liked it on her skin.

She'd gone to bed like a good little kid and tried to fall asleep. It was impossible at first, but once Nate had knocked and then poked his head into the room to tell her that Vi was safe and away from Saratoga Springs with Max, heading for a safe house, she finally did take his advice and succumb to the adrenaline crash and sleep. She had nightmares about her and Vi running away from an invisible bogeyman, fingers grasping at her as she ran. She had jolted awake, her heart racing.

Now, she was enjoying some truly divine coffee in the living room, the smell of bacon cooking filling the penthouse.

Nate was at the stove and had already baked some type of muffins. Brian was in the shower in a different bathroom down the hall. She had counted three bedrooms, meaning the guys must have each had their own last night.

"Do you stay here often Nate?" she asked him.

He'd removed the bacon from the oven and sat the pan on a hot pad. He grabbed a bowl of strawberries and began cutting the cores out before he answered.

"I do. How did you sleep? Are strawberries okay? I hope you like bacon," he replied.

Another stall tactic she noticed. And yes, obviously she loved bacon and strawberries.

She let the subject drop. That worked better for her plan, anyway. Gotta build up that sense of security, false though it would prove to be. She smiled to herself. These guys were wonderful, they just weren't willing to cross Luke to tell her what she wanted to know.

"What are we up to today?" she asked instead.

"I thought that after breakfast, you could order some clothes and I could go pick them up for you. Toiletries, clothes, shoes, whatever you need," he said.

"What if we made a quick stop over at my apartment?" she asked him.

"I'm not sure about that yet, but maybe," he demurred.

"Okay, I'll put together a quick Athleta order if that's okay. And then maybe a pharmacy run," she said.

"Whatever you need Hazel, we'll take care of it," Nate said, as Brian walked out.

They ate a quiet breakfast together and then she created an online order in Nate's name for pick up at both Athleta and a Duane Reed close to the condo. Brian cleaned up from breakfast while Nate took a quick shower and then he ran out to pick up her items. It was a pretty uneventful day, really.

Hazel decided that the lulling was working, she only needed more time. She'd give them the day, even though they had cautioned her that they needed to lie low, no online presence, no socials, etc. She spent her time writing on a laptop that Brian had given her, eating her meals with them and sleeping. She went to bed early that evening, after another incredible steam shower.

After a yogurt parfait for breakfast the next morning, she went back to the couch while Brian took his turn in the shower. Nate had already cleaned up and was working at a laptop at the kitchen counter.

"Nate, would it be okay if I had some privacy? I hate to ask, but it's weird to be around you guys twenty-four seven and I need to watch trashy TV without someone judging me." She gave him a sweet smile as she flipped on the TV and turned the volume up just enough to not be obvious.

"Sure Hazel. I can go into the office and work there. Although, I do love some trashy TV too," he said as he got up and walked down the hall to the office. He left the door open, but that was okay, she'd grown up sneaking out of her parents' house with Vi, she could be a damn ninja if she needed to be. They'd already taught her the security system in case of an emergency so she was good to go.

She also wasn't stupid, she didn't intend to go far. She had no desire to get hurt by whoever was after Violet and whatever was going on and if Luke had sensed something, that was good enough for her to stay put . . . ish. Strong emphasis on the *ish*. No, she wasn't running away, she was showing Luke he needed to treat her like an adult and get his ass over there. From wherever he may be. Or, talk to the guys openly so she was looped in. She didn't care which at this point, but she was done with being kept in the dark. This was her sister, and she deserved details.

She slipped on her shoes, grabbed her phone, her purse and

headed for the door. She paused to listen, her guilt almost making her stop. She steeled her spine in resolve, it was time.

She went through the security system and was in the elevator heading downstairs in moments, quiet as a church mouse. She gave a small fist pump, excited about her victory. She'd escaped from highly trained Marines. Ha! 'Take that Luke!' She thought.

She was smiling to herself, resplendent in victory when the elevator door opened to the underground parking garage. She looked up smugly, right into Luke's furious, albeit handsome face.

"Going somewhere Hazelnut?"

FOUR

LUKE

WHAT IN THE FUCK WAS THAT LITTLE MINX DOING? HE GROWLED AT the live security feeds showing the foyer of the penthouse. Those fuckers had no idea either. goddamn it! Two of his closest team guys and they'd been had, buffaloed as his grandpa used to say, by his Hazel. He had to tamp down the sense of pride that was pulling the corners of his mouth upward.

He switched to his phone, pulling up the feeds and ensuring she got into the elevator. He took the stairs down three at a time so he could cut her off when the elevator opened.

He caught her completely unaware that she'd been detected, a smug smile on her gorgeous face as the elevator doors opened. She startled when he spoke to her, physically gasping.

"Luke! You scared the hell out of me," she exclaimed.

"So scared that you are running away from my friends?" he asked with no small degree of snark.

"Well, I'm tired of being left out of whatever is happening. I called you. Remember?" She had crossed her arms against her chest, pushing her breasts up. He fought to maintain eye contact.

"No patience huh, Hazelnut? I could have sworn the guys

were taking great care of you too. Nate made you his famous banana chocolate chip muffins and everything." He made a tsking sound at her and shook his head sadly, as if disappointed.

What he felt had nothing to do with disappointment. He was damn impressed at her ability to get this far from Brian and Nate. He was slightly stunned at being face to face to her after so long too, her clear eyes on his and spitting fire. God, she was incredible. It was always like this when he saw her though, that hit right to the solar plexus, a warm, a happiness that just knocked him on his proverbial ass.

He heard the heavy footsteps right before the assholes rounded the corner of the stairwell. They looked hysterical, coming around the corner so fast that Brian ran into the back of Nate, like a couple of stooges.

Both men shot accusing eyes at Hazel, after clocking that everything was fine.

"You didn't like my yogurt parfaits Hazel?" Nate asked.

She looked the tiniest bit contrite in that moment, like a naughty girl caught with her hand in the cookie jar. Fuck, that was a turn on.

He turned to the guys. "Hazel here would appreciate being kept in the loop more guys. That's on me. Thanks for taking excellent care of her. And Nate, your parfait sounds awesome, did you use the homemade granola?"

"I did," Nate huffed.

"Then it's settled. I'm hungry, I need to update you guys and I miss my shower, let's head back up." He ushered the guys into the elevator where Hazel was standing and they rode up together, Hazel's reassurances that she hadn't intended to go far quietly spoken throughout the quick ascent.

Brian and Nate stepped out in front of them but before he allowed Hazel to step into the apartment from the foyer, he spun back to her. He pinned her with his eyes, his arms physically caging her against the brick wall next to the double doors.

"Do something like that again Hazelnut and I will spank

your ass," he growled against her ear, his lips vibrating against the sensitive skin there.

He watched her throat swallow and she let out a shallow breath. She reached up on her tip toes and spoke against his ear, the way he'd done to her, "that can be arranged Luke." She dipped under his arms and went inside of the apartment.

Holy shit. She had taken the upper hand so fast, he couldn't breathe. His dick was akin to a spike against his jeans. He laid his forehead against the cool bricks in front of him. She was going to kill him. He took a deep breath and followed her inside.

They settled at the island in the kitchen to talk, each with a fresh cup of coffee in hand.

"Vi and Max have made it to a safe location in Little Compton, which you already know from the updates earlier. They're good for now and hunkered down. You also know that I've got your parents covered," Luke said to Violet.

"However, I still don't know what we're dealing with completely yet. I know that whoever is now after Vi is well organized and well-funded, deadly, and fairly skilled to have killed Brandon Mills so quickly. I don't know if she was the original target, or became a target. She can't think of any reason anyone would want to kill her, so there isn't an easy solution here, and Mila has combed through every recent article that Vi has written and nothing stands out to her either." He met Hazel's eyes, "I didn't want you to worry while we were searching for the puzzle pieces." He added.

"Thanks for that, Luke, but I'm a big girl and Vi is my sister. This is my life," Violet said, her voice low but firm.

He knew better than anyone that she was a big girl, that knowing was actually his problem. He sighed and spoke again. He needed to regain some control here.

"I know, Hazey, but it's my job to protect you and Vi as much as possible. Give me that as the older brother type I used to be," he said to her. "If not for that, give me a break in front of my guys okay, or they'll never listen to me again." He smiled at her.

She inspected him then, her eyes drilling into his. She must have found some version of what she was searching for, because she nodded. "Okay Luke, I trust you. You know that, or I never would have called you. Tell me how bad it is, please. I won't freak out or run. I promise," she said.

Man, he felt a kick in the gut at her pleading. He'd tried to keep his distance since that phone call, knowing she was his undoing and he needed to focus. Seems as if his willpower had skipped town the moment he saw her give the guys the slip.

He laid out everything they knew at that point, every plan he had in place, and what he was thinking. Well, almost every plan he had in place, some contingencies didn't bear mentioning yet.

"Are we safe here?" she asked when he was finished.

"We are for now. We have an alternate location here in DC in case that changes. It isn't quite ready yet, or we'd be over there now. I can promise you that we will keep you safe," he assured her.

He saw her glance around the table at the other guys, both of whom nodded at her their own assurances. He knew his guys, they'd protect her with their lives.

"What can I do to help?" Hazel asked him, her shoulders squared. She was tough, ready for anything. He loved that about her.

"Let's get to work guys. Hazey, follow me," he replied. He stood up and carried his mug to the sink. He turned for hers and found her right behind him.

Before he knew what was happening, she had her arms wrapped around his waist and was looking up at him with those deep namesake eyes of hers.

"Thank you Luke, I knew you'd help us," she said. He watched helplessly as she then lowered her head back down and squeezed him tighter, her eyes shut and those luscious curves flattening into his own chest. He felt his arms come around her of their own volition as his eyes met Brian's over her head. That asshole was smirking at him again.

"I've always got you Hazel," he murmured down to her as he squeezed her back and then stepped away from her. Too much longer and his dick would think it was finally go time with the object of his obsession. Less than an hour in her actual presence and he was already softening. He internally shook himself back into focus.

"All right now, let's go," he said as he ushered her to the door to the foyer.

FIVE

HAZEL

HE SHOWED HER THE NEXT LEVEL DOWN, ONE STORY BENEATH WHERE she'd been for thirty-six hours, completely oblivious that these guys were renting both units. She was taken aback by the space these guys had in this part of DC, one of them must have some type of inheritance to be able to rent both spaces like this.

She was in awe of their set up. It far exceeded what she'd seen on TV that NASA had set up, screens and computers everywhere.

She had barely sat down in one of the cushy swivel chairs when one of the video monitors started ringing.

"Hey, Mila, find anything good?" Luke said as he answered the video call.

"Luke-a-licious! Sadly, not a digital arrow pointing to the bad guy, yet what I do know is that whoever is on the other end of the keyboard is really digging into Violet and that level of skill is not normal my beefcake friend," Mila said back in a singsong voice. She went on, "everything within her digital footprint has been scanned. I can see that they are running through her bank account, socials, you name it. They haven't taken anything though, which is bad news. That tells me they are looking for her, for where she will spend money based on where she has spent money before."

Hazel saw Luke grimace. "I expected as much," he replied.

"Oh hello beautiful friend! You must be Hazel." Mila started, looking away from Luke.

"Yes, this is Hazel, my little 'sister' neighbor, Mila," Luke cut Mila off before she said anything more.

"Hi, Mila, nice to meet you via screen." Hazel smiled Mila's direction.

"I met Vi earlier and you Burke sisters are my new fave. I'm making Vi my new bestie, but we could totally have a bestie throuple too if that works for you," Mila went on.

Hazel shot a glance to Luke, her smile growing wider.

"Yes, she is always like this. Yes, you get used to it," he murmured under his breath to her, his back to the screen.

"Anyway, I'm checking in because the level of tech strength I'm seeing on the other side of this screen is considerable. They've gone so far back and are accessing stuff I'm shocked by trying to locate her. They've pinged her cell phone, yet thankfully, we still have that off. However, it is getting trickier and trickier to fend off these bad guys. Luke, I know my own limitations and all, but I am pretty freaking good and this is taking all I have," Mila went on, her sunshine-y voice dimming slightly.

"Mila, you are one of the best in the world, I know this. Don't be too hard on yourself in this. We don't know who we're dealing with, but hell, this does narrow it down some. Is Wills around?"

Hazel watched as Luke and Mila talked more and then another gorgeous face filled the screen with Mila's. Geez, where were these guys coming from? she wondered. He had that Clark Kent vibe going strong.

"Wills, this is Hazel. Hazel, meet Wills, also on our team," Luke said. "Wills and Mila are the tech wizardry portion of our team, my favorite nerds as we like to call them-all in love of course," he went on, a smirk ticking up the corners of his lips.

"Remember that I am a better marksman than you my guy," Wills laughed and snarked right back at Luke.

"Hey, Hazel, nice to meet you. We've heard lots about you over the years," Wills said to her while Mila clacked away on her keyboard in the background.

She laughed and said hello, all while surprise was tightening within her.

"You've heard of me?" she asked quizzically.

"For years. I tried Le Diplomate for the first time because of your article. You made a devotee out of me!" The handsome Clark Kent lookalike replied after a beat. Was it just her or was there an awkwardness happening?

"Oh, that's amazing, it's stupidly good right?" Something about his answer still stuck out in her mind, yet she *had* written an article about the restaurant, and it had been one of her most well-received. He was kind to mention it and she was overly keyed up with what was happening. She looked over to Luke for reassurance.

"Wills loves food, Hazey. You've got a big fan in this one," he replied and then turned back to the video screens and asked Mila for an update. Mila nodded her head and began laying out what she'd created and what was happening as she typed.

"The worm holes I was using to discombobulate them appear to be holding for now, but every time I fire a zing of lightning from my fingers, they seem to dodge them and they're dodging them quicker and quicker. It's making me nervous and I don't know what else to do, so . . . I called in some help," Mila said.

Hazel briefly wondered if every damsel in distress called Luke. She herself certainly had. Wow, she had this sinking sensation that she was one of many who called him for help. That did not settle within her as great at all, but she didn't know why that made her sad. She shook her head at herself and refocused on the conversation on the screens. It had gotten very technical, and it was clear that Brian and Nate had also zoned out to a degree.

Luke was peppering questions at the screens and between him, Wills and Mila, technical terms were flying like a flurry of snowflakes in a good old-fashioned blizzard. She heard words such as 'wormhole,' 'black hat,' and, "inside man," before Luke nodded his head affirmatively and moved to wrap up the call.

"Thanks Wills, let me know if I need to take action," Luke said to Wills before clicking off his video feed.

"Well, now what?" she asked. She was ready to dig in. Surely there was something she could do to help. "I need to help Luke, this is Vi we are talking about. I know her life better than anyone," she said.

"I agree, Hazey. Let me get you connected online through a secure channel and you can start combing through what you know about the Vi's life and maybe the last thirty days of her activity. There could be something going on around her that she didn't even clock. We just need to be careful to not alert whoever else is watching online," Luke agreed with her and motioned her over to another section of the desk, the two of them hunkering into work.

SIX

HAZEL

LUKE HAD SET HER UP WITH A SECURE LAPTOP HOURS AGO NOW. IT was only the two of them in the 'command center,' as he called it. Brian and Nate had both gone upstairs a while ago, leaving her alone with Luke for the first time in literal years.

She'd cyber stalked Vi's life with a fine-tooth comb when she noticed him stretching out of the corner of her eye. Although they'd talked about different angles, they'd also had comfortable stretches of silence.

It had been years since she'd been alone with him, yet it still felt so easy to be with him. He was Luke. The boy next door, the guy she'd grown up with, the cute guy seven years older than she was, the one she had loved as a brother for years. The boy who had cried himself to sleep for a week straight when his mom died and his dad had wanted to uproot them further and move them to DC. Luke had stayed with her family from that moment on, so he could finish high school with his community before going to college and then the Marines. She'd heard him that first night, crying as quietly as possible in the office her parents had turned into his bedroom. She'd been unsure of what to do, God-she'd been so young back then, but she knew he was hurting, and she didn't want to embarrass him, so she'd sat down in the hallway, her back flush to the door. She'd stayed in case he needed her, but never said anything. She remembered those nights now, and how close they'd been. She had always assumed that they'd all grow apart once they grew up, but it had still hurt when their relationship became mostly holidays, emails and infrequent texts. She'd written to him early on after he left home, and he always wrote back, even if it was an email to say hi and let her know how his classes were going, then basic training, followed by deployments she learned about after they seemed to be over, and then his training for special ops.

It seemed as if in every big thing in her life, she'd thought of him first. He'd always been a piece of her heart, whether he was around or not.

"Luke, why don't we hang out more?" Her softly spoken question a lion's roar in the still room.

He looked up, eyes intense and raw. She could have sworn she saw something flicker in his gaze, but it was gone, and the laughter was back before she could examine it too far. "We hang out, Hazey. We text, hell . . . you're the only person I still email occasionally," he said.

"Right, but never alone. I think that this is the first time in years we've been alone together," she pushed further, dug a little deeper. She felt it in her bones. She knew there was something there. "Since Virginia Beach."

"Is it?" he questioned, trying to come off innocent and bewildered, which really wasn't a good look on Luke. He always had an answer. He was always in charge. It was one of the things she found incredible about him. Hell, it was hot to have someone who looked like Luke and acted like Luke always knowing what to do.

Whoa. Shut the front door. Had she really just had that

thought about how hot it was? Shit. She did. He was hot. She guessed that she'd never really let herself think about it too much—he was just Luke. But huh, he was the whole package. Thick lashes framing those deep brown eyes, burnished blond hair, dimples, all of her favorite things. He was tall and broad, his chest wide enough to lie on. She remembered that week at the beach when she realized how gorgeous of a man Luke had become. Her heart sped up and her eyes glazed over. Shit. Shit! What was she thinking?! This was Luke! Her boy next door. Her partner in crime! Luke, who felt like the other half of her for most of her life. The man she could call when she needed help immediately with the most important person in her life. Luke. Holy shit. She'd seen Luke in Virginia Beach, but had she really *seen* him? Her eyes were open now, that was for dang sure.

Okay, she needed to slow her roll. These crazy thoughts were crashing around her like wave upon wave of the sea, an onslaught of water and salt clouding her perception, and she needed a reprieve. She needed to get her head above the water-line on this.

"Okay, yeah. Hey, I'm kind of hungry, are you?" She stood up, fidgeting with the edge of her sweatshirt.

"If you are cooking, I am starving. Or I could order something for us. Nate is upstairs, but Brian is out and could grab something," Luke replied. He also stood up and stretched his arms above his head, showing off a good chunk of his toned stomach and that crazy V line of muscles. Shit! She caught herself staring.

"I'm cooking!" she practically shouted. She needed something to do and needed it right away. She turned for the door.

"Hang tight, Hazey. Let me lead the way," he said.

She nodded in the affirmative at him and kept her eyes on the door. "Cool, yeah, thanks," she said. Shit! Her voice was getting higher and higher.

"You good Hazelnut?" he asked her. He was right behind her

now, practically against her back. She could feel the heat coming off his body, hear the concern in his voice. His hand was on her elbow, gently squeezing. Wicked thoughts coursed through her, making her shiver. It took every ounce of willpower she had not to lean back into him, to sink into his warmth.

"Um, ya, good. I sat too long, I think," she rambled off. She needed space. Thinking about Luke like this was terrifying to her. Thrilling? Terrifying. Both and? Shit, she needed a moment or ten. She let him lead the way upstairs and while she rummaged in the refrigerator and pantry, he poured wine for them. One of the guys had been grocery shopping and one thing was certain: They knew how to cook. There were plenty of things she could make, and she settled on some shrimp scampi.

She put the frozen shrimp in a bowl and left the cold water running over them to thaw while she got everything else out. The guys had naturally gravitated to the island in the kitchen and were talking about potential leads in the mess that Violet had found herself in.

"Want me to share my favorite recipe?" Nate asked her.

"Nah, man, my little sis can cook. She's got whatever she is making handled," Luke said. "But if you need a sous chef, let us know," he said to her.

Great, back to 'little sis.' It had never bothered her before, and she needed to examine why it stuck in her mind now. She *was* like his little sister, or at least she had been until college. Did little sister neighbors find their closest friends hot now? Was that normal? Shit! She wished she could talk to Vi about this, but Vi would likely laugh at her relentlessly. She didn't care, she needed her sister . . . she needed advice here.

"Hazey, tell the guys about your work," Luke said. He was watching her closely, as if he knew what was going on in her head. Shit. She sincerely hoped he couldn't read her mind.

She told them about her articles, her content writing for some clients in the industry, and her dream of writing a cookbook featuring the lost dishes of cultural groups and specific parts of the world. The conversation flowed through the rest of her cooking, the dinner and cleaning up the dishes.

"Hazelnut, you kill me," she heard Luke's low, rumbling voice. She sensed it across her skin, goosebumps left in the wake. "No one cooks that as well as you do."

"No wonder that dish is his favorite, Hazel. I have never had it done that well before. You have ruined shrimp scampi for me now too!" Nate said.

Shit. She had even subconsciously made his favorite meal. How she could have done so on autopilot, she didn't know. At least it had turned out okay, she supposed.

Brian left to take a shower and Nate left to go back downstairs and monitor some of the programs Mila and Wills had running on guests from the event Vi had been to.

"Let me get the rest of the dishes, Hazey. Go take a hot shower or bath," Luke said. He had come in to the kitchen from the other side of the island and was gently pushing her toward the primary suite again, his hands taking the dish from hers.

His fingers slid against hers in the sudsy water and she gasped. She almost dropped the plate she'd been holding. Her fingertips were singed, but in the most pleasant and buzzy way. Her nipples had puckered under her sweatshirt and her heart was galloping. Arousal slammed into her, her stomach muscles clenching.

He reached one of his hands up, lightly grasping her wrist as she still held on to the plate. The water was warm and silky with soap around them and she felt his thumb brush across her wrist, her pulse point.

"Are you okay?" he asked, his voice low in his throat. She gave a peek upward and became fixated on the strong, tan column of his throat. She missed his next words, stunned into silence as she watched his throat work and felt his thumb against her pulse. She shuddered. She had to get out of here before she embarrassed herself by kissing him. His lips were so close, his beautiful body practically flush to hers.

"Yes, sorry, was sleepwalking there for a minute. Sorry. Thanks. Yeah, I'm going to go take a bath. A shower. One of those. Clean, yeah." She released the plate into his other hand in the water and scurried to the bedroom and bathroom she'd been using, her mind filled with getting very dirty instead.

SEVEN

LUKE

HER PULSE MIRRORED THE WILD FLUTTER OF A BIRD'S WING UNDER his thumb. Her skin was flushed and her eyes had taken on a sheen of something he'd never before seen in her eyes, lust.

His dick was rock hard. He'd been so close to kissing her. It had taken one look from her and he was ready to go. Ready to throw caution to the wind and consume her. He'd wanted to slide his hands to her hips, push her against the counter and worship her. He could have had her leggings off and been tasting her in three seconds flat. He groaned. Okay, those thoughts weren't helping.

Fuck! He could smell his own soap on her skin all damn day. All damn day, he'd smelled her, heard her little noises while she worked, cast furtive glances at her. All. Damn. Day. He took a deep breath, counting in and then breathing out. He willed himself to finish the dishes and finish cleaning the kitchen.

Once Brian was done in his shower, Luke put him in charge again and went downstairs to the gym. He ran for miles and miles on his treadmill, lifted and then stretched, his mind on Hazel the entire time.

She was goodness, she was everything. She was smart, driven, kind, funny. Not to mention, Nate had nailed the smoke show comment earlier. But it was her heart that he loved the most.

He'd been a lost boy there for a while when his mom had died. He had come from a wonderful, loving home that had been filled with laughter, meals around the table, cheering parents at his games, to nothing. To broken. In one cruel twist of fate, his mom had died of an aneurysm way too young and his heart-broken dad had given up. His dad had been gutted. He hadn't wanted the life they'd built together if his wife wasn't in it, so he left. Luke's entire world was irrevocably changed in a matter of moments. Cherished only child to orphan with one fell swoop of fate.

Thankfully, Lawrence and Nancy Burke had asked him to stay with them until he graduated. It allowed him to stay with his friends, his teams, his hometown. His dad had too readily agreed, and that was that. Their home office had become his bedroom, their dinner table his dinner table.

The Burkes had been wonderful neighbors, wonderful best friends to his parents. They had never tried to replace what he had, but to honor it. His heart clenched thinking about them. He owed them everything. They'd cheered him on, talked about his mom often, sent photos to his dad, everything they could do to help him, they did.

But it was Hazel who had helped the most. He'd never told her that he knew she sat outside of his new room while he cried himself to sleep that first week. At first, he was slightly embarrassed. He was a teenager after all, so close to graduation. But that wash of embarrassment had faded quickly in his heartbreak. She had always been there for him, never pushing, simply there if he needed her.

When his muscles resembled liquid, he staggered back up to the penthouse he called home. The space was quiet, with Brian asleep on the couch. He took a hot shower in the guest bathroom, put some sweats on and staggered back out to the living room. He woke up Brian and sent him to the guest bedroom he knew Brian had been using.

He took the space on the couch and fell asleep facing the wall of windows, his dreams of Hazel and how it would have felt to cage her into the counter earlier.

He awoke to Brian brewing coffee a handful of hours later, the rich smell rousing him from lurid dreams of his fist wrapped around copper strands of hair and eyes like kaleidoscopes on his as he worshipped her body.

With a deep groan, he rolled off the couch and padded to the kitchen.

"You could try with Hazel man, tell her how you feel," Brian's low voice whispered across the silence.

"And when something happens, as it inevitably will, the other would rather die than continue on? Maybe leave our kids alone to fend for themselves? I know myself Brian, I know that I would destroy anything around me if I had her fully and then lost her. It's in my blood." Luke's voice was quiet, yet clear conviction rang in his words. He clapped Brian on the shoulder and headed for the door to go back downstairs to work.

"Or it could be a wonderful and rich life, Luke, where you get everything you want and deserve as a truly good person. One where you've been through the fire and you come through it together, stronger," Brian's voice followed him.

That thought was too tempting to dwell on. Brian couldn't know the heartache and abandonment that came with that kind of love. He couldn't understand what that did to people. To families when the worst happened. And shit, the worst had a higher likelihood of happening than anyone realized. It could be an aneurysm while a person is gardening, or it could be some demented motherfucker coming back for vengeance after an op. With both his former line of work and with what he and Tad had recently begun building, the stakes were incredibly higher. They certainly weren't getting any better either, not with the type of ops they'd agreed they'd cover for Uncle Sam. He hadn't even told his team all the details yet, and they could opt out, but he knew they wouldn't. A few more items on the list and they'd be ready to share their plan with the rest of the guys. He felt the rightness of what they were embarking on in his gut. He'd seen too many assholes in the world that governments couldn't touch. So, why not use his wealth and special skills to help? He knew he was likely indulging in some white knight syndrome, but he didn't really care too much about that if he was able to rid the world of some of the truly evil motherfuckers they'd seen in their service.

And risk Hazel's heart in the process? Or expose her to one of those truly evil humans coming for him in retaliation?

Not a chance in hell. Not even when it killed him a little each day to not be with her.

EIGHT

HAZEL

SHE'D TALKED NATE AND BRIAN INTO TAKING HER BACK downstairs around mid-morning, and they'd all been working quietly since. Mila had created a safety net for her to be online again without tipping off anyone else who was monitoring hits on Vi's name in searches and she'd wanted to help more, and was using her journalism training to dig into each person on the guest list for the event Vi had attended. She had to be helpful in some way to whatever was happening or she'd go insane. She'd spent hours reviewing screens and bios with the guys before she asked to go back upstairs. Nate had run out for dinner and altogether, it had been an uneventful day. She supposed that was better than anyone getting hurt. She was just grateful that she had one of those jobs that allowed her to set her own schedule. She was also grateful that her gig as a food writer who loved food meant that she had a library of work she could churn out if she had to.

It had also been kind of a weird day with Luke. She was prickly around him, her skin tight and her heart beating faster every time she hazarded a peek his way or he came close to her.

She wasn't the most experienced woman out there, hell . . . she was still a virgin. She just hadn't met anyone who felt worth it to her over the years and now she was a twenty-four-year-old virgin, unintentionally. And then yesterday happened and all she could think about was Luke. Luke caging her to the counter, his lips dipping to hers, his hips pressed against her. His stormy eyes drinking her in. Her heart rate kicked up.

Shit! Her nipples had tightened again, and she clenched her thighs together, the friction was amazing, heat spreading within her. Could they do this? She wanted him, she trusted him, she knew him so deeply. It all just felt so right. If Vi were here, what would she say?

These were the thoughts that had been zinging around her brain all day. She was alternatively giddy and then guilty. Vi was in trouble and Hazel wanted to jump the man they'd grown up with who saw her as a younger sister.

She jumped up from her chair, three pairs of melty eyes springing to her in surprise as she did so.

"I need to do something, guys. I'm not used to being cooped up, please, let's get outside and do something," she pleaded as she stretched her arms above her head and twisted her back.

"Luke, man, why don't you and Hazel get some air or something and Nate and I will cover here," Brian said.

She turned pleading eyes to his. "Pretty please, Luke?" She hadn't necessarily wanted to be one on one with him right now because she didn't trust herself to not jump him, but she needed to move around. Maybe a run on the Mall?

"Hazel, I'm sorry, we can't take you out. Mila has created an online trail showing you in Europe, but we don't know who is watching. One glimpse of you and we could be fucked. The amount of cameras in this city that anyone with cash and capacity can access is too dangerous. I can't risk you," Luke said. "We can't risk anyone seeing you," he amended, his eyes downcast.

Well shit. She really needed something here. She pursed her lips and rolled her shoulders back.

"But come with me. I think I know something that will help," Luke said next, standing.

She pumped her arm into the air. "Hell yeah Luke! Thank you! Show me the way!"

All three guys laughed as Luke led her through the doorway and out into the hallway.

"You'll love this, Hazey. I'm sorry I haven't shown it to you already," he said as they walked. He stopped in front of another door and opened it, motioning for her to go through.

The view inside made the air catch in her lungs. "Luke!" she gasped.

The opposite wall of the room was all windows, that special glass again. There were a few treadmills, some ellipticals, weight machines. Hell . . . there was even a Pilates machine! This was a dream gym situation. There were a few TVs mounted in the room, but they were all dark. She wasn't an avid gym rat, but she was always in motion and worked out enough that she knew she needed movement to settle her brain.

Luke stepped around her and walked over to a credenza built into the wall. It resembled a wet bar, but with water bottles and a dispenser, Drip Drop packets, sports drinks, protein bars and fruit all stocked. A fitness bar set up. He pressed a couple of buttons on a remote and music filled the cavernous space.

"Race you!" Hazel yelled as she skipped over to the treadmill overlooking that incredible view and fired it up.

She heard him laugh behind her and the next minute he was on the treadmill next to hers and jogging right along with her.

She felt like a happy puppy. She was not someone who could sit still for too long and the not walking the city part of her life these last few days was rough. As expected, even the warmup brought a calmness to her thoughts, and gave her a lightness she hadn't felt in days.

The smile was so big on her face, it practically hurt. "Luke, this is incredible. Thank you."

"Sure thing, Hazelnut. This is my favorite space here. If I have to be inside, I'm typically here if not at my desk," he said. He smiled over at her.

"I would be too. It's a gorgeous space," she said.

She didn't hear what he mumbled under his breath, but that was okay. She already felt better, and they were just getting started. He took off his shirt and amped up his incline and speed. Holy shit, the man was built. She had to work to drag her gaze away from his battle honed body. His beautiful muscles, that slightly tan skin. She almost stumbled on the treadmill. Crap, she had better pull herself together.

She pointed things out they could see through the wall of windows, drawing him into conversation. Before long, they were both running at their full speeds, him much faster than her, and laughing. It was easy and natural. They talked about everything and nothing. He shared stories of his ops, funny little quips about the guys, heartbreaking anecdotes about those they lost. She peppered in questions and replies about her own life along the way, reconnecting in a way that felt like coming home for her.

She had sweat practically pouring out of her by the time she slowed to a walk to cool down. The sun had started to set, casting the entire world in that golden hour hue that glowed magically. She could feel the music through her body, her muscles happy to have been worn out. She could have stayed in those moments with him forever. Her heart was lighter as she stepped down from the machine.

She heard Luke turn his machine off also and glanced up to see him staring at her as she bent over, stretching her arms down her right leg, extended out a little wider than her shoulders.

His eyes were hot on her skin. She'd ditched her sweatshirt miles ago and was only wearing a black sports bra and black leggings. Her skin pebbled under his gaze. Her mouth had gone dry. She slowly raised the top half of her body back up, straightening under his gaze. She dropped her shoulders, bending her arms to place her hands on her lower back. She wasn't an idiot, she knew that thrust her chest out, and she felt not one bit bad about it. She wanted him.

She wanted Luke. Her best friend growing up, the older boy she'd known her whole life. The warrior. The man now.

NINE

LUKE

THE LITTLE MINX WAS TRYING TO KILL HIM. HIS MOUTH HAD LONG since dried up. The saliva gulped down his throat the moment he'd seen her bent over at the waist. Probably a good thing he had been in front of her and not behind; he would already be dead.

He dragged his gaze up from her belly, across those gorgeous breasts, up that beautiful neck and right onto her own. Those hazel namesakes were fixated on him, an unspoken challenge in their depths. God, she was perfect. She had no idea what she did to him.

He stepped off the machine and stalked toward her. The light in her eyes never once changing, the setting sun streaking across her skin, painting her in oranges and reds. His world narrowed to a golden time continuum where only the two of them existed at this moment.

He stopped barely shy of her body, a deep breath from either one of them away from their bodies brushing against one another. He felt her pants against his bare chest as he ever so slowly raised his hand. He used his middle finger to skate along the edges of her bra, starting in the deep vee between her breasts and painstakingly dragging his way lightly upward, across her collarbone, and up to her lips. His eyes never left hers, his calloused finger barely skimming her skin.

She shivered, sending her own body against his in the lightest caress. Her eyes dropped closed as he pushed her lips open and repositioned his hand, dropping it back down. His strong fingers gently gripped the back of her neck as his thumb rested at the base of her throat.

She trembled, her nipples poking through her bra to scrape against his chest as he lowered his own lips to hers.

It was madness, he knew that, and yet he couldn't have stopped if enemy insurgents were breaking down the doors to the condo. He had to have one taste of the heaven he knew she'd be.

His gentle grip firmed slightly as his lips hit hers. It was as if he was in a dream, the speed of movement around him happening in slow motion. His other hand came up to her hip and rested there. His lips coaxing hers open, his tongue sweeping inside.

Need consumed him. She was everything he knew she would be. He swallowed her gasp as she notched more firmly against him, her hands coming up his chest gently at first and then digging into the ridges of muscle.

He devoured her, his lips everywhere. She matched him, their inferno blazing hotter and brighter as their hands roamed and caressed, dragged and gripped. He nibbled on her lips, working his way down her throat to the top of her breasts, tasting the salt on her skin.

Her hands were in his hair, tugging through the strands as she murmured his name. He backed her up to the glass windowed wall they'd been facing earlier and pinned her against it with his hips, his erection pressing against her belly as his lips claimed hers again.

The sky had turned deep shades of lavender and blue

outside. His heart was hammering. He knew he could keep going, but this was Hazel. His Hazel. She deserved more from him. She deserved everything. And he could give her nothing but heartache. Their metaphorical golden hour had faded to moody purples and stormy blues, heralding the close of something he should likely never have started with her.

"Hazel, sweetheart, you're absolutely beautiful, and I'm sorry. I shouldn't have taken this from you," he said, his voice hoarse. He stepped back from her and dropped his hands. His erection hadn't gotten the memo, and he stepped back even further.

"Taken from me? I freely gave you everything we shared, Luke. What in the hell are you talking about? What is happening in your head right now? Why are you stopping?" Hazel was getting pissed, her skin flushing with anger now and the glaze of lust fading from her eyes.

"I can't be what you deserve, Hazel. Ever. I'm broken. Shit, Hazel, I should never have taken those moments for myself and I won't take any more. I'm sorry. I can't do that to you," he said.

He raised his eyes back up to meet hers directly and saw the hurt, the pain, there.

"Bullshit, Luke," she spat at him. "I gave, you didn't take. And I gave it freely. Whatever lies you've built up in your head, you're wrong. You are a good man. You are a whole person. And, Luke?" She stabbed her finger into his chest. "You need to pull your head out of your own ass."

With those parting words, she stomped off to the door. He gave himself one more moment, his forehead dropping to the glass as she waited for him to take her upstairs. The colors around him were cold now, like him.

She barely spoke to him the rest of the night. Hell, she barely spoke to any of them. She immediately went to shower and barely ate. He didn't even see her again before she went to bed and he realized that was for the best.

She'd been wrong earlier. He was broken. He knew, without

a shadow of a doubt, that he would love her forever. She was it for him, but he could never get closer. He'd ripped his own heart out in that gym, but it was better now than later, when it could kill them both.

He settled onto the couch and had just flipped on an old rerun of Matlock when his phone started beeping out an alert. Concerned, he grabbed his phone from the coffee table and quickly opened the video feeds he had for the Little Compton house. What he saw there had him jumping from the couch and yelling for Brian and Nate. He needed to get back downstairs to his command center, but he wasn't leaving Hazel upstairs by herself, and he needed Brian and Nate with him.

All hell was breaking loose for Vi and Max in Little Compton. They were under siege and as he watched, small explosions were lighting up the night sky.

Brian was able to wake her quickly as he and Nate went downstairs. Less than ten minutes later, she followed Brian into the room, still rubbing the sleep from her eyes.

"What's wrong? Brian wouldn't say," she asked, only half awake.

Before he could answer her, her eyes focused on the screens he was working on and her brain must have finally registered the other voices streaming into the room from the partners he'd tied into their comms systems.

"Holy shit! Vi! Oh my God. Vi!" she screamed, her eyes going wild.

Brian tried to console her while Luke spoke to Seb on the line, but that was a losing battle. Hazel was a mess. She couldn't stop crying and he couldn't go to her. He'd planned an exfil for Vi and Max in the event they were found, yet Max had been shot trying to get Vi to the boat they'd provisioned as an alternate getaway, and he was losing a great deal of blood.

Violet had gotten him on the boat and was working to stop the flow of bleeding, but she needed Luke's full attention to get them to Narraganset on the water. It took everything Luke had not to go to Hazel, and his focus was absolute shit.

Thankfully, they had a team, or they'd all be fucked. With Brian and Nate helping Hazel, Luke was able to guide Vi along the coast in near darkness down to where she could dock outside of Narraganset. He'd sent Seb up a few days ago, and he was ready for them. He'd also picked up Lauren, Tad's sister, who lived there and was a surgeon. It sounded like Max was going to need the help as fast as possible.

He heard Hazel's silent sobs throughout the room, gathered them in his heart. He wanted to go to her, wrap her in his arms and promise her that everything was going to be okay, and yet he didn't know that. Lauren needed to get Max to her home and get the bullet out.

With Vi's quick thinking, they'd been able to get away, but Max wasn't out of the woods yet. While Lauren worked on him, Seb kept them updated.

"What in the fuck happened?" Tad's voice boomed across the comms.

"I don't know, but we are sure as fuck going to figure it out," Luke replied, exhausted. He rubbed at his eyes. God, they burned.

"Guys, it's on me. I've failed you, failed Max and Violet. I thought I had it covered, but they beat me. I am so sorry." Mila's voice caught on the last of her words, turning into a cry. "I'm sorry. So sorry."

"Mila, it's going to be okay. No one blames you. We are all in this together." Tad had collected himself and now that he knew how Max and Vi had been found, he would focus on reassuring Mila. Tech oversight could be finnicky and it was on him as Team Lead to have only had one person active on that when Mila had already told them that whoever these assholes were, they were more than solid in cyber activity.

"I'll never forgive myself Luke, I am sorry I let them slip past me. And poor Max!" she started crying again.

Mila was not the only person crying in the command center of his townhome. He swung his focus over to Hazel and saw the tears streaming down her face, although she had quieted down. Those silent tears were killing him, but they weren't through this yet.

"Mila, we've got you, sweetheart. Max is going to wake up and tell you it's all good, you know that. And Vi is already telling me to tell you not to worry," Seb added.

"Vi is okay? May I talk to her?" he heard Hazel's quiet question.

"Ya, hang tight. I need to go back and get her. She's in with Max now. Lauren has him patched up, but Vi won't leave him. I stepped out to let you know that he's going to be okay and relay what they learned before the shit storm started," Seb replied.

"Oh, okay. It's okay, let her stay with him. But she's okay, right? She's safe?" Hazel asked, uncertainty ringing in her voice.

"She's solid. Saved his ass. Her and Blitz," Seb replied.

Hazel didn't respond, she simply nodded her head. She murmured to herself, but didn't seem to be fully aware of what was happening. Before he could stop himself, he'd crossed over to her and pulled her against him.

Her body was stiff and unyielding against his at first. He could pull her in physically, yet the distance between them emotionally stunned him, as if she held him away from her. He squeezed tighter and murmured in her ear about how Vi was okay, she was safe now, and Seb would protect her until Max was back on his feet. He felt her nod against his chest, but still no words came from her pretty lips.

"Luke, man, we need to talk about what happened," Tad's voice broke across the comms. Shit, they really did. He hugged Hazel harder to him and then stepped back. He tried to meet her eyes and reassure himself that she was coming around, yet she wouldn't meet his eyes.

"What did they learn?" Brian asked while Luke collected himself.

"From what we can tell, when Max and Vi powered up Vi's phone to check a hunch about a snapchat that Vi took at the party, yet couldn't send, those assholes nailed their location and come in extremely hot," Seb said.

"Was she was the target, after all?" Nate asked.

"Maybe not originally, but when Vi thought she was taking a snap of the party for Hazel, she inadvertently filmed something that she could destroy some very powerful people with, unbeknownst to even herself. That's the only thing that makes sense with what we know, and she said she panned around the crowd. Figuring out who that was is the tricky part."

"Figuring that out will be a needle in a haystack. It was a DC fundraiser. Everyone who wants to be elected in the next decade was there," Brian pointed out.

"True. And we can't do anything tonight. Tad sent some of our FBI contacts to the Little Compton house and, as expected, no one was left behind. They're going to comb through everything and see if they can find anything and in the meantime, I owe a buddy a house," Luke said.

"Agreed. Let's call it a night and then we can all talk tomorrow when Max is up to it. Max and Vi could have details we're missing right now." He paused, thinking for a moment before adding, "Mila, will you see if you can access a seating chart from the event? We have a guest list, yet maybe there is a clue in who was sitting together."

"Yes, of course. Anything I can do, you know I will. I am sorry guys. Seb, please tell Vi that," Mila said. Her normal sunshine-y expression was so forlorn that Luke made a mental note that he needed to talk with her more, offline. She'd be beating herself up for a while, he knew that, but he wanted to assure her that they worked together even when a mistake was made. She was human after all.

They said their goodbyes as a group and then Luke turned to Hazel. It was as if the light typically within her was turned off.

She was a shell of the Hazel he'd known his whole life, and that scared him.

"Hazel, I need to stay down here and work for a few hours, but you should get some rest, okay?"

Still no verbal response, only a slight nod. He glanced over her head at Brian and Nate, nodding to them.

"Hazey?" He waited for her to look up at him until her wounded eyes met his directly. "Babe, Brian and Nate are going back up with you. I'll be up in a few hours, but if you need anything, just ask. Okay?"

More silent nodding, and then she was turning to leave the room. A deep sigh slipped past his lips and he dropped his head back on his shoulders. He was exhausted, and there were a million things he needed to focus on, but shit. Hazel was breaking his heart.

He set about following up with Mila, then he checked in with Seb. Max was sleeping and was fever-free for the time being, which was great news. Vi was also asleep and Seb was getting ready to get in some rack time too. They decided that Lauren would go to work at the local hospital tomorrow, as planned. Any time you were hiding something, which Lauren's house guests qualified as wanting to stay hidden, you should stick to your normal programming as much as possible. Seb didn't like it, but Lauren also insisted.

"Let give it a day or two, talk more when Max and Vi are up to it later and then we'll fly up for you. Just take care of them until we can get you, and take care of yourself too. We don't need anyone else out of commission right now," Luke added before Seb hung up.

"Copy. I've got them, don't you worry. And Luke, Max is in deep with Vi, he's a goner for her and from what I can tell, she's got it just as bad."

That was the good news that Luke loved to hear. "Well shit. That's the best news that could have come from this clusterfuck. Two of my favorite humans. Good."

"I thought you might be glad to hear it. Might have to start calling you cupid from here on out." Seb laughed.

"Hell ya, you will. I take full credit. They better have a son and name him for me," Luke snarked right back. "Night, asshole. Stay safe."

"Ditto, asshole. Love ya, brother," Seb replied before hanging up.

Well, that news was unexpected, yet like he said, it was great news. He loved Max, and he loved Vi. He hoped that Seb hadn't misread the situation, but Seb rarely did. His emotional intelligence was freaky good.

His last call of the night was to Tad, who was the night watch in their plan. "Hey man, I'm going to hit the hay, you good?" he asked when Tad picked up.

"Ya, I've got you. Sounds like we both also talked with Mila. She'll be okay. If anything, we might need to add someone to help her on software pieces. She's only one person and she could use a work life balance in this brave new world of Titan Group we're building."

"Great point. Let's talk with her about it after this and see if she wants someone on her team. I don't want her to fill as if we are adding because we don't trust her," Luke replied.

"Exactly. I want to add so she stays forever, I don't want her burned out," Tad said.

"I'm with you there, man." Luke sighed again, the hours and the stress catching up to him. He said his goodbyes to Tad and headed back upstairs to the quiet condo. He found Nate asleep in one of the large club chairs and decided to leave him there and let him get some rest.

He checked on Hazel, who was also asleep, and then made his way back out to the couch. Laying down, he wondered about how she was holding up. He was surprised that she'd fallen asleep, but grateful. He'd never felt so torn in his life before tonight. He needed to go to her, to comfort her, yet he couldn't. He had a job to do. His focus may have been shit, but Max and

Vi had needed him, and thankfully, they'd made it out alive. The last thought he'd had before sleep claimed him was that of gratitude for his team.

The next day, they pieced together that the snap Vi had taken accidentally caught the US Ambassador, Ambassador Neil, meeting with her date, Brandon Mills, heir to a weapons company dynasty *and* the Speaker of the House's son, and the Scott brothers, one of which was a prominent NYC society type, and one who was a current board member of the New Jersey and New York Port Authority. She'd then unknowingly told her date about the snap that wouldn't go through, right in front of Ambassador Neil.

They had to assume there was some reason those people didn't want to be seen on film together or that something else was on the video, and that they couldn't risk her snap going through once she was back in cell service. Vi relayed to them that no phones were allowed at the party, but she hadn't known that, and had hers off when she got there to save some battery. Because it wasn't on originally, only being powered up when she decided to take the snap, the working theory was they'd tried to jam cell phone towers all night, but they were only successful at that in the environment they expected to control, not the hotel Vi was staying at. Turning on her phone with the little battery she'd had left and calling Hazel from the lobby of the hotel had saved Vi's life. Luke had a hunch that she was never intended to be allowed to get back to the hotel, but he wasn't sharing that idea with Hazel, she still seemed to be a dimmer version of her normal self.

After some supposition about why that was worth killing for, they had some leads to follow, but first, they needed to bring the team back together, in the safety of DC and the fortress he'd built in Georgetown. They'd been working on finalizing a large home base there for years, fully outfitted with every safety, defense and tech measure known to man. And, some unknown to anyone else. Wills was a hardware genius after all.

Luke took a few of the team and Hazel, and flew up to Narraganset to pick them up and bring them home while Tad reached out to their FBI contact for help.

The flight up in his Learjet went by quickly and by the time that they loaded Seb, Max, Vi and Blitz up in Narraganset, Hazel was starting to act more like herself. He was beyond grateful to have everyone together, but he was also anxious to get them back to DC.

The entire trip was blessedly uneventful, except for a reckoning conversation about how they could afford the level of safety and accommodations they were enjoying, including the plush Challenger 3500 they flew in. He hadn't meant for it to be a secret, there just hadn't been a good time to talk about before. Hazel had that wounded light in her eyes again and he could only imagine she thought he'd lied by omission.

He resigned himself to her anger, which frankly, he would take. He much preferred her anger to her sadness.

TEN

HAZEL

SHE COULDN'T EVEN LOOK AT LUKE WITHOUT HER HEART CLENCHING painfully and thudding against her ribs. He was courteous, kind, laughed with her, fed her, tried to care for her but his smile never quite reached his eyes. She just felt so numb. Her emotions were a mess, and her mind was fuzzy, as if she'd been swimming under water and everything was happening on the shore above her. She could hear everything, but in that distorted and distant way. She was part of what was happening, but separate from herself in a garbled world.

She shivered in the seat of the private plane they were on to pick up her sister, Max, his dog Blitz, and Sebastian. The flight up to get them was quick and before too long, she was faking calmness and hugging her sister tightly. Her happiness at seeing her sister safe lifted the boulder of worry from her chest, and the hug they shared was the balm her soul needed for the moment. Her sister, safe in her arms. Internally, she likened it to her head breaking above the water and her ears finally popping. Everything was in real time again.

She met Max, the beefcake who had been sent to save Vi in

Saratoga Springs, and who seemingly, was head over heels in love with her sister. By the looks of it, Vi was smitten with him too, which gave Hazel her first real smile in days. Max wasn't a single package either. Along with Sebastian, one of the guys on Luke and Max's team joining them, Max had a black lab named Blitz. Hazel was immediately slobbered on, Blitz's tail wagging a million miles per hour. Real laughter bubbled in her throat, God she had needed this. Why she hadn't gotten her own dog yet, she had no idea. She loved them.

All too quickly, they closed the plane up and shot back up into the clouds, Luke wanting to be as fast as possible on the ground. She knew they were flying back to DC, but that they weren't going back to the luxury condo they'd been hiding out in. She had heard the guys talking around her about the place in Dupont Circle and she knew Brian had stayed behind to handle a few items. She'd just mutely gone along for the ride, her emotions too jumbled to focus.

Having Vi, Max, Seb and Blitz in the plane with Luke sitting up front made the bands of tension wrapping around her body ease slightly. They were the safe space she needed to ask about the private jet and holy shit did she get an answer she wasn't ready for. Luke owned it, he owned it all. The plane, the condo, apparently he owned lots of real estate. He was some secret gazillionaire, and she hadn't known. She didn't even care about the money but she felt like he'd driven a knife more deeply into her bleeding and tender heart. He was a man she really didn't know anymore. A man she thought she could love, the other half of her heart and yet, had realized maybe she didn't even truly understand him, or know him.

She latched onto Vi before they stepped on to the tarmac at the FBO outside of DC, waiting until the others had disembarked.

"Are you okay Hazey? What's wrong? Other than the murderous web we're trapped in I guess," Violet whispered to her.

"Do you wonder if we ever really knew Luke at all Vi? He has this whole other life that we knew nothing about. I guess I'm rocked by it all," Hazel whispered haltingly back to Vi.

"I hadn't even considered that honestly. Luke is practically a big brother out living his own life and I know he has my back whenever I need him, but I guess I hadn't thought about him as a man necessarily," Vi said as she met Hazel's eyes.

"Vi?" Hazel whispered to her sister. "I've considered him all man for far too long." Hot tears leaked from her eyes at the admission. "And now I realize that I'm not even important enough to be on his radar as a woman. A woman is someone who knows him, and whom he knows. I'm only a bratty little sister." She sobbed into Violet's arms.

"Woah, Sis. It's okay. Shhhh." Violet hugged her tightly.

"What the hell ladies? What's going on here?" Luke came from the cockpit and took one look at them, his eyes snagging on Hazel's face. "Hazelnut, what happened?" he asked, his voice going tense.

Violet looked over Hazel's head to Luke. "It's okay Luke, she's just relieved we're both okay. We'll be out in a minute, you go," Violet said.

He waited a few beats longer. "Are you sure? Hazelnut, you good?" he asked her.

She stepped back and rubbed at her swollen eyes. "Yeah, obvi. Relax, Warden Luke-a-licious," Hazel added some snark to her watery voice, hiding the crashing waves of pain constricting her heart.

Luke didn't seem convinced, he walked over to the door leading down the stairs and waited for them. "Rejoice in the safety of our home base please. Our time here has to be fast."

Violet nodded her head and then squeezed Hazel tightly to her chest. "We'll finish this later."

Hazel squeezed back and disengaged from her. "No, thank you."

They descended from the plane to find both Max and Luke at the bottom of the stairs, both slightly perplexed.

Seb had opened the door to a waiting black Yukon Denali, loading Blitz in first. "Ladies, your chariot awaits." He shooed them in.

Thankfully, the drive to the townhome in Dupont Circle was uneventful. The large, Georgian property had underground parking, and it appeared as if they were driving right up to it until a door hidden mostly by clever landscaping opened and they pulled inside quickly. It shut behind them immediately and Brian, who had been driving, waited a beat to ensure it was safe before he jumped out and then held the door for Violet and Hazel to climb out of the back seat.

Hazel took in the structure she found herself in, the inside better than her imagination could ever have dreamed. The property wasn't one townhome, but three massive townhomes conjoined on the inside and made to seem as separate units on the outside. She and Vi took in the walnut paneling as she smoothed her hand along the gorgeous dark wainscoting on the wall.

Sconces glowed brightly from the walls as they passed a library on the main floor with a fire blazing in a hearth that easily took up half of the wall. The windows on this floor were mullioned but were thicker than she'd ever seen before.

"They're bulletproof," she heard Max say to her sister next to her.

"Who owns this place? How in the world did you find it?" Vi asked.

Max cleared his throat. "Actually, we all kind of own it. We bought it to be a headquarters of sorts, but we weren't sure what type of headquarters. At the time we bought it, all of us were alive and making so much money with Luke's investment portfolios, we wanted to have a home base here big enough for all of us. Being guys, being Marines, we've added the security layers over the years. We've hired different contractors for different pieces, we've done lots ourselves, we've masked parts of the insides so those hired only saw bits and pieces, you know . . . kind of just some boys with access and some paranoia," he explained, sheepishly. "It had the last safety measures put in place so being here now, with you ladies, is like a homecoming," he went on.

Hazel wandered into the library as she heard Max and Vi head for the stairs. Seb had warned her on the plane that the two of them were all hearts and rainbows and he'd been right. Her incredible sister was in love with a gorgeous man who would die for her. A pang of jealousy slammed through her as she walked to the fire. Fall had hit, and she shivered. She stepped closer to the bright flames and held her hands out.

She felt Luke at her back before he spoke, his voice over her left shoulder.

"Are you mad, Hazelnut? I'm sorry I didn't tell you about the money," he said, his voice quiet.

She shook her head but didn't turn to him. She couldn't, he'd see the pain too clearly in her eyes.

"I don't care about the money Luke. I'm really, really proud of you. Of the two of us, I seem to be the one who sees the best in you so no, I'm neither mad, nor surprised."

She heard him take a deep breath behind her but before he could say anything else, Brian's voice carried across the cozy room.

"Bossman, we're rolling in command center," Brian said.

Hazel took the opportunity to run metaphorically. She wasn't a coward per se, but she couldn't do this with Luke right now. Her emotions were too raw and that proverbial water was rushing in her ears again, quasi-drowning her.

"Brian, where am I bunking friend? Will you take me there? I'm freezing and need a hot shower," she said as she stepped around Luke.

She saw Brian's eyes meet Luke's above her head, whatever

he saw there being enough that he smiled easily at her and said, "Of course, Hazey. Right this way."

She followed him to a gorgeous space on one side of the property. Her room had its own fireplace and was done in rich jewel tones. She had a small bag of clothes the guys had gotten for her that first full day and she sat it on the bed as she explored the connecting bathroom. It was stunning. Carrara marble, warm brass fixtures, plush taupe-y-colored towels laid out for her. It had a huge bathtub and a glass bottle of bubble bath sitting on the side. A crystal chandelier hung above the expansive bathtub, the light low and glowing.

She decided to leave the brighter lights off. The low glow fit her mood better. She filled the enormous bathtub up as high as she should with water as hot as she could stand it. She'd added a few drops of bubbles and sank down into the steam with a groan. She needed a minute to herself and that luxurious bathroom was just the place for it before she rejoined the group in other parts of the massive house.

The hours after that passed quickly. They had a plan now, a party to infiltrate and a good handle on who the players were on this scary chessboard they found themselves on. The alarming hunch they were following was that Brandon Mills had been supplying weapons from his family factory to Phillip Scott at the port authority board, who was overseeing them loaded on to ships to Tunisia, where Ambassador Neil was paying to have them come in without inspection. Once the weapons were clear of the port in Tunisia, they hit the black market in the war-torn countries of the Middle East. If their hypothesis was correct, it was pretty clear as to why the Ambassador was willing to kill to keep it secret and moving forward. Something had to account for the massive amounts of money moving into Swiss and Bahamian accounts Mila and Wills had just tracked.

Ironically, the Ambassador had over-reacted. By freaking out, he set a chain of events in motion to lead Luke and his team, along with Vi and Hazel to start asking questions. Why did it matter if the US Ambassador to Tunisia was in deep conversation with Pell Weaponry, via Brandon, and a member of the New Jersey and New York Port Authority board?

It seemed that Titan Group had walked into their first case without planning to, but their partners at the FBI were very interested in what they'd uncovered, and obviously, that angle needed a delicate touch of investigation . . . perfect for Titan Group. When Tad had checked in with their contacts, they'd of course given them the green light to pursue. The FBI would start their end of work with the Port Authority, bringing in a SEAL team, and Luke and Titan Group would focus on Ambassador Neil to get more proof of what they thought might be happening.

The entire group had come together in the command center, a truly impressive room that any agency in the world would love to get their hands on. They ran through Luke's planning, the positions everyone would take, potential distress signals and some hand signals a dozen more times and then all went upstairs to eat a late dinner together.

Dinner was a light affair. They were easy in each other's company, telling stories about their tours together, and their leaves. They talked about the fun times, the wild times, and the sad times. They all drank a toast to those brothers they'd lost. She saw Vi and Max always touching each other in some way.

At dinner, she met Theo, the consummate flirt. Another one of Luke's guys, Theo was built, tan and had clear green eyes. His dimples were deep, and he smiled readily, teeth bright against his olive skin. He flirted shamelessly with her, which brought a lightness to her night. She even flirted back and made a joke about her own virginity. Her friends from college had always teased her about it, so she didn't think the joke was that big if a deal.

Unfortunately, that joke had landed awkwardly and Luke was pissed. It was apparently tough to hear his "little sister" talk about sex. She rolled her eyes as she stood up with the others to clean her dishes, but inwardly, she felt so foolish, childish even.

After dinner, everyone went their separate ways. She could tell that Vi wanted to talk with her more, but Hazel had waved her off from the couch in front of the main fireplace. She felt like a cornered badger and her emotions were too high. She didn't want to unleash on her poor sister while she had everything else going on and ultimately, she didn't even know what to say. She was angry at herself for her own awkwardness, hurt by Luke's big brother behavior and straight scared of what they were facing. Everything they knew about this insane plot to distribute weapons was based on tenuous threads and supposition, gathering proof still lingered over their collective heads.

"Vi, please let me read for now. I know we're going to talk about it but not here. Not yet. I'm too raw on this right now and frankly, one of us should be upstairs getting more nakedly acquainted with their tall dark and handsome man." Even she heard the little thread of bitterness in her voice as the words flowed out.

"Hazey, for blurting out the virgin bit, you sure are comfortable talking about me getting some," Vi chided her gently.

"Ya well, I have to live vicariously though you. I've been reading the same smutty romance novels you have, Sis. One of us is now living it so please, do us both a favor and go live it," Hazel grumbled at her but had softened her tone. Her sister didn't need her anger or confusion. "Seriously Vi, savor this for now, we can talk about all the other stuff tomorrow."

Her sister kissed her on the forehead and went up to Max's apartments within the large house. Blitz, Max's dog, stayed with Hazel, looking up at her pleadingly.

"Staying with me, huh? Get up here, I could use the snuggles." She patted the couch next to her and Blitz jumped up and wiggled into her body, pressing against her leg. Blitz laid his head on Hazel's lap while Hazel stroked his soft fur. Dogs were amazing, he must have known Hazel needed the comfort. Or, he preferred the comfy couch. Either way, she was glad to have him wedged against her.

She was thrilled for Violet, even if the jealousy was taking hold of her in a small way. What would life be like with a man who worshipped you for all the world to see? A man who was proud to love you, and told you regularly in his actions and with his words? She imagined Luke then, as he had been that night in the gym, with his hand gently wrapped around her throat, his lips skating across her sensitive skin.

She snuggled more deeply into the couch, her eyes on the flames in the fireplace. She'd snagged the blanket off the back of the couch and felt warm and safe with Blitz curled up against her legs. She was able to close her heavy eyelids and think of Luke. Of his kisses, how different their life could be if he saw her the same way she saw him. It was as if a switch had been flipped in her heart and now she knew Luke was the man for her, but he'd shut her out.

The fire had died down to embers hours later when she felt her body lifted, floating and then tucked against a hard chest. Ropes of muscles held her tightly, as she was carried to her room. If this was a dream, she refused to wake up fully. She'd fallen asleep thinking about the what ifs in life and was dreaming up how wonderful it would be to be cherished by Luke.

Lips brushed against her forehead as she was nestled into a pillow cloud. Airy and warm blankets were tucked against her shoulders and she sighed more deeply as she turned to her side. Dream Luke was dreamy indeed. She reached for him then, running her fingertips along his warm skin. His skin against the pads of her fingertips was solid, real, fading the vestiges of her dream.

She rolled against him and sat up, bracing herself on his chest.

"Luke?" she asked, the sleep still heavy in her voice.

"I just need to hold you Hazel. I'm sorry, I wish I was a

stronger man, but please give me tonight to hold you close," he said. He pulled her lips to his then, deepening the kiss as she sank into him. She dropped her knees to each side of him, straddling him fully as his kisses became hungrier and hungrier.

"Please Luke." She sat up and pulled her t-shirt off over her head. His eyes darkened to nearly black as she reached behind herself and unfastened her bra, letting it fall beside her in the bed. His hands were hot and calloused at her waist.

"I need you too Luke, please give me tonight. All of you. Give me everything," she said.

She saw the indecision in his eyes then as his hands swept down and gripped her hips.

"Are you sure Hazel? I don't know if I am strong enough to stop or say no to you right now," he murmured.

"Then don't. Give me everything," she said as she sank back on his bare chest. His skin was incredible against hers, warm and satiny, encasing those gloriously hard muscles. She ran her fingers down her own body and pulled her leggings off as she went. "Please." She nibbled her way back up his chiseled chest, nipping along the dips and ridges of muscle.

He must have heard the desperation in her voice because one second she was in charge, kissing along his chest up to his throat and the next second he had flipped their positions.

He stared down at her, his arms locked at his sides as her nipples puckered under his watch. His eyes were scorching in their slow perusal of her. Liquid heat gathered at her core and she lifted her hips ever so slightly and wrapped her legs around him.

"I ache, Luke. Please." She wouldn't beg him necessarily, but she wanted this. She wanted him to be her first, her everything.

He groaned and then capitulated, feasting on her mouth. They became a tangle of tongues and hands as he shed his sweats and boxer briefs. The first moment his skin moved against hers she wanted to weep with the pleasure of it.

His lips fastened on her clavicle and began working downward, her body squirming under his. He praised her as he went, murmuring words of wonder at her body and kissing along after each compliment. She was ragged with need, something she had never felt to that degree before. There was an urgency gathering within her, an impatience that only Luke had ever inspired.

Her thoughts vanished the moment his tongue licked along her opening. His hands had kneaded their way down her body with his tongue and words and now he held her hips, playfully licking at her most sensitive skin.

"Hazel, you are the most beautiful woman I have ever seen," he whispered against her. His mouth was heaven. She writhed against him, his tongue becoming more insistent as he added a finger deep inside of her heat.

"So wet baby, that's right, so good," he praised as he worked her into a frenzy. Her hands were in his hair, her mind racing to catalog all the feelings crashing through her.

"Luke, yes, Luke. Please," she whimpered, grinding against his mouth and hand.

"I've got you Hazelnut, come for me." He said against her, his finger crooking back just enough. She had been so close, that little extra pressure causing her to shatter against him then, euphoria seeping through her veins, leaving her limbs heavy and buzzing. She'd never felt so deeply connected to another human before.

Luke began kissing his way back up her body, skating his lips across her belly and then working upward to nip and lave at her breasts. No sooner had she started to come down from her first orgasm, than another, more powerful wave began building within her.

She ran her hands down his muscled back, nails digging into his cheeks when she reached them.

"I need you inside of me Luke. Now," she said hotly against his mouth.

He rolled over to his nightstand and opened a new box of condoms. She noticed that he had to take the packaging off the box before opening it. He saw her face and leaned down to kiss her again, the box forgotten in his hand.

"I've never had anyone in this place Hazelnut, only you. Only ever you." His words were a promise to her and she shifted out from under him then. She grabbed the condom from his hand and opened it herself. She reached over and fitted it on his length instinctively, bringing her hand flush to his groin to secure it before dropping her fingers to caress him gently. He groaned and rolled her back under him.

"The less touching you do right now, the longer this will last Hazelnut. I've wanted you for years." He smiled at her then, a shy smile against her lips.

His words floored her. She wanted this moment to last forever. "Then show me."

He laughed then. "There's my sassy girl." He sank into her slowly at that, filling her as cautiously as possible, stretching her, completing her. He pushed all the way into her wet heat and waited for her to adjust to his size.

"Hazelnut, are you okay?" He kissed her more deeply again, getting lost in her but still not moving, willing her to be okay.

She felt the pinch of him within her, but she'd been more than ready, she was eager for him to move. It was as if that wave was crashing into her again, and she was ready to be pulled into it, under it, along with it. She shifted her hips and kissed him back, the urge to move causing her to lift her hips up to more fully engulf him.

"It's perfect, you're perfect. I'm so much more than okay," she assured him.

"You're perfect." He moved within her, wringing pleasure from her body, the waves pulling her under. This man owned her body. He owned her heart. They came together, words of adoration whispered in the night.

ELEVEN

LUKE

NOT STAYING IN BED WITH HAZEL THE NEXT MORNING AND PULLING her back against his chest was one of the toughest things Luke had ever done. He physically ached to hold her. He had a job to do though, and they needed to see this through to move on. The sky outside of his window was as tumultuous as his thoughts, and as chaotic.

He kissed her on the lips and slid from their cocoon. They'd made love three times in the night and he knew she needed sleep. Her body had to be tender after that, whereas he imagined he could take on world. He took a quick hot shower, and seeing her still sleeping, he went down to their command center to get this fuckery figured out. He was renewed by her. Could this work? Could he be the man she deserved and kep her safe? He'd spent months talking through those previous tough ops with the team doctor and felt at peace with his service leadership, but he still questioned if he could love someone as completely as Hazel deserved to be loved and not destroy everything in the process. Was he like his dad? The thought brought him up short. Was he?

He'd always gravitated back to Hazel his entire life. Could they have it all?

Would he end up leaving her alone if something happened to him? His heart clenched at his next thought, his ultimate fear, that someone from his past would come for her. A guy didn't get through what he had in his service record without serious enemies. He caught himself before those thoughts spiraled. Maybe, just maybe, they could have what he'd had as a family unit before his mom died. Before his dad simply gave up. He was reasonably certain he could protect her and himself. He knew that she was worth it, if he had the courage to try. He didn't think he could live without her now that he knew what they were like together. He really didn't.

Resolving that they'd talk after the party and he would lay it all out there, he set to work preparing and before long, it was time to leave. Hazel had worked side by side with him and the team, as had Vi, all day preparing for contingencies and talking about what would constitute the proof they needed for their handler.

They'd staggered the arrival times to the party at Ambassador Neil's townhome and each had a cover, him playing the role of the drunken playboy version of himself for this op. He'd pretend to be the tanked heartbreaker with more money than brains and see what he could learn.

Because they had agreement from their handler in the White House, their role was to find proof of their hypothesis while a SEAL team looked for the weapons they believed to be in shipping containers along the Port of New Jersey and New York. That part of the joint operation was a giant shell game, and he was glad to be on the ground in DC, blocks away from where Hazel would be so they could finally talk once this was wrapped up later that night. His buddy Callum was on that SEAL team and so far, they hadn't found anything in the search but crates filled with clocks and baking supplies stuffed into different shipping containers.

"That just means that we're on to something," Luke relayed to the questioning faces around the room.

"How so?" Hazel asked.

"Everything sounds like a bomb and looks like drugs, messes with the dogs and the humans." Max answered. "Luke is right, we're in the right place, but they don't know what we know or think we know, so it's cheaper for them to just try to mask what is there than to move it at this stage of their game." Max added.

"Right, because if they have to move it, then they risk it not going out, which Ambassador Neil isn't willing to risk," Vi said.

"Bingo. We stay the course," Tad said, looking around the room.

The tension had been mounting all day, but it was finally time to leave. Vi was really struggling with staying behind while the others went into a potentially dangerous situation on her behalf, yet Luke wasn't willing to put her in harm's way and even if he was, Max wasn't. It seemed to Luke that his buddy Max was truly smitten with Hazel's older sister, and he couldn't be happier for both of them.

Max being up in Lake George, working through his grief at losing Alex had been sheer luck on location, being that close to Vi when Hazel had called him. They'd almost lost Max too in that last op when it went FUBAR, had Seb not pulled him from the rubble just in time to save his life. Luke knew that Max would rather have died there with Alex, and he'd mandated couch time with the team doc, which he knew was helping. And now, Max had found Vi in all of this mess.

Max was coming back to himself, in a different way, but more like the guy Luke had known since he enlisted. He couldn't think of a better partner for Vi, the only Burke sister who he thought of as a sister. Hazel, on the other hand, had always been different in his heart.

He was glad to see Max coming back, the light in his eyes warm again. He made a mental note to talk to Max about staying retired being completely fine, versus continuing with the plan to be part of Titan Group.

He refocused his thoughts and mentally walked through their plans. Mila and Theo would be at the party as guests, along with him and Tad. Nate was on overwatch, but Max was staying behind to cover Vi and Hazel, along with Wills on tech and comms, in case anything went haywire, so he wasn't on his typical spotter duties or overwatch himself. One sniper would have to do for this plan. Brian was driving Mila and Theo. Seb would also stay in their command center and Mila had even arranged for two female FBI agents she knew to be fake dates for Tad and Luke. That part sucked for Luke. He could see the fear and unease in Hazel's eyes and they hadn't had a chance to talk much that day, which was ramping up the tension between them.

"Luke, man, let's roll. The Uber will be here soon to take us by a bar before we hit the party," Tad said. Part of their plan was to play the part, with them being seen at a bar before heading to the party.

Luke lifted his chin to Tad, signaling him to go ahead, before he made his way over to where Hazel was watching him. She seemed wary, and nervous, not that he could blame her. He and the guys were used to this prep, the calm before the craziness, the planning for every potential problem. He planned to fail and had plans for each fail point they could come up with. It was time.

"Are you sure this is the right idea?" Hazel asked when he reached her side. "We don't have to do this. We can leave it all to the authorities. Right?" She raised pleading eyes to his.

"It's the best idea we have, and we are almost out of time. If we miss this shipment, we don't know when we'll have a chance to get proof again. This is the perfect job for Titan Group, for me, for my guys. We know what to do, Hazey, and we'll be safe," he reassured her. "Without proof, Vi will always be in danger, which means you will be too, and I can't live with that."

ONLY EVER YOU   89

Lifting her hand in his, he pulled her against himself gently. The others were all preparing and in their own worlds, and in the midst of the chaos, he felt her sigh into him, her body plaint against his own. Her anxiety palatable.

"Come back, okay?" she asked. "Promise me."

"Always, Hazelnut." He shifted, notching her curves more perfectly against the hard planes of his body, bringing his lips to the shell of her ear and gently kissing there. "Then, we'll talk."

She nodded against his lips, prompting him to steal one more moment for himself, closing his eyes and nuzzling against her before squeezing her hand and stepping back. She didn't say anything, but before he released her hand, she rushed to squeeze his back too. It was what he needed to turn and head out for their mission. He'd take care of this asshole and then they'd move forward.

TWELVE

HAZEL

THE PARTY WAS IN FULL SWING WHEN LUKE AND TAD ARRIVED, BOTH playing their parts perfectly. Perhaps too perfectly, as she saw the woman she knew to be an FBI agent squeeze Luke's arm and whisper in his ear before he headed to the bar. Watching that unfold certainly wasn't how she expected to spend the evening. She'd be so glad when this was behind them and they could talk. She felt like she'd tipped over some invisible line into a land of Luke, a land she was excited to be in. A little bubble of happiness had worked its way into her throat and she kept telling herself to focus, but listening to herself on that advice was next to impossible, and her heart hadn't stopped racing. What if he didn't come back to her? What if something happened?

She shivered in her chair.

"Are you okay, Hazey? You seem quiet today, but more settled than when I saw you last night. Are you worried?"

"I am. I'm ready to get this behind us and move on, but I should be asking you if you're okay. You've been through so much in the last week," she replied nodding her head in Max's direction, not wanting to talk about her situation yet.

Her sister smiled then, a soft look coming over her face. "He's the one, Hazey. I have no idea how something like this could happen so fast, but I feel like I've known him forever, and yet I'm on this mountain top of hope, with the whole world in front of us. As if I'm starting this crazy fun vacation with my best friend," Vi said, her eyes watering up. "It's crazy, I know. I sound like a bad poetry student," she laughed.

Hazel laughed with her sister and then leaned in for a quick hug. One tight squeeze and she sat back, taking her sister's face in her hands. "Potentially bad poetry aside, I'm happy for you Vi. Who cares if it's soon? He seems crazy about you too, and he's seriously hot, and he has a dog! You love black labs! See, it was meant to be," she added, laughing along with Vi.

She was seriously so happy for Vi, and Max was all of those things she'd said he was. He also looked at her sister with a naked look of longing and adoration on his face, which was all plain to see. Would Luke look at her like that soon? Would it be obvious to his team the way it was for Max?

It felt secretive to not tell Vi about what had happened with Luke last night, yet she wanted to have him with her when they did. Vi would be floored at first, yet also happy for them. She loved her family, and now Luke would also be by her side. She was practically bouncing back in her seat at that thought, Vi's bad prose in her head. She knew exactly what the top of that mountain top of hope felt like. Day one of vacation with your best friend, airport drinks in hand, an incredible adventure ahead of you and no worries in the world.

They just had to figure this thing out with the Ambassador, the Scott brothers, and the guns. Guns! A black market in Tunisia! What in the world had her life become in the last week? She was a food writer, Vi was a newspaper journalist who was trying to write a young adult mystery and now they were in a command center of sorts in a swanky Georgetown neighborhood, two hot former Marines by their sides and an international war crime unfolding. She just needed Luke to come home to her, she thought as her eyes found the screen of him again.

Wills had created some prototype tech that looked like little clear patches, roughly the size of a nickel, and they'd planted some earlier in the day inside of the Ambassador's townhome by Nate pretending to be part of the catering crew. The little patches of video allowed them to see what was happening, in addition to hearing what was happening through little devices hidden in their ears. Seb had called it "serious spy shit," as Wills was describing the tech, and she thought that was the perfect description. Again, she had a moment of wonder at their current situation, not realizing that kind of technology had existed. She prayed they worked.

So far, the party hadn't turned up any proof, yet her eye was caught by Luke appearing to stumble down a hallway. The guys had decided to move onto the next phase, which was searching the house. She knew the stumble was an act, and judging from what she was seeing on the screens, he did a convincing job of appearing drunk. No sooner had she thought that than a beautiful woman entered the hallway from the other end, heading straight for Luke. The woman seemed to be in distress too, maybe even crying. Hazel scooted her chair closer to the screens to get a better look.

Hazel studied the woman. Something was off, but she couldn't put her finger on it. At her side, Vi had also scooted her chair closer for a better look.

"Wait," Vi breathed out. Such a simple word and yet her sister's tone made the hair raise on the back of her neck. "She looks familiar."

Hazel whipped her head around right as Vi gasped and then yelled, "That's Illyana! She was with Brady and Phillip in Saratoga Springs! She was there that night too!"

Hazel saw it before she even processed what Vi had yelled. The woman had held a knife close to her side and, without a moment of hesitation, had plunged it into Luke's gut, a deep red blooming immediately across his stomach. His hands flew to the knife, blood coating his fingers as Hazel screamed at the screen.

"Hazelnut," Luke whispered as he hit the ground, unconscious.

She heard screaming as Wills and Seb scrambled around her. Vi and Max were both talking on the comms again, planning. The screaming continued as Vi turned to her. "Hazey, we're going after him. Hazel, you have to stop." Vi's firm voice and arms tightening around her jolted her into awareness. The screams were hers.

"No, don't go. Please, you can't," she begged her sister. The water was rushing in her ears again, damn it. She was not okay with this plan. Why them? Where were the authorities? Why had they agreed to this?

"Hazel, I have to go. You know this. If you could see clearly right now, you would know that I have to do this. Ambassador Neil is holding the others until I show my face, but we have a plan, Hazel. You have to trust me, trust the guys," Vi pleaded with her.

"You don't have to, Violet! You aren't some military badass, you're a writer!" she cried.

"I am, but I'm also going to see this through. I can't leave them, and we're going to be okay. You have to believe that," Vi replied, her tone allowing no more room for argument.

THIRTEEN

LUKE

Fuck, he hurt. Awareness, consciousness, both had slammed into him and he fought to keep them without opening his eyes or changing his breathing pattern. He could hear Tad from somewhere directly above him, and before he could stop himself, a groan of pain slipped from between his lips.

"He needs medical care, please," he heard Tad pleading for him to whoever else was in the room and he worked to open his eyes. FUCK. That sucked. He blinked a few times to clear the cloudiness from his vision and focused in on Ambassador Neil, Phillip, and the woman from the hallway. Of course, she had stabbed him. He could feel her handiwork draining the life from him, but he was helpless to stop it. They'd never considered that Illyana wasn't a date, she was a player. Luke felt so stupid, and he may pay for his mistake with his life.

"This isn't fucking amateur hour, Luke. We know you're connected to Violet Burke. You may think you buried that connection, but you can't bury physical photographs in frames along random mantels, now can you?" Neil pulled Luke's head back viciously by his hair to punctuate his rant.

The waves of pain from his head being yanked back increased the searing sensation in his gut and he fought to not throw up, to stay awake. Bile was in his throat while Neil continued on about the once a year in person meeting that Vi accidentally caught on video. He kept his chin up, swallowing shallowly, his brain sluggish.

A memory of Neil's rant was on a loop in his mind, a photo? He'd seen a photo? Neil's voice interrupted his thoughts again as he continued on about seeing a photo of Vi, Hazey, and him in Vi's apartment. Shit, they really had walked into a trap tonight. His vision swam again. He needed a hospital and soon.

"So now, we're going to wait for our little friend to arrive. She'll come out if you tell her to, and that's what you're going to do," Neil said.

"Over my dead body, asswipe," Luke raged, his pain threatening to overwhelm him, pull him back into the darkness.

Neil continued on while he faded in and out of consciousness, threatening Tad and speaking as if he knew they were on comms with the team. Time was getting harder and harder for him to track, but he was jolted fully cognizant by Vi's voice yelling his name and her hands on his head.

"What the fuck, Max?" he gasped, barely conscious.

"It's okay buddy, she wanted to help." Max winked at him. He must be dead, he thought to himself. There was no way Max would have brought Vi into this clusterfuck, even if they had a contingency plan for one of them being caught.

The dimming was getting worse and worse, he was losing the battle to stay with it. He really may die here, in this library, Hazel watching it on the screens from his home blocks away from where he lay. He'd had his perfect moments, and now he would leave her—alone—just like he had always feared he would. Worst of all, he was powerless to stop it from unfolding as he lay dying.

He heard shots, and more yelling, hands grabbing him under

the arms, felt himself being dragged. Tad's face swam in front of him when he tried to open his eyes, a look of concern there.

"Don't die on me, man, we're clear. Bad guys are dead. Going to get you fixed up." Tad's voice was strong, but he heard the fear there. It was impossible not to.

"If you fucking die on me, man. I swear to God, I will never forgive you," Tad said.

"Hazel," he croaked out.

"Hazel will meet us at the hospital. They are on their way now. Don't be soft and die in some library in the middle of Ambassador Row right when it seems you're going to get over yourself and be happy," Tad continued.

He could tell Tad was trying to keep him awake, but he just couldn't do it. His mind went back to that day in Virginia Beach, Hazel turning toward him in the waves, the sun setting behind her. Only that time, she reached for him and started back to him. He reached out his hand to grab her, a smile ticking up the corner of his mouth.

FOURTEEN

HAZEL

SHE WASN'T SURE WHAT LIFE WOULD LOOK LIKE WHEN SHE ARRIVED at the hospital. She knew from the comms that both Luke and Vi were unconscious and that both had lost tremendous amounts of blood. Both could die at Illyana's hand, their blood shed to keep a profitable shipping route open for black market guns. Thankfully, her sister had also taken Illyana out in the melee, and the Titan Group guys had taken out Ambassador Neil and Phillip. Luke had created a few safety nets in case something went wrong. He just hadn't planned on bleeding out while the others executed those backup plans, or that Vi would have to join them in that hellscape for those plans to work.

The hospital was chaos around her. Machines were beeping and people were racing past her. The sterile lights were so bright that they hurt her eyes. Seb's grip on her hand was tight as he pulled them to the OR waiting room. Numbness had overtaken her the moment she'd seen Luke go down in that hallway. Then, Vi and Max had rushed into that insane trap and all hell had broken loose. She'd never be able to get those sounds out of her head, or the visions out of her memory. Luke down, Vi down. Vi being held by that crazy bitch, her knife at Vi's throat.

Her skin felt clammy, her face hot, her own vision iffy. She tugged her hand out of Seb's and sprinted to the trashcan in the waiting room, emptying her stomach into it. She vomited until there was nothing left in her stomach, until the soothing voices and hands at her back stopped and a cool washcloth was tucked into her hand.

"Hazey, they're going to be okay. Shhhh, they're going to be okay." Seb had stayed with her, summoning Theo to help with a cold cloth. His words were reassuring, his tone more so, yet he couldn't know, couldn't promise her that the two most important people in her life would live through the night.

The thought made her wretch again, but her stomach was empty by then and painful shudders racked her body. She felt weak, and like she wanted to sleep and wake up when the nightmare was over, yet she couldn't close her scratchy eyes.

"Hazel, honey, the doctor just came in," Seb said, helping her to stand. Thank God he was holding her up. She didn't think she could stand on her own.

"A great deal of blood . . . clean . . . stable . . . not out of the woods . . . " Hazel didn't really know what the reports were exactly, just that she felt Seb relax against her, a tension breaking in the room.

She heard Theo from somewhere behind her, "Oorah!" Relief robbed her of breath, the gratefulness at the words caught in her tight throat, the adrenaline crash making her weaker.

She saw Mila coming around another hallway into the room, was gathered in the other woman's embrace and held tightly. Heard Mila murmuring against her, yet she was still out of her own body, as if she was watching everything happen, a sleep-walking version of herself. She let Mila lead her to a bathroom and allowed her to help her brush her own teeth, wash her own face, brush her hair for her. Mila led her back through the waiting area and down the hall, machines still beeping everywhere, FBI agents lining the hallways, cops speaking with guys in dark suits. She saw Theo with an agent and a cop, their heads nodding. She saw one of them slap him on the back. A feeling of jubilation existed in the hallway and yet she still felt asleep with her eyes wide open, as if held that way by tiny cartoon toothpicks.

"Luke is still out of it, Hazey, but he's going to be okay. He didn't survive multiple deployments to die in a stupid party back here in DC," Mila said, nodding at a door to her left.

"Vi is waking up in here." Mila turned her to the door on her right.

She mindlessly followed Mila into Vi's room and went to her sister, clutching her hand in her own. "Vi . . . " she whispered. Vi's eyes were open, crinkled at the edges where she tried to smile. Thick bandages covered her throat and IVs ran along her arms. Her skin was pale, but she was alive.

Vi squeezed her hand, a wordless reassurance. She reached down to hug her gently. "Rest, Vi, you just rest. I'll be here."

Another squeeze to her hand and Vi's eyes blinked slowly a few times before drooping closed. Hazel stayed with her until she knew Vi was asleep, Max acting as sentinel over her sister.

"Go to Luke. I've got her," he said, his voice low to not wake Vi. How he knew what she had needed to hear, she didn't know. Max seemed to be a very emotionally intelligent guy, and extremely observant.

"If you're sure," she whispered back. "I'll be right across the hall. Get me if anything changes, please." Her voice broke on the please. Before she could turn away, Max had stood and hugged her gently.

"She's a warrior. She will be okay. I'll grab you if she wakes up again, but right now, Luke needs you."

Hazel whispered, "Thank you," to him, gave her sister another check and left the room as silently as possible. She knew Max would protect her sister, would die himself before he let anything happen to her. She only hoped that Vi was completely okay after nearly having her throat slit. The visual hit her memory again before she could brace herself, knocking the breath out of her. Her sister was definitely a warrior. She mentally braced herself and crossed the hall to Luke's room.

The door was open slightly, and she saw Tad sitting next to the bed while Theo stood at the foot. She'd seen Brian talking to one of the guys in suits in the hallway, and Nate was heading their way with two cups of coffee in his hands.

She pushed the door open, two pairs of eyes coming to her as she did so. Seb gave her a small smile, and Theo crossed to her.

"He's been awake, asking about Vi. He just fell back asleep and the doc says that's normal. He's going to be okay. They're just letting his body heal. Making sure he continues to react well to the blood he was given, watching for infection, that sort of thing," Theo updated her. She nodded to him as he spoke, but her eyes were on Luke. His normally tan skin looked pale and waxy, but the machines beeped steadily.

Tad had stood up and crossed over to them, and Nate had joined the room with the coffee. "You stay, Hazey. We'll check in on Vi and then finish up taking care of some of the legal aspects of this. Seb has talked with our contacts in the White House, and Callum and his team located Phillip's brother Brady for questioning," he said.

"Are we in trouble? Did something happen?" she asked, her mind going to worst-case scenario.

"Not at all," Tad assured her. "This is standard practice and because we are newer to this aspect of join operations, I want to make sure everything is buttoned up. My business partner would kick my ass if we messed up on our first op of this kind," he said, a smile on his handsome face.

She exhaled a knot of tension that crept up, worried about how Titan Group worked and what it all meant to do joint ops, with a handler at the White House, working with the alphabet soup of contacts. In the insanity of the last week, she really hadn't stopped to consider what it all meant. Her eyes flew back to Luke, assessing.

"He's good, Hazey. He just needs the rest," Tad reassured her, serious again.

She didn't think she could talk at that moment, emotion overwhelming her. Without another word, she stepped toward the bed and sank into the chair next to Luke. She heard the guys file out of the room, heard the snick of the door as they closed it behind them. Contrary to the hallways of the hospital, the rooms were dimmed at this hour. IVs pumped meds into Luke and his chest rose and fell in a steady rhythm.

She laid her head down on the side of the bed. She'd called Luke a week ago and now he was laying in a hospital bed, after almost dying before her eyes on some screen in DC. He'd survived war, leading special forces, that last op that had gone bad, the loss of some of his team, the loss of Alex, Max's brother. And yet, there he laid, strong. Alive. Hers. Tears leaked from the corners of her eyes, the physical manifestation of her jumbled thoughts and wild emotions. She had called him. He'd come for her, keeping her safe, helping save Vi. He was her past, and now he was her future.

She curled into him as much as she could without jostling him or waking him. Her tears were wet on her cheeks and her body was drained. Weariness weighed her down. At first, she thought she had imagined the tug on her hair. Then another tug. Luke's hand had curled around her face, his thumb attempting to dry her tears.

Her head popped up, her eyes wide on his sleepier ones. "Luke!" she whisper-yelled. "Oh, Luke, thank God you're okay." A sob caught in her throat, her head lowering back down to his chest.

"Hazel." His voice was groggy, and yet firm. He tipped her chin back up, meeting her eyes. There was a seriousness there, a finality that she didn't understand.

"Hazel. I can't do this. You should go to Vi," he said, his finite words ripping her heart in two.

"Can't do this?" she asked. "Can't do what?" She sat up more fully.

"This. Us. You, I just can't. It's too much. I can't do my job when I'm worrying about you." His words were so simple, so direct, and yet they pinged around her brain in tumultuous pangs.

"Worried about me?" she parroted him.

"I can't do it, Hazel. I've made my decision, and it's final. You should go to Vi," Luke said, his hand dropping to his own side. He closed his eyes, shutting her out.

She didn't know what to say. *He'd* decided. He'd considered, thought about them, and that was final? He'd decided. All on his own. He made the decision that they weren't happening. There was no *us* because he said so.

She stood, backed away from the bed, confusion, anger, pain warring within her. She waited, waited for him to say more, waited for words to come to her own throat to fight this craziness. They'd just found this in each other and now nothing? She waited and waited, and the words didn't come. Luke held himself still and refused to open his eyes, refused to say more. She knew he was still awake, she could tell. He simply shut her out. Turned away from what she had thought they were building, from feelings she had thought he shared, a future for the two of them. Did she really know him at all if he was willing to do this?

She turned from him and, in a daze, staggered for the door, trying not to cry. She ran smack dab into a broad chest on the other side of the door. Hands flew to her shoulders, steadying her. "Hazel, did something happen?" Tad asked, moving her slightly to look at Luke in his hospital bed.

He must have seen something then. Luke must have been willing to open his eyes for Tad, just not her. She heard Tad huff out a, "Dumb fucker," under his breath before he released her.

She stepped around him and left the room, crossing the quieted hallway to her sister's door. She heard Luke's door shut behind her, a finality to the future she had dreamed about with the only man she had allowed herself to dream of.

She looked in the window, brought up short by the sight in front of her. Max was lying in the hospital bed with Vi, his lab Blitz somehow smuggled into the hospital and tucked against her other side. All three were sleeping, the machines beeping in the patterns they should. Safe. Protected. Alive. The perfect matches for each other.

She dropped the hand that had gone to the doorknob, pulling up short. She paused, looked back down the hallway. The agents were gone, the cops were gone, only a night nurse could be seen charting in the lowered lights. She was alone. All alone, and so weak. She'd been sleepwalking these last hours, not strong enough to stand on her own when shit had gone sideways, not strong enough to even yell at Luke. So weak. She'd been tested, and she'd failed. Failed herself, failed Vi, failed Luke.

She glanced back through the window at her sister, Max and Blitz. "Love you Vi," she promised. She turned then and headed down the lonely hallway, toward the coming morning, her heart broken, her disappointment in herself propelling her forward.

PART TWO
JUNE

FIFTEEN

HAZEL

HAZEL HAD NEVER SEEN ANYTHING MORE BEAUTIFUL THAN THE sight laid out before her, sparkling like the lost city of Atlantis, rising from the sea after falling from favor of long-departed deities. The walls of the fort, lit with brightly flaming torches, reflected on the rippling water outside of the moat. Boats anchored in the dark waters with party lights stringing across their bows glittered against the waves. The stars sparkled in the inky, clear sky overhead and the jewels, my God, the jewels on the guests were stunning.

It was the perfect place to put her past behind her and move on. Finally, move on. Her heartbreak over Luke had lasted long enough, and it was time to grow up. Here, she could do that. Here, for tonight, she was Hazel Burke, lauded food writer gaining national popularity for highlighting the cultural foods across the oceanic state of Florida, date of Dan Perry, the dashing and rich son of Miami royalty.

She shook herself slightly and stepped away from the edge of the boat. The breeze off the water was incredible, but in her satiny dress, held together with the thinnest straps crisscrossing her back, she should go inside the walls of Fort Jefferson. Their boat was one of the largest berths in Garden Key for the event, and because of the sheer size of the vessel and the fact that the Perry family hosted the festivities, they'd taken priority and were able to dock directly versus anchor and take smaller boats up to the narrow dock.

Dating Dan was new, and not a serious, nor a long-term thing, yet he had insisted she join him for this lavish affair, something his parents hosted annually. She was glad she had joined him too, as the feast for her senses was truly stunning and she needed to lose herself a bit. She couldn't help it if the deepest corner of her heart wished she were there with someone else, and that they were the only boat there, exploring the sea and sand alone under the night sky. Luke would have loved this place. He had loved the water, always. They used to joke as kids that he was part fish. She guessed that was what had made him such a great Marine; he was at home in the water.

She sighed deeply, once again, and stepped down onto the wooden dock. Fort Jefferson, located on Garden Key in the Dry Tortugas, was the southernmost National Park in the United States. It had once held Dr. Samuel Mudd, the physician who saved the life of Lincoln's assassin, James Wilkes Booth. Mudd had been tried and convicted, then imprisoned in this island fort. It was most accessible via Key West, which is where she'd been for the last week learning about the cultural foods and practices of the islands for the book she dreamed of writing someday. She and Vi had that dream in common. Her heart gave another little clench at the thought of Vi back in DC. She missed her sister, but she needed to be decidedly not in DC. Her gaze shifted back to the sight before her.

The torches seen on the walls and walkways overhead were more for necessity and safety for the arriving boats than for lighting the path for visitors, as they'd been asked to remain on the main floor. Hazel had thought that the torches visible as they arrived seemed to glow out of nowhere. The boat had been on

dark water for a few hours when it slowed and an announce-
ment had been made that they were near. Hazel had made her
way to the bow and was struck breathless as the fort appeared
on the horizon. It was practically mythical in how it rose out of
the deep sapphire waters upon the sand bars.

She imagined the stories these walls could tell. The lighthouse had recently been repaired and shone brightly over the
fort, grounds, and surrounding waters. The Perry family had
gone all out for their annual affair, with lush, tropical flowers
and large, glass hurricanes protecting flickering candles lighting
the path from the dock to the inner courtyard of the fort. There,
they had a large ballroom floor recreated for dinner and dancing.
The arched hallways of the fort were also lit with the hurricanes
and candles, casting deep, swaying shadows across the brick.
They'd roped off much of the actual fort past the main story
courtyard and halls, likely meeting the extent of what their
money could buy for an event in the National Park.

She wished Violet and Max could see this, her sister and new
brother-in-law. Violet would love this place and how beautiful it
all was. Vi loved history and had been super jealous when Hazel
described the party to her during their FaceTime call this
morning.

She'd had to cut her sister off about the historical facts
surrounding Fort Jefferson. Yes, it was a stunning marvel of
brick masonry, yes, it was one of the largest forts in America, and
yes . . . it had never been finished before it was rendered obsolete
with the arrival of the rifled cannon. Her sister's windy words of
wonder were nice to hear. Hazel herself just didn't care as much.

Alas, Vi and Max were in newlywed love and awaiting the
birth of their first son. Hazel was insanely happy for her sister,
and she herself loved Max. She just needed some time away
from their glow of happiness and, well, time away from the
home they shared and constant presence of Luke. Her heart
clenched painfully again.

Luke, the boy who always been the other half to her, turned

into the hardened Marine who led special forces teams through six tours abroad. Luke, the man she'd always love, but who would never see her as anything more than the little sister he needed to look after, or maybe even worse, a distraction that could get him killed.

Luke, who had sent her away from him, hours after practically dying at the hands of a crazy person and whispering her name as he hit the ground. At least he was alive. He had survived, and that had to be all that mattered.

She'd begged an unconscious Luke to live, to come back to her, to open his eyes, to move his hand on hers in that hospital bed. And when he did? It was to push her away.

She was jolted from her inner pain by a warm hand across her back. "Hazel, darling, come and meet some more of my friends," Dan said as he handed her a cold glass of bubbly.

She needed to forget Luke, and this was the place to do it. Dan was a new thing for her, and while she wasn't sure she'd see him again after tonight's fun date, she might as well enjoy the evening. She shook the shadows from her mind.

She smiled brightly at Dan and linked her arm across his back. "Absolutely, lead the way!"

SIXTEEN

LUKE

WELL, SHE'D DONE IT. SHE'D LEFT DC, HER SISTER AND MAX, HER home, him, and flown south. He didn't know if he should be grateful or if he should wallow in the agony of not seeing her face every day, hating himself for taking something so precious from her, only to push her away when he had to. He supposed he'd settle on gratitude, as he had been the one to push her away, even though it gutted him to do so.

He didn't think he could handle being so close to her and not being with her a moment longer. After being nearly killed, that old fear had taken over and he felt like a shell of himself, watching his life from a black hole. A waking coma. He worked out, he recuperated, he wished things were different. He died a little more each day knowing he couldn't ever have a future with her, even as his body physically healed and got stronger, sharper.

Maybe in a different life, they could be together, but with his track record, he couldn't do that to either of them. Even if he had started to wonder, trepidatiously, if he could break free from his family patterns of trauma, a relationship with him would only put her in danger and he would not stand for that. Loving her, protecting her, laughing with her had been air to him. He'd relished having a reason to keep her close. Hell, they'd shared the hottest moments of his life in the days before it all went to shit. He'd never had anything like that with anyone else and he knew without a shadow of a doubt, she was the best thing that would ever happen to him. And he'd fucked it up.

His throat tightened again thinking about that moment in the hospital, watching her walk out of his room and wishing he could die then, or wishing he wasn't such a broken man.

He needed her to move on, though. His career in the military may be over, but the new path he and Tad had been building was going to be more dangerous than ever before. If almost losing Violet last fall, whom he considered a sister, had almost gutted him, he could never love and then lose Hazel. Not after his mom.

He was startled at the knocking on his office door. He'd been ensconced in his space inside of the Dupont Circle mansion home base he shared with Max and Violet, although they lived in the western wing of the property.

"Luke, man, you in there?" he heard Tad knock again and ask.

"Ya, c'mon in," Luke replied. He'd healed physically from the attack on his life and he stood up to hug Tad without a wince as he greeted his brother in arms. Max trailed in behind him and he nodded at his housemate before sitting back down. Thank God for good physical therapists and treadmills. And Tad, who had carried him out of the hellfire. "Drink?" he asked them both.

"Obviously," Tad replied. He waved Luke back into sitting. "But I know how to pour myself your expensive whiskey, so sit back down." He grabbed the bottle of Johnny Walker Diamond Jubilee from the bar cart and filled a deep green, heavy glass decanter for each man while Max watched silently. Luke would have to make a note to thank Violet. Those Estelle glasses really were a nice Christmas gift. He felt Max's eyes on him and prepared himself for whatever intervention his guys thought they were about to have. Tad had poured from one of the rarest bottles in the house, which meant he was in for a doozy of a lecture.

"You should have taken the service while you can get it asshole, I'm completely healed and I'm fine now," Luke groused.

"All except that broken heart, right?" Tad poked, but his face held a concerned edge. No one knew him better than Tad. Tad, who had not only carried him out that night, but had practically been his shadow over the last months while he worked his way back to form. His gaze swung to Max, still silently watching him.

"Fuck off. Subject closed," Luke barked out. Shit, he knew these guys cared, but he wasn't going there with either one of them again. He'd heard a version of it when he first sent Hazel away from his hospital room. He'd seen the silent fucking version of it every time they looked at him with pity in their eyes. And didn't he deserve that? He'd taken from her and then sent her away, heart breaking and believing the words he'd spewed at her to get her to walk away, the only words he knew she wouldn't argue with. The lies he told.

"The subject is not closed, Luke. Look, I know what you are thinking. I know what losing your mom and then your dad walking away did to you," Tad said, diving straight into the complicated subject with his trademark clarity and directness. "And before you lay into me, just hear me now. You are a good person. You deserve to be happy. You deserve a family, you deserve Hazel."

Sometimes it really sucked that your brothers in arms knew so much about you.

"And when something happens to one of us? Will you stand by me when I burn the world down if something happens to her?" Luke asked angrily. "How can you even suggest this when we are hard launching this business?" His voice grew to a roar.

"A business that will demand we are directly in danger each

and every damn day." He felt anguish curdle in his gut, the hopelessness he'd carried since he told her to walk away, piercing his heart. "He has a pregnant wife and can barely leave her side for ten seconds and you expect me to love Hazel freely and still lead Titan Group?!" His shout would have reverberated through the walls of a lesser house, it would have caused lesser men than the other two grown men in the room to shrink as he'd raged and pointed to Max.

He saw Tad's face tighten in his own anger but couldn't make himself look Max in the eyes. It hurt too much.

"I can suggest this because we do not live in fear, Luke!" Tad yelled, his face inches from Luke's own, his own muscular frame towering over where Luke was sitting.

"You are a goddamn Marine. You do not make decisions in fear. Every single day, men and women like us go out and fight the assholes of the world, leaving behind loved ones, walking away from our families to take care of the boogie men. Every single day, man. This is who we are, what we do," Tad continued, his tone leaving no space for argument.

"You cannot continue to choose fear, Luke, that can't be who you are." Tad's words piercing the fog in Luke's brain, his eyes begging his friend to truly hear him.

"Luke Stratton does not let fear win. He does not let fear pull him under and make him a shell of a man. Luke Fucking Stratton is a Raider and he will not fuck up his life any more out of fear." Tad's heated voice had gentled at the end of the rant, the softness of the words belying the strength in them.

Fuck. Tad and Max knew him better than anyone. He stood blinking at Tad then, his words a cooling mist over the haze he'd been drowning in throughout the months without Hazel.

Was he right? Shit. Yes, he was. Luke hung his head down, shame washing over him. He had been living in fear. His mom had taught him better than that. Could it be that easy? Could he just decide to put his fear on the back burner and man up? Was he strong enough to do the work to get past his fears?

Max's voice finally broke the silence, the timber rolling across him.

"Get some altitude on this, brother. Ask yourself why you are completely fine with me being with Vi, but you become murderous thinking about any other guy with Hazey. If they're both like 'sisters' to you, you'd be happy to have someone from the military love her. We are all your brothers, your men, your team, Luke. This is Titan Group, man. You'd be thrilled for one of them to be looking out for her long-term," he pushed on, forcing Luke to look over and meet his own eyes.

"Nothing really hard here, buddy, and I'm saying this with all the love in my heart. Think about why it isn't ok for one of them to be with Hazel. I'll fill you in, because Hazel isn't 'like your sister.' She's your endgame. She's it. I love you, man, but you need to get your shit together here." He rose, laid his big hand on Luke's shoulder and squeezed.

"My pregnant wife needs me. It's been longer than ten seconds and I need her." His smile flashed across his face, nodded at Tad and left the room. Trust Max to feel absolutely comfortable in not wanting to go ten seconds without being with his new wife. Jealousy rose hotly within him at what his buddy had. Violet here, happily pregnant with Max's baby. Protected, happy, living her best life. Blitz tucked along their respective sides.

Fuck. He was an idiot.

He needed to call Hazel. Hell, he needed to go to her in fucking Key West. He looked back up at Tad.

"You're right, you know that. Fuck, I hate it when you're right." He felt lighter after saying the words. Hope began to trickle through his nerves, tingling along his fingertips.

"Ya, man. I am always right. Don't forget that either. But for now, let's get down to business." Tad laughed lightly. "And Luke, then you can run off to beg forgiveness for being a dumbass, but only after you talk to the team doc so you can move past this."

He stood then and hugged Tad. "Thanks man. You can bet your ass that's my plan, so talk fast. You've got about thirty seconds before I call for the jet." He laughed and stepped back, dropping back into his chair to go over the next steps in their business plan as quickly as possible.

They had created something incredible, and potentially incredibly dangerous. They had the capacity, the knowledge, the contacts and the skills to do what Uncle Sam couldn't. They could leverage those things to take care of what the government couldn't or wouldn't. Not vigilantes, the real off the books stuff that happened every day, out of the scope of the alphabet agencies. Tad's family had been in the business for years, and now Titan Group would move into the sector officially. The situation late last fall had slowed them down some, but they were full steam ahead again, and all the guys were in. After what went down with Wills and Mila, the guys were champing at the bit to get back out there actively. Titan Group was about to be a reality.

His thoughts drifted back to Max briefly, and to what he had said, the rightness of the words settling in his gut. Max's new baby was going to be his nephew practically. The man never wanted to be separated from his wife and yet, he was all in on Titan Group, as was Vi. He also knew that if anything happened to Max, Violet would kill him herself. There was that fear talking again. He pushed through those dark thoughts and re-focused on what Tad was saying, mentally flagging it was time to see their team therapist again asap.

The ringing of his secure cell interrupted them. Tad looked up at him questioningly and shrugged his shoulders when Luke showed him the name on the caller ID. Luke tapped the green button and placed Commander Cullins on speakerphone. Cullins had been one of his superiors in the Marines and had gone on to serve in a leadership position of secretive scope at both the Pentagon and the White House. He was Luke and Tad's primary "handler" for Titan Group, whether they operated independently or as part of a joint operation.

"Commander, to what do I owe this honor? Kind of early in the business plan for a courtesy call, yes?" Luke said.

"I think you'll want this assignment, boys. We've gotten word that a party at Fort Jefferson has been attacked. One of the attendees was able to put a call out as masked men were swarming, weapons drawn. Unfortunately, the call was cut short, but intel picked up Farsi being spoken in the background and we know there were gunshots. The party is being thrown by a prominent Florida-based family and we aren't sure why they were targeted yet, but we do have a guest list," Commander Cullins shared.

"Okay, that does sound bad, but we aren't ready yet, sir, with all due respect. I can get you contacts that speak the language . . . " Tad started to speak but alarm bells were ringing in Luke's ears. A Florida-based family? Why hadn't Cullins just called the guys at Naval Air Station Key West?

"Hazel Burke," Commander Cullins barked out. "Hazel Burke is at the party, or was at the party. Hazel is now a hostage of whoever raided the party," Cullins went on, but Luke heard nothing but those damn proverbial alarm bells ringing in his ears.

Luke felt like he'd been stabbed again, as if ice water was flowing through his veins, chased by fiery gasoline. "How in the fuck is that possible?" he shouted.

"We know the location, the language and some approximations, but we don't know why or how many assholes we are dealing with. We've decided to go in quietly. There are too many VIPs at that party to risk at this moment," Cullins was telling Tad.

"Copy, we're on it. Send us everything you have," Tad told the Commander. Cullins agreed and hung up.

"Luke, man, we're going to get her, you have to breathe," Tad assured his friend as he quickly tapped out a message on his phone. "Breathe, brother, we're going to get her back."

Tad's voice faded into a rush in his ears. He was not reassured, he was enraged. He didn't know what the fuck was happening, but he was going to kill anyone standing between himself and Hazel.

SEVENTEEN

HAZEL

THEY'D BEEN ROUNDED UP INTO SMALL GROUPS AND WERE BEING guarded by four men at each group. Each group had been also separated from each other, creating an isolation factor to the fear. She didn't know if others were alive, where they were, she knew nothing about what was happening outside of the horror around her.

Her group had been taken to the third level of the fort, deep into the dark recesses of the brick structure. She could see the ocean outside of the window, a swirling and dark mass crashing against the outer walls. She guessed that maybe three to four hours had passed. The once sparkling night sky had clouded over slightly and she shivered. The water had grown choppy and gray outside of the key, mimicking the darkness descending over the once glittering party.

The guards with her group spoke very little to them, herding them around with grunts and guns. Dan was in her group and had been rendered practically catatonic with fear. She wished Luke was here. He would know what to do. She sent up a silent prayer that Luke would come for her, although she didn't see how that was possible. There was no way to call him, or her sister, or Max. She thought of her heavily pregnant sister and tried not to cry. She wanted to be an aunt. She wanted to hold Baby Alex as soon as he made his debut. She wanted to fight for Luke. She cursed herself for the seventy-ninth time since being ushered to this dark corner by crazed gunmen for leaving the safety of DC. For listening to Luke in that hospital room when he woke up and pushed her away.

The guards were clearly aggressive and well-armed. She heard cries in the night from other guests, occasional shouting, and a few shots peppering the eeriness. She wondered if coming upon a fort typically inhabited more by sea turtles than people to find it flush with people in full party mode was not on their agenda. It seemed like they were in a holding pattern until they reassessed, and she wondered what they were holding for. Had they intended to raid the party or the place? She wasn't sure which. Something was off about their captors. She felt the right-ness of the thoughts in her gut as she tried to catalog as much about the attackers as possible. Seb had talked about doing so as they watched that party at Ambassador Neil's townhome all those months ago, and it had stayed with her.

A woman in her group was yelling at one of the guards again. She'd been particularly brazen in telling them all how important she was and how they'd pay for this. "You can't keep me like this for long asshole, let us go," she slurred. Shit, the woman was drunk and did not understand the gravity of the situation.

"Silence!" one of their guards shouted at the woman.

"If you want money, this is a shitty way to go about it. No one can help you in this dank hallway," the woman continued. "Seriously, you assholes . . . " Her rant was cut off by the piercing of a bullet.

Oh my God! They'd shot her! Hazel gasped, reaching for the woman as she went down, but she was already dead before she hit the ground. Hazel caught her against her own body right before her head hit the ground. The lifeless weight heavy in her arms, she glared up at the accuser. She didn't know this woman, but she didn't deserve to die. Hazel had also acted without thought, reaching for the woman before any self-preservation instinct had a chance to kick in. She also opened her mouth before that instinct caught up with her.

"Why? Why are you doing this?" she softly asked, fear streaking through her, but unable to stay quiet.

The guard who had shot the woman leaned down to her and used the butt of his gun to strike at her face. She couldn't move quickly enough with the woman's body in her arms and took the brunt of the hit on her cheekbone. Pain exploded through her head as she fell wholly back onto her butt, her arms shaking from still trying to hold on to the woman so her head didn't hit the hard ground.

"No more talking!" the guard shouted then in a heavily accented voice. God, she'd hear that voice in her nightmares if she ever made it out of this alive. She tried to bank down her fear and sent another prayer up for help. She had to learn when to keep her mouth shut and when to speak up, something that had failed her so far in life. Her courage felt new and tenuous, like she wasn't quite sure when to flex that muscle.

The other partygoers in her group were crying and whispering nervously among themselves. Dan was at the edge of the group, and she couldn't see his face. He was going to be zero help, obviously. She shivered again. She'd known there was something off about him. What an ass. Violet laid the woman down gently and pressed herself against the bricks at her back again.

She sent up another prayer that somehow, someway, Luke would find her before it was too late.

EIGHTEEN

LUKE

THEY WERE IN THE AIR TWENTY ONE MINUTES AFTER COMMANDER Cullins hung up the phone. They had no time to waste. If whoever had raided the party had already left the little island with Hazel, the chances of anyone seeing her again were less than zero. Fuck! This was on him! He'd pushed her away and now he may lose her forever. He worked to push that fear back down.

Tad had called in Calder Gray, a buddy from their college days. Calder had joined the Coast Guard and had served in the watery graveyards of the world's oceans in heavy search and rescue. He was back in his native Keys now and was mobilizing ground support there while the DC group made their way south.

Max had been in papa bear mode, thankfully containing Violet to their home and command center. Tad had rounded up the others, and they were en route via helicopter to Key West. From there, they'd refuel before dropping onto a boat they'd deployed right out of range from the island fort. Calder would join them if all went according to plan, yet was ready to roll ahead of them in case they needed him to go out sooner. It was tricky. Farsi was not a common language in the Keys. No, something major had pierced the safety of the island chain and the beautiful old fort.

They had to go in quietly, and they needed to understand the scope. He knew they could handle most things, but there were only so many of them and so many weapons available. They needed to get to Hazel and the other hostages as their primary objective, but they didn't even know how many hostages there were, their status, nothing.

His gut tightened in fury as he watched the miles race by below them. The Coast Guard was mobilizing to rescue the party guests as well. A team from Naval Air Station Key West was deploying and local Key West cops were on standby. Cullins wanted to go in quietly which, combined with his knowledge of Luke's ties to the Burkes, was why he called in Titan Group. From what Luke had overheard from Tad telling Seb as they loaded up, there were some serious VIPs also in attendance and delicacy was the name of the game for the first wave of response. Luke gave zero fucks about Cullins and his orders at this point. All bets were off, knowing Hazel was involved. If they could carry this off quietly, it would be a miracle.

"Mila, tell me what we've got again," he said tersely.

"Okay Luke," her typical sunshine dulled, knowing they were racing against the clock to save one of their own.

"I've sent the small fleet of drones with Wills. Once you are on the boat, you can send them in for closer recon. They don't have the payload for weapons, but we're working on that and I hope to have a few of those UAVs available by the time you hit Key West," she went on.

"The smaller drones will give you heat signatures and locations. I've sent the schematics of the fort to your iPads and Wills will have everything running once on board the boat," she said.

"Good. Thanks, Mila," he replied.

"Tad, talk to me. What else does Cullins know?" he asked Tad.

"Still no word on who is behind the attack. They have limited chatter, and no one is claiming responsibility for it yet, which scares the fuck out of me. If this was the end game, they'd be all over about what they'd done as soon as they had the island locked down, which should have been fast work. However, speaking of drones, the government has been using carbon fiber, remotely crewed boats to patrol our southern waters for the last ten to fifteen years. Essentially, drone boats. They call them barracudas. The boats closest to Key West are unbothered and haven't picked up anything. One of the boats closer to the midway point between Key West and the Dry Tortugas was disabled about four hours ago. They'd been trying to bring it back online, but hadn't been too concerned until the initial hostage call came in," Tad said. "Cullins is sending four more barracudas now, but the timing might not help us," Tad replied.

"Coast Guard ready, Calder in play, and he's got guys mobilizing as well for anything you personally need-separate from the Coasties," Mila said. He felt a measure of pride in that; the Coasties were badasses. Hell, they'd been the only armed forces until the Navy was formed in 1798. Knowing he had Calder and a team of practical fucking fish ready, he was ready to take on whatever was out there to get to his Hazel.

Seb waded in, "Violet said that Hazel told her the party was a formal thing, hosted annually by the new guy's family. They essentially rent out a portion of Fort Jefferson and their extremely exclusive guests arrive by boat."

"What do we know about Fuckstick's family?" Luke ground out.

"If Miami had a royal family, this would be it. They own more land than anyone else along the southern seaboard and made their fortune in oil and gas out of Mobile. Fuckstick is the only son. He's a partier and a ladies' man," Wills spoke from his laptop.

"AND WHAT IN THE FUCK IS SHE DOING WITH HIM?" Luke roared, his voice echoing over the headphones they'd donned in the helicopter. His team silently regarded him for a full minute, and he knew he needed to get a handle on himself. He needed to be at this best to save her. The flip of the switch from stoicism to rage was bound to happen, and it seemed that he'd finally cracked. He dropped his head back and squeezed his eyes shut to focus.

"Luke, honey, you told her to go," Violet's quiet whisper spoke up from command central back in DC, crackling across the airwaves.

He rolled his shoulders back at her words and took a deep breath. She was right, damn it. He had sent her away from him.

"Well, I am the dumbest motherfucker out there, aren't I?" he asked as he looked down. No one replied. They didn't need to. He was absolutely the dumbest motherfucker alive for letting her leave him and when he got to her, he would tell her that too.

They touched down in Key West right at the three-hour mark from Commander Cullins's call. Refueling and loading the single larger UAV with added payload capacity took less than five minutes. Luke had never before been more grateful that he was good with money. His fortune had moved mountains at the speed he'd needed them to move. They were already ahead of the official agencies on this joint op, making him glad once again that he didn't operate in the bureaucracy any longer. Not that he would have listened to any of that bullshit with Hazel in danger.

They'd landed on his yacht and before the propeller blades had quieted completely, they deployed the smaller drones for recon off the bow of the ship. They were running right outside of any radar capabilities from the fort, and they were using a new tech that Wills had created that acted like an umbrella of protection. They had jokingly called it the 'cloak of invisibility' when they were testing it, and yet Luke hoped to hell it held. They'd never tried it on such a large coverage area and he didn't want them to be found or seen. They believed they were undetected, but they also didn't know exactly who they were dealing with.

He wasn't the only rich asshole in the world, and he wanted to be careful.

The plan was to understand the numbers and locations of people inside the fort, how it was being guarded, enter via water and then extract Hazel while killing as few of the assholes as possible so that information could be beaten out of them. He was looking forward to that part, as well as the part when he killed anyone who had touched Hazel. Depending on numbers, rescuing hostages was the priority immediately after getting Hazel off that island. That was his order of operation, although probably not Cullins's preferred order of operations.

Wills and Nate would stay on the boat in their mobile command center, Max had command center back in DC with Mila and that left the rest of them gearing up for battle. Sebastian, Tad, Theo, Brian and himself. Calder had jumped in with them and was prepared to slice through the crashing waves to save whoever needed saving. Luke sent up a silent prayer that it didn't come to that, that they didn't need the search and rescue skills he knew his buddy was the best at. Commander Cullins had pulled the Coast Guard and Callum, their old Navy SEAL buddy, with his team, in too, all of them currently en route to Miami.

Luke gave zero fucks about every single hostage and every single asshole on that island other than Hazel. His team knew that their collective and primary mission was extracting her safely and getting back to this boat unharmed. He locked in on the midnight horizon in the direction he knew the fort to be.

"I'm coming Hazelnut, hang on," he vowed, his stony words lost in the wind.

"Luke, we've got eyes in flight," Wills said over their comms. He left the bow of his yacht and made his way to the command center to watch the feeds.

"Commander Cullins is on the line, Luke," he heard Wills say.

"Commander, what do we know?" Luke asked.

"The good news is that it appears they've been releasing hostages. Coasties just picked up a few boats trying to sail together with no navigation. The guests were stripped of their phones and the boats have been wiped of all technology. They are saying they were taken to different parts of the fort and almost immediately thereafter, returned to random boats and allowed to leave. Most of these people are still tipsy or completely in shock, but they all agree that the largest yacht left there when they were pushed out was the yacht at the dock, belonging to the Perry family," Cullins went on. "Based on the numbers of people we are picking up now, there can't be that many left on the island."

"And Hazel?" Luke asked tensely.

"No sign of Hazel, nor any of the Perry family. It sounds like they were separated into smaller groups and no one has seen any of them since the initial raid." Commander Cullins replied. "Reports of gun shots, yet no one saw anyone actually go down, so we're hoping it was a scare and control tactic versus outright murderous."

"And any idea what is going on?" Nate asked into the speakerphone.

"None, but there does seem to be a general sense that the captors were after specific people. NAS Key West is locked down and guys are ready for airstrikes when we need them. If we need them, which I am hoping we don't. That will get messy," Cullins said.

Luke met Tad's eyes. That was not good news, considering the boat belonging to Fuckstick was still there. An airstrike was also a very loud way to alert the media and set off a chain reaction of congressional hearings. An airstrike on US soil was never a good idea. And an airstrike with Hazel in the vicinity? No fucking way was he going to allow that to happen.

"Copy commander. Our eyes are overhead and I see confirmation that only one large yacht remains tied up at dock. There also seem to be three smaller motorboats, like what we've seen modern day pirates using in the Middle East. One is patrolling and the two tied to the Perry yacht are empty," Wills started, zooming in on what the drones were streaming back to them.

"Confirming the two boats tied to the yacht are empty, but they've got some guards onboard the actual yacht, counting twelve, all armed," Seb relayed verbally to Cullins.

"Heat sigs are moving, one group left inside the fort. Four heat sigs with guns, eight without." He cleared his throat, tersely uttering, "Shit. Guys, we have one down."

"Repeat, there is one body down. The heat sig has cooled enough to indicate deceased. The live camera feed is too grainy at this height to tell if it is a woman or man," Wills relayed.

Luke swallowed down the bile threatening to rise in his throat. If he lost her, he would burn the world down to kill every single motherfucker who had any part of this clusterfuck.

"We don't know it's her, Luke. Focus, buddy. She needs you right now," Tad murmured to him, his hand on his shoulder. "We do not lead from fear."

"We stay the course via water. Let's get our asses on that island," he ground out.

NINETEEN

HAZEL

The guards were moving them, but she didn't know if she should be thankful for that or not. They hadn't shot anyone else, but no one else had said a word. The woman's blood had pooled beneath her and created a halo of red around her body. Hazel was sick to her stomach with the metallic smell in the surrounding air, taking over the salty freshness and dank brick smell originally there. She'd wedged herself as tightly against the brick wall and as close to the open window arches as possible. Every time the guards shifted into her direct line of sight, she shifted ever so slightly to stay a bit hidden. She needed to think. There had to be a way to get help. Her head was throbbing, the hit to her cheek already swelling. She'd been fighting to stay mentally alert, awake enough to be ready if an opportunity presented itself. Her only idea was to get out of the window, but that still left her to drop several feet, straight into the moat surrounding the fort. She hadn't decided yet which path was worse, the moat or another option.

Dan had not said one word to her. She may measure everyone against Luke from here on out, but she'd rather quietly pine for him than date this sniveling asshole. She rolled her eyes to herself. Great intentions . . . if she made it out alive. And also, she was done being quiet. If she made it out of here alive, she had something to say to Luke. He may have decided all on his own to break her heart, but she sure as hell wasn't going to stand there mute ever again. He was going to hear from her all right. *If* she made it out of this.

Her muscles were stiff, and she was freezing. The dress that had seemed so sexy earlier made her feel so exposed now. She'd braided her long reddish hair in a fishtail braid over her shoulder for the party, leaving her back exposed to the elements. She tried to ignore the scratching pain from the brick wall behind where she had been pressing herself tightly, but it had caused the straps from her dress to dig into her delicate skin, tearing it every now and then.

One of their guards spoke to her then, "move!" he commanded. He lifted the gun from where it was resting along the shoulder strap and pointed it at her. She fell into line behind Dan's mom and followed her along the path the guards were directing. They were in a single file line, winding down the old fort to the main entrance.

She could see other guards milling about, guns trained on the snaking line of hostages she was in, but she couldn't see any other groups of hostages. She wondered again what was happening.

As they neared the shore, a smaller motorboat bobbed against the rocks with two guards in it. The guards leading their line began to push people in line ahead of her to the boat. Were they letting them go? Hope rushed through her, making her lightheaded. God, please let them let us go, she prayed internally.

When they got to Dan's mom, though the guards began yelling to each other in some foreign language even louder. It sounded Middle Eastern, but she couldn't be sure. She thought again of Luke, and wished he were here with her, even though she was still mad at him.

Dan's mom, a delicate woman in her mid-sixties named Celeste, was roughly shoved in the direction of her own yacht. A guard had peeled off and was pointing the gun now directly at Hazel, motioning for her to follow Celeste. She lifted her open palms up and nodded her head, causing pain to sear through her. She needed to go along with this as long as possible, hoping there would be an opportunity to escape down the road so she could get some damn Tylenol.

She turned her head more slowly the next time and saw two more guards directing Dan and his father Ralph toward their own yacht as well. Oddly, it was only the four of them being herded back to the Perry family yacht. The four of them and a guard for each one of them.

The others were placed in the little motorboat and shoved off the shoreline, with a guard telling them to leave or be killed. The two guards who had been onboard the smaller vessel jumped to shore and started walking her way. The boat full of the other partygoers left as fast as they could, not one of them even glancing back at the Perry family or Hazel.

She was about to step onto the wooden dock leading to the yacht when all hell broke loose.

She saw the guard next to her go down in her peripheral vision, and she turned in time to see a figure rising out of the dark waters, completely covered in a wetsuit, goggles covering the eyes. The figure appeared as a modern-day Poseidon rising angrily from the sea. He was huge and terrifying, and coming right for her. She heard bullets pinging around her and more yelling in that foreign language. Two more guards dropped around her, dead before they finished yelling. Shit! She refused to freeze again, to watch while life was happening around her. She turned to run back to the fort. If she could get there, maybe she could hide long enough for help to come.

She'd made it one full step before Poseidon grabbed her and

turned her back for the water while she thrashed against him. What in fresh hell was this?! Terrify her and then drown her? Why not just shoot her? She clawed at the neoprene arm banded around her.

Dan and his parents were shoved onto the yacht by the remaining guards as she saw more figures emerging from the sea. Another small motorboat came rushing at her as she was dragged through the water and held tightly against the strong figure. She couldn't get loose, no matter how hard she fought.

"Hazelnut, knock that shit off, it's me," she heard Luke grunt into her ear.

He'd come for her! Oh, thank God, they'd found her. How? She started to ask him, but he cut her off, "later." His hands tightened around her for the briefest of a moment before she was practically flying through the air. For an arrogant asshole, she was definitely glad to see him.

He had tossed her into the boat, another pair of strong arms coming around her to pull her in and then push her to the floor of the small vessel. Three more figures dove into the boat as the driver opened speed toward open water. Luke was formidable against her body, pinning her to the floor and returning fire at the Perry yacht and the guards firing on them.

"Keep down!" he shouted.

Bullets hit the water around them with a *thwap, thwap, thwap*. She worried that they were surely done for but before too long, the hail of bullets stopped, and they were surrounded by darkness. The slicing waves beneath them and the inky sky above them. Earlier the stars had sparkled like a blanket of diamonds, but now it was completely clouded over. She didn't know which way was up and which way was down. It was dark everywhere.

Luke eased his body off hers, pulled off his goggles and unzipped the top of his wetsuit, revealing his face and head. The other five men in the boat did the same, and she looked around at each beloved face, hardly believing they were real. She clocked a new face, but he seemed friendly.

"Shit, Hazey, that was a dramatic way to hit the dating pool in Miami!" Seb laughed.

Luke glared at him, but Seb was undaunted and continued, "Sure glad to see ya, little sis." He reached over and gave her a one-handed hug. She peeked up to see Seb glance over her shoulders at a glowering Luke.

"Stop molesting her and let her talk, asswipe," Luke demanded. Seb just laughed.

"Hazel of hotness, girl, are we glad to see you!" Theo added.

"Tell us what happened," Tad directed her.

"Start with why your face is swollen and cut," Luke said, his voice low and harsh. His eyes were hard on her. His hand had reached up to cup her swollen cheek tenderly. She was dizzy with the sheer dissonance between the harshness of his voice and the tenderness of his touch.

"We'll get you checked out once we're on board. One of my crew guys was an Army medic. I want him to check you out," he said.

"I'm okay, just shaken up. I could use some Tylenol and an ice pack, and I'll be fine," she replied. She told them about the events of the evening, just getting to the part where they'd been split up at the dock when a huge yacht came into view, towering above them.

"Guys!" She looked up at Luke quickly, unsure if she should be scared or relieved.

"It's okay, Hazey. That's Luke's baby," Tad told her.

As they neared the enormous yacht, she saw the scripted letters spelling out, *Copper Goddess* scrawled in large black letters along the back.

They boarded the yacht and tied the smaller motorboat alongside the lowered swim deck.

"Hazel," Luke lifted her hand in his own. "Brian is going to show you to a room. There should be clothes there for you. Take a hot shower and get warm. I'll get you some coffee and then I want Tom to check you out, make sure you aren't concussed.

Brian will be right outside your room if you need anything while I get the coffee and brief Tom. You need to warm up." His hand squeezed hers before letting go.

His eyes dropped to her chest. Her midnight blue satin slip dress, with the gorgeous straps crisscrossing the back, was now drenched and ruined. She shivered and knew her puckered nipples had to be plainly visible to anyone looking at her. She tried to care, but she was too tired at this point and fighting off the crash of adrenaline, the throbbing pain in her face and a splintering headache.

She watched him swallow and fight to raise his eyes back to hers. "Go get warm and grab a sweatshirt Hazel," he said.

"Luke, thank you." She reached up on her tiptoes and kissed his jaw before turning around to face Brian. She had seen Luke's clenched fists. She knew he was simply tolerating her gentle kiss to his jawline, but she didn't care. He'd had to come save her again and while that knowledge broke her heart a little wider open, standing there shivering on the back of his *Copper Goddess*, she'd had to say thank you. He had saved her when she didn't know how that was even possible. She'd think about all the rest later, post hot shower ideally.

"What. In. The. Fuck. Happened. To. Your. Back?" he bit out as she turned.

Her once pale skin was abraded with bloody scratches and deep welts from being pressed against the brick walls while being held captive. The thin, satin ribbons of her dress were stuck to the open wounds in places and hurt like hell. She hadn't said a word the entire time, but man, the salt water in those cuts hurt.

"I can't tell why it hurts so badly, but it's my own fault. I was trapped against the brick wall of the fort, and I didn't want to turn my back to any of the guards. Luke, they shot the one woman who demanded they release us. She bled out in front of me. I tried to catch her, and I asked the guard why, that's when he hit me." Hazel had turned back to him, tears rolling down her cheeks. She'd reached her breaking point.

"Shit, Hazelnut, I'm sorry." He gathered her gently in his arms and picked her up, holding her against him as closely as he could without hurting her further. His eyes met Brian's over her head.

"I've got her."

TWENTY

LUKE

HE WAS GOING TO GO BACK THERE AND KILL THOSE MOTHERFUCKERS. Dead. With his bare fucking hands. He needed to get his ass back to the bridge and call into Cullins but he'd be damned if he didn't take care of her first. He'd tried to give her a moment before he was all over her, but that was before he'd seen her back. After seeing the damage to her gorgeous skim, there was no way in hell he would leave her. Tad would know what to do and would take command while he was with Hazel. She was his primary focus.

She was his. He had tried to push her away for her own good, but he didn't know how he could survive without her. The last five hours had taught him that it didn't matter if she was with him or not, she was always going to be his. He'd never be good enough for her, but right now she needed him to help her clean her wounds and be cared for. He'd start there. No one else was going to touch her right now.

He carried her to his large cabin. This was his favorite place in the world. The hardwood gleamed in the low lighting and the entire room was done in shades of creams and soft blues and greens. He led her into the large, private bathroom adjacent to his cabin and sat her on the vanity.

He turned on the hot water and as the steam filled the room, he turned back for her. She was quiet, watchful, in shock by now he guessed.

"Hazel, I need to get your dress off you, but it will hurt you to get the straps out of your skin. Baby, I am so sorry, but I have to hurt you to help you," he said to her, meeting her eyes.

She nodded her head and gingerly jumped down from the vanity. He handed her some Tylenol to take before he got started on her straps and she downed them quickly.

When she turned her back to him, he had to bite down a slew of very bad things. The added light in the bathroom showed him that it was worse than it had looked on the swim deck in the darkness.

"Hazel, sweetheart, this is terrible. I'm so sorry for what I'm about to do," he muttered. He grabbed a clean washcloth from the drawer in front of them and got it wet with the hot water running in the shower.

He gently placed it along her cuts, holding it for longer where the thin satin pieces were stuck to the bloody and raw wounds. He moved ever so slowly, cleaning, rinsing out and wiping away her blood.

Finally, he could loosen the satin without it tearing more deeply into her. He untied the bow at the base of her back, his hands sweeping along her shivering skin.

Fuck, there was no way she had on underwear or a bra. He wanted to kill Dan for seeing her like this and his mind was running rampant wondering if that Fuckstick had tied the bow low at her back for her, his hands gripping her hips, his lips nuzzling her neck as he tied. It was what he'd do if he'd been the one to take her to the party. He never would have left her side. He would have had her dress pushed up around her hips and his cock sunk inside of her every twenty minutes of that party, using the darkness of the hallways around the fort as his personal playground. He mentally reigned himself back in, taking deep breaths to calm his own mind.

He really needed to get out of this small space with her if he was going to have any blood left in his brain and not act like a crazed animal with her. He trailed his fingers slowly along the satin straps, pulling on them ever so lightly as he went to free them from her skin. Once he had unthreaded them all from her back, she held the front portion over her breasts so the dress wouldn't fall to her feet.

He stared up at their joined reflection, his hands dropping to her satin-clad hips. Her gorgeous hazel eyes were ablaze on his in the mirror. Before his brain could talk him out of it, he kissed her upper shoulders and along her back, whispering his lips along her wounds to not hurt her. His large palms open, skimming along the sides of her hips and snaking around to her belly, pulling her more tightly to his lower body and bending her forward ever so slightly.

He continued his ministrations upon her back with his lips while his hands inched slowly upward, his thumbs rubbing along the undersides of her full breasts.

She shuddered against him and moaned quietly. His eyes flashed back to hers in the mirror as he kept his hands moving up, up, up, fully encompassing her breasts in the satin dress falling off her shoulders. He swept the top of the dress down and watched as the material gathered at her waist, held up now only by his own body, flush to hers.

He cradled her breasts in his large hands, a whisper of a caress. The need to possess her drumming though him.

"Hazel, baby . . . " he quietly murmured against her. Fuck, he needed to get her warm and stop groping her. She was in shock and didn't need him all over her right this second. He stepped back slightly.

Hazel was entranced, like she'd do anything to keep this moment forever and yet confusion skated across her face. He dropped a kiss to her exposed shoulder and gently swept his palms down, taking the satin with his hands. He helped her step out of the dress and then turned her toward his own body. He righted himself slowly, running his face as gently as possible along her bare skin as he stood. He fought for control.

He brought his hands up and helped her to the shower. "Get warm baby, I'll be right on the bridge with your coffee when you're ready to come up. I still want Tom to check you for any concussion or wounds, and he'll meet you there. If you want, I'll bring coffee to you. Whatever you need."

He forced his hands away from her chilled skin and stepped outside of the bathroom. One of his crew had miraculously been fast enough to stock the built-in dresser for her while they'd been on the chopper on the way down to Key West. There were enough clothes for every season, swimsuits, undergarments, sandals, socks and tennis shoes for her. He'd have to remember to thank his provisions team for that later. He laid everything out, added two more Tylenol for the pain and then left the room before she came out. If he saw her in only a towel at this moment, he'd be buried so deep inside of her that they'd never figure out what was going with Fuckstick and his family. And truly, he couldn't go there until he was sure she understood that it meant more than once. Until she understood how badly he had fucked up. Until he groveled. If she could ever forgive him.

TWENTY-ONE

HAZEL

SHE THOUGHT THE SHOCK OF THE NIGHT HAD BEEN WEARING off . . . and then Luke had seen her back. He'd gone from somewhat still cool operating cucumber to alpha hero in a heartbeat, which had been thrilling and confusing. After shredding her heart from his hospital bed like an arrogant prick last fall, he had left her pride shattered and her heart bleeding at his feet. She had known he was as much into whatever had been happening as she was, and she knew it was her he had called out for as he thought he lay dying. But then he woke up in that hospital room and coldly stated *his decision*. That tone, those words, how he had shut her out at her most vulnerable moment, he may as well have killed her himself.

She'd known Luke her entire life. She'd loved him for almost as long, and never as a little sister should love their older brother. Never like Violet, her actual sister, loved Luke. They had always had a sibling relationship and although she was only nineteen months younger than Vi; she had always felt differently about Luke. He was seven years older than she was and she'd given him her heart years ago in hindsight. Last fall had opened her eyes, only for him to cruelly cut her out of his life.

Last fall had been the start of forever in her mind. They'd shared everything that last night together and while she didn't regret it, it had shattered her to hear his words almost as soon as he woke up in the emergency department.

She had clearly seen him, and everything had clicked into focus for her. She sighed deeply and remembered the pain of his speech. His decisions. The finality there. The coldness with which he had shut her out. Her own inability to process, to fight for them.

So resolute was he, that after he returned to the Dupont Circle headquarters home from the hospital, he'd barely spoken to her. She'd had her entire existence rocked, her sister hunted by madmen . . . that wound was still fresh, and she sighed, thinking about losing Violet, losing Luke, what could have been.

To reign her errant thoughts back in, she pictured her favorite meal in DC and methodically worked her way mentally through that experience. By the time she had reached the dessert, she felt better . . . and warmer in the shower. Her skin was shriveled, but she was finally ready to face whatever was on the other side of the shower door. She'd let him push her away once, but she didn't know if she could do that again. Not after the events of the night. She was also working through how she had simply frozen when shit hit the fan last fall, being completely incapable of functioning when it mattered most, then how she'd allowed him to make his decision and not even stand up for what she knew. She wouldn't be that scared girl again.

She stepped out and dried off, paying careful attention to her back. Man, now that some of that shock had worn off, her back was throbbing. She hadn't even realized she'd hurt it that badly while being held captive. She had been too terrified, she hadn't thought about the rough bricks at her back.

She put on the whisper thin tank top, sleep shorts and cash-mere cardigan left on the bed and took the extra Tylenol, grateful for Luke's care. Did he mean it as an operator rescuing a hostage? A brother figure? Or as the man who had made her body hum not forty five minutes ago? She shook her head at herself. She needed to get to the bridge and see what they could do to save the Perry family.

When she opened the stateroom door, she found a smiling Brian waiting for her.

"Hey, Hazey, feeling better?" he asked her.

"Much better, thanks Brian. And really, thank you so much for coming for me. I don't know what is going on, but I'm glad to have friends like you. You guys saved me. Again," she replied.

Brian chuckled and put a warm hand on her shoulder lightly. "You're family Hazey, we'll always come for you." He pulled his hand back.

"Oh no, not the little sister treatment from you too, Brian! Max and Vi are overprotective enough!" She laughed.

"Sorry, Hazey, you are my little sister now too, and I'll always have your back. But hey, give bossman a break, okay? He was sick about this, alternating between raging at everyone since we got that call to broody silence. I've never seen him like that, and if I had to make a wager, he wasn't promising to 'kill every single motherfucker responsible' because he felt nothing." Brian winked at her.

She shrugged, not wanting to get her hopes up. Her heart couldn't take any more pain like Luke had dished out over the last year and now did not seem to be the time to have that conversation. She also hated that all the guys had known something had happened between them both before Ambassador Neil's party and afterward in the hospital.

"Thanks, Brian." She sighed. "I think I'm ready to face the music now."

He chuckled and led her to the bridge.

Thank the sweet baby Jesus, there was a pot of hot, fresh coffee waiting on her there. She did not care what time it was, she was drinking a cup or three. She needed the comfort and grounding of the warm mug in her hands, and she wanted to be as alert as possible to help in any way she could to help Dan and his parents.

"Hazel Ann Burke, thank God you're okay! But your sweet face!" she heard her sister exclaim.

"Vi! Oh, Sis, hi! I'm so glad to see your face!" She glanced at Wills and murmured a 'thank you' before turning back to the video monitors.

"I'm sorry to worry everyone. I have no idea what happened." She shivered. "I'm sorry, Sis, but please go to bed. The stress isn't good for Baby Alex cooking in there," she said, smiling into the camera.

"A woman after my own heart, Hazey. Thank you for telling my wife to get her gorgeous ass to bed. And Hazel, we are glad to have you back and safe. Luke mentioned you have some injuries on your face and on your back. Are you okay?" Max spoke next.

Her eyes flashed to Luke's. He was watching her intently but hadn't said anything since she'd entered the bridge. "I'm good guys, it's nothing really. I am incredibly lucky and deeply grateful to have you all come for me," she said.

There was a chorus of, "Always," resounding throughout the room and from the screens with her loved one's faces. She loved them all so much. At that moment, she couldn't believe that she had thought moving to Miami was a good idea. It had been running away, plain and simple. Cowardly, and she was done burying her head in the stand when things went wrong.

As she studied all of those beloved faces, she knew that she was strong enough to be back in DC, come what may with Luke. She was done running from her collective family. Her eyes landed on Luke's last. "I'm good, Luke," she reassured him. Whether he understood her comment's hidden context or not, he nodded at her.

"Hazel, we need to call Commander Cullins and talk through

what you saw, what you know, anything you can tell us. Our primary objective was to rescue you, obviously. The secondary objective for Cullins and the Coast Guard is to rescue the remaining adrift hostages and the Perry family, which they've been working to do," Luke said.

He continued, "First, though we need to make sure you don't have any more injuries we can't see. Tom is also here and can check your head." He nodded to another man standing close by.

What was it with these muscle-bound hunks?! She wondered. They were everywhere she turned, not that she was complaining one bit.

"Hi, Hazel. Nice to meet you." Tom shook her hand, his eyes already assessing her face. "Next time, let's meet in more fun circumstances, yeah?" His eyes crinkled with his broad smile.

She laughed and agreed. Ten minutes later, she was given the all-clear, and Tom headed back down to check on something for the boat.

Hazel walked back to Luke then, ready to get that call with Cullins over with. She walked them through everything, from the boat ride to the island, details about the party and then the raid and guards. She answered countless questions about the guards, the language she thought she heard, every single detail in her brain. They even asked her about her week in the Keys and what that had been like.

"You Burke sisters are always tumbling into trouble!" Seb laughed as he refilled everyone's coffee. He was right. They did seem to have both gotten entangled in some mysterious happenings in the last year.

"Tell me again how Dan acted with the guards," Luke commanded.

"It was weird. He immediately seemed to shrink into himself. He didn't talk to me once we were taken hostage. He didn't try to talk to anyone else. Really, he was practically catatonic. He was close to where I was, but he never even spoke to me again. Even when our guard shot that woman and hit me, he never moved a muscle to help. It was very weird, come to think of it," she told the group.

"So let me get this straight. You start dating him what, seventeen days ago, he takes you all over Miami practically salivating over you every step of the way, laying it on way too thick, invites you to this party and then as soon as trouble hits, he abandons you? He watches you get hit in the face with the butt of a gun and doesn't do one fucking thing?!" Luke was incredulous, his rage making his voice go nuclear.

"Um, yes?" Hazel responded quizzically.

"Played your hand there, Luke." Tad laughed as Luke kept at it. He patted Luke on the shoulder. "Easy buddy, we've got her now."

"So, why does the guy who brought you there act like he doesn't know you as soon as the shit hits the fan?" Luke demanded. He continued, "Such a fuckstick move for such a fuckstick coward . . . "

"What if he was protecting her? Maybe he didn't want the kidnappers to know they were connected," Sebastian said, cutting Luke's rant off. "If my girl is there and I'm in some shit, the least I can do is act like I don't know her. That takes their eyes off her, right?" he mused.

"I like this train of thought," Theo mused. "His smoke show of a girlfriend." He paused to wink at Hazel even though Luke was glaring a hole through his forehead. "Your smoke show of a girlfriend is in danger so you ignore her. It's the dumb ass thing to do, but if you're a dumbass, maybe that's all you can come up with," he went on. "Not that any of us is okay with any woman getting killed or hit and then ignored." They all nodded at that, mumbling throughout the bridge about dead assholes.

"Right, but it didn't work-did it?" Tad added. "They had her with them when they were moving to the yacht," he pointed out.

"And why was the Perry family separated out from most of their guests? There had to be a reason that everyone else was let go," Mila said from the screens.

"Well, he's a dumb fuckstick motherfucker dickhead," Luke responded flatly.

"Got it, Luke. You don't like Fuckstick. Check," Tad said, rolling his eyes at his buddy.

"Guys, we've got bad news," Commander Cullins cut in from the video feeds. His face was turned to the side, reading a brief before he turned back to the video feed. "The Coast Guard has lost the Perry's yacht from radar. Whoever is behind this is smart and well-funded also to make that happen. That's next level tech."

"Fuck," Luke said. "Wills, how are we on our detection bubble?" he asked.

"I think we're holding well." Wills checked a few things and then nodded back at Luke, indicating all was good.

"You're the best, Wills. I love you, man. You know that. You can wrap me in this invisible bubble and I will walk through a hellfire of bullets trusting that protection." Luke turned and glanced back at Hazel and lowered his voice. "I'm less risk tolerant with our current guest. Let's get this boat to the Bahamas until we know where else these assholes could be lurking in the waters around the Keys. If nothing else, we can move any engagement that we need to lead away from US soil."

TWENTY-TWO

LUKE

HIS INITIAL RESPONSE WAS TO TRY TO PURSUE THE PERRY YACHT AND figure out what the hell was going on. It took him a deep breath to hear Cullins and understand that the scope was larger than they could tackle immediately, and they needed to regroup and get more data. The Coast Guard would work to track the Perry yacht, along with a team from NAS Key West on aerial support. The Keys police had assistance from the FBI and would process the guests as fast as they could, gathering intel and ruling out potential avenues. That guest list was stacked with potential targets. He needed to figure out what to do with Hazel, how to make her as safe as possible.

At that moment, his part of the joint op was to protect Hazel while trying to figure out if she knew anything that could unravel their current clusterfuck.

Could he hide her somewhere safe? The helo could pick her up and take her to Max, but they needed to talk through Fuck-stick and his family more to understand what was going on. And in reality, his gut tightened at the thought of sending her away again, even if it was short-term. The last time he did that, it had nearly gutted him and it had landed her in Miami. In the hands of Fuckstick. The safest place for Hazel was next to him. If she even forgave him and didn't demand to leave.

Luke also knew this clusterfuck that had hurt her was on him. He hadn't trusted his own mind in how to be with her, and his mind seemed to be warring with his scarred and barely beating heart. When he'd nearly died in the ambassador's library, he'd only been thinking about Hazel. How the sun hit her hair in the late afternoon sun scattering across the waves in Virginia Beach, how his heart had changed it's pattern in his chest seeing her like that. All woman, all gorgeous curves and long, deep red hair. It was similar to a linebacker sacking him on that beach on a blind side. One moment Hazel was like a younger sister he cared deeply for and would die for, and the next, she was all he could see. The woman he would kill for.

He remembered the softness of her skin against his that last night before it all went FUBAR in DC. How her gasp of pleasure had tasted when she came undone around him. Her eyes on him as he held her that night were the last thing he saw in his memory before he lost consciousness.

In his mind, he marked time as before and after. Before he realized who she was to him, and after he knew she was it. The problem was in the knowing. After losing his mom so young and seeing his dad self-destruct with her loss, he wasn't sure he could live through that kind of pain. Losing his mom was bad enough. She had been a fantastic mom, better and funnier than what you see on TV, the kind of mom every kid should get. Warm chocolate chip cookies, unabashed cheering at his games, strict homework time at the dinner table. Her loss changed everything. She was gone, and so was his dad. One without a choice in the matter and one with a choice in the matter, sure, but both gone. He barely spoke to his dad now. And hell, he got it. He wouldn't want to live without Hazel by his side either. But geez, he'd been a kid, a kid who needed his dad.

That pain meant that in the *after* times, he'd panicked and distanced himself completely from Hazel. His heart had been raw, and he didn't trust himself to understand how to navigate through the past pain and fear of the future. He hated the rage that overtook him when he thought of Hazel dating through college. He didn't appreciate the constant hard-ons she inspired and so he had stayed away while she was in school. He timed his visits back home to her family when he knew Hazel wouldn't be around.

He sent gifts during the holidays and . . . unbeknownst to them, when he'd proven to be really good at investing his modest trust and the team's "hazard pay" during their tours, he'd paid for both girls to finish college. Both had received 'surprise scholarships,' full rides that covered everything. That hadn't been that hard to finagle. They had good grades, volunteered often, were great students. Each member of that family also had a trust in their respective names and were his beneficiaries on almost everything. He planned. That's what he did.

His plan of avoiding Hazel to avoid further heartbreak and temptation had been rolling along decently well until she called him frantic for help for Vi. She never called him. She texted him, she replied to family group chats via text, she emailed him, but she never called him. Ever.

He shuddered, grateful that he'd had the balls to answer her call.

Hazel, the one person it seemed that he couldn't keep at arm's length. Especially now that he knew what her body felt like notched against his own, what her lips tasted like on his tongue, how her heat enveloped him. He knew the sounds that came from low in her throat from pleasure.

He'd let his fear triumph over his heart once before and he wouldn't make that mistake again. Tad had been right. He would not be ruled by fear any longer. He would not give her up for anything. She just didn't know it yet.

They were inevitable, just like the certainty he had felt in his gut that day at the beach. She was his. Now, he had to figure out how to make it up to her after his behavior last fall, to convince her to take a chance on him. He'd certainly dug himself a hole with her, but he'd spend his life digging out of it if he had to.

No time like the present to get started digging.

TWENTY-THREE

HAZEL

AFTER THE TERRIFYING NEWS THAT THE PERRY'S BOAT WAS MIA, she'd asked to call it a night. It had to be almost dawn, anyway. The guys had all agreed and had divided up a watch system while she went back to the room she'd showered and changed in earlier. It was stunning, and she couldn't believe it was so stunning on a boat. Tomorrow, she was going to poke around Luke's boat more. Tonight, she was dead on her feet.

She shrugged out of the cardigan, brushed her teeth with the new toothbrush left for her and crawled under the fluffy blankets. The bed doubled for a luxurious cloud and before too long, she was able to settle her racing thoughts and fall asleep, sheer exhaustion pulling her under.

Her dreams betrayed her that night. She dreamed as if life had unfolded differently, like Luke hadn't sent her away all those months ago. She felt his warm arms gathering her close to his chest, gently cradling her and pulling her into his hard body. She dreamed of his large hands on the back of her head, smoothing her hair down and across her shoulder. She dreamed that he whispered words of love and care across her ear, his lips tracing those promises. Dream Luke was the safety and security she needed to slide deeper into sleep. Dream Luke had always come for her when she needed him most.

She awoke several hours later, energized as if she had slept for days. The blinds and drapes had been closed in the room, making the stateroom a personal luxury cocoon. She barely noticed the gentle motion of the yacht as she rolled out of bed to brush her teeth, pull her hair back, and get dressed.

After opening the drapes, she gasped at the clear turquoise waters and miles of sunshine. She opened the dresser drawer across from the massive bed to poke around for clothes and found endless options of beautiful women's clothing. Bikinis, cover-ups, shirts, tee shirts, jeans, tanks, sweatshirts, socks, bras, and underwear. Her heart clenched thinking about who the clothes may belong to. Jealousy almost choked her, and she shuddered out a ragged breath. She did *not* want to be wearing some other girl's clothes, left behind on Luke's sanctuary. The idea that he cared enough about a woman to have her clothes settled in on his boat made her almost wretch. She knew she needed to move on. It was simply easier said than done. Particularly while in this space that was his. My God, she could smell him in here.

She decided to stay in her tank top and sleep shorts and go find some coffee. She'd ask one of the guys what the plan was and if she could borrow a tee-shirt for the day. What she wouldn't allow herself to do is to wallow, or hide out down there. Especially if there was any possible way that she could be of help to whatever was happening.

Coming up the steps, she found it was indeed a beautiful day on the water. The air was balmy against her skin, the sea smelling of fresh salt and the sun bright against her eyes. She made a mental note to ask to borrow some sunglasses, too.

"Hey, gorgeous!" Theo called to her. "C'mon over here and give me some sugar." Theo smiled widely at her and held open his arms. He sat at a round teak table on the upper deck, different pastries and fruits in front of him, along with his iPad.

"Morning! Wait, is it still morning? I've been a real Rip Van Winkle," Hazel said.

"It is still morning, barely though. It's good to see you topside in the sunshine. You want some breakfast? We've got some fruit and there is always a fresh pot of coffee on pretty much twenty-four seven around here," he replied.

"I could kiss you, Theo. Yes, to all of that." She laughed.

"Ah, sweetheart, you earned it last night. That was probably scary as shit for you," he said.

"It was. I can't believe that I slept at all. I can't get that woman out of my head, and I'm scared for Dan and his family."

"I get that, Hazey. Let's get you fed and watered like a happy puppy. After that, we'll check in with Luke to see what our plan is for the day. He's on the bridge now," Theo said.

"He needs sleep, Theo. You need to make him get some rest," she admonished. The damn man forgot that he was human and needed to sleep. No matter how upset with him or confused by him she was, she couldn't turn off the need to care for him.

"Ahhh, Hazel? He did sleep, sweetheart. He slept with you," Theo said, somewhat bashfully.

The bottom of her stomach dropped. He'd slept with her? Was Dream Luke real? She was confused and she sure was *not* getting her hopes up after their silent implosion last fall.

"Oh, I guess I must have been out of it," she demurred.

Theo smirked at her, as heat climbed up her neck and across her checks. He took pity on her and didn't pursue the conversation, instead patting the seat next to him for her to sit and make a plate. He poured her a cup of coffee while she helped herself to some breakfast. Brunch? She wasn't exactly sure.

"Theo, this is certainly the lap of luxury. A girl could get used to this! I could live here." She smiled over at him. But, as soon as she said it, her memory flashed to the woman's clothing in the stateroom on the main deck she'd stayed in. A frown marred her face before she could stop it from forming.

Seeing her frown, Theo asked, "Woah, sweetheart, what happened there? No lies allowed. Remember that I'll be able to tell." He smirked at her. Theo and those dimples.

"It's nothing, Theo. I'm grateful for everything . . . it's just that there are women's clothes in the stateroom I slept in on the main deck and I . . . " she trailed off.

"I can't help but think of that poor woman from last night, no matter how hard I try. And then being back here, with you all, with Luke, it's like last fall, only it's different now. I've worked really hard to try to move on and here I am, thrust back into God knows what and needing you all to save me. Except this time, Luke rides to the rescue on a mega yacht that also has another woman's clothes on it. And hey, I get it, I'm just fried right now, okay. I'm really, really fried, and I am trying my best to keep up mentally and help those other guests as much as possible. So please, ignore my heartbreak right now. I am trying *so* hard to ignore it myself and think of any details whatsoever that may be helpful to understand what happened last night."

Her voice had risen throughout her escalating emotions, and she felt herself shaking slightly after that diatribe to Theo. God, he must think she was insane. At this point, it was an accurate read of her. She was a food writer, for crying out loud! And now, for the second time in a year, she was part of some weird life and death mission. Was this the standard day for these guys?!

"Hazel. Look at me," Theo commanded quietly as he lifted her chin with his hand, all playfulness fading from his face. "You are currently living on Luke's yacht . . . the *Copper Goddess* . . . and slept in the only stateroom on the main deck, with Luke, whether you remember that part or not." His eyes drilled into hers. "The clothes belong to you. Luke had the provisions team purchase them all for you, not knowing what you'd need. They loaded everything for us, including the clothes and any other crap for all of us, and food to last for quite a while. He had them provisioning while we were still in the helo down to Key West to refuel. There is no other woman who has ever been on this boat. And Hazel, pay attention here. There will never be another woman on the Copper Goddess." Theo finished his speech and smiled again, softer on his face this time, more genuine than the smirk he threw out constantly.

"You ever stop to think about the name of this sanctuary that Luke loves so much, Hazel?" he asked, his voice barely above a whisper.

"I . . . " she started.

"She's awake!" Brian's voice cut her off unknowingly. He was coming down the stairs from the bridge deck, with Luke close behind him.

"Morning gentlemen. Thanks for letting me sleep in." She jumped up to hug Brian good morning and then stepped back awkwardly, unsure if she should hug Luke or not. The decision was cut off in her brain as Luke stepped around Brian and braced his hands on her biceps, pulling her into him. He leaned down and kissed the top of her head.

"Are you trying to make me kill my brothers Hazelnut?" he asked her, for her ears alone.

She stared up at him, confused. When her eyes met his, she was taken aback by the sheer lust shining in his brown eyes. Those melty chocolate eyes dropped then, right to her nipples. Ohhhhh, that's right. Thin tank top . . . no bra. Yikes, good morning boys indeed.

He kissed the shell of her ear as he whispered again, "you're lucky I don't want anyone else to see you like that or I'd have you laid out on that table and those gorgeous fucking nipples in my mouth in my next heartbeat." His hot tongue traced her ear lightly. "Please go get dressed. Please." He pulled his face back from her and kept her body almost flush to his.

"Hazel is going to run back down to our stateroom to get dressed for the day and then we can all catch up," he announced to Brian and Theo, without ever taking his eyes off hers. She stepped back from him and crossed her arms over her chest. Thankfully, neither of the other men had glanced down. Her skin resembled a path of flames racing from her ear to her nipples, straight to her core. She sincerely hoped that no one could see how his words had affected her on her face.

He spoke directly to her, "Hazel, we'll be on the boat for a handful of days at least while the Coasties, police and FBI process through the guest list and potential leads, and until whatever asshole planned this is found and stopped. Right now, we are safest on this boat, so we're staying put on this boat. If you want to swim, it is safe to do so and there are suits for you in the dresser across from our bed. I know being able to move is important to you, and you aren't a prisoner or anything here, Think of it as your floating home, whatever you want or need should be here but if not, let me know and we'll get it."

"Ok, thank you." She addressed all of them as she started down the stairs, "Thank you all so much. And, Luke's right guys, I'll be back in a jiff."

Geez, he was messing with her head, not to mention her heart. And well, heat had gathered at her core with that little tongue slip he'd traced on the shell of her ear. He acted this way the last time they'd been pushed together by danger, and then he'd pushed her away with a broken heart. She wasn't going there again with him. She was going to have to tell him to stop with the push and pull. She couldn't take the whiplash again. She would stand up for herself this time around.

TWENTY-FOUR

LUKE

"Luke, you dumb fuck. She didn't get dressed before she left the room because she thought the clothes belonged to some other woman. She was sick with it. Grow the fuck up and embrace your big boy feelings," Theo hissed at him as he watched Hazel make her way back to their stateroom.

"What? Why would she think that?" he asked Theo. Brian was shaking his head at him too now.

"Because you've made her think you don't care for her, as if she isn't the one woman this has always been about. The *Copper* fucking Goddess and you've made her so uncomfortable that she doesn't want to put on clothes from some mythical woman you've had on this fucking love boat. Fix this. For her, and for you, man. I personally am not going to let you push her away again and I garun-fucking-tee that none of the rest of the team will either," Theo ripped into him. "Go get your girl, you dipshit." The younger man glared at him, his eyes as serious as he'd ever seen them.

He couldn't believe that she would think he'd had a woman on his boat, in his bed. He couldn't even see other women. He'd only ever seen her for so long. He'd had sex with other women over the last ten years, but few and far between and never repeats. He certainly hadn't looked at another woman since she'd called him, needing help for Violet last fall.

Shit, he hated himself for making her doubt herself. He wanted to kick his own ass.

"Hazel?" He knocked on his stateroom door before he opened it.

She twisted toward him and the breath caught in his throat. She'd put on an emerald green bikini, the rest of her creamy curves on full display. Her nipples were still hard and poking into the little triangles that covered her breasts, her skin pebbled in the cool room. The bottoms tied at the sides and were cut high on her ass, with those cheeks just begging for his hands. He'd go to his grave with this visual in his brain. He quietly closed the door behind himself and locked it.

"Hazelnut," he groaned. "It has come to my attention," he stalked her way, "that I made you feel like this," he swept his arms out wide at his sides, "wasn't made for you." He brought his arms to her biceps again, his calloused palms making her shiver even more.

"This is the *Copper Goddess*, Hazel, it's yours. It always has been." He dipped his head down and stared deeply into her eyes. "Forgive me?" he pleaded with her.

"Forgive you? For what exactly? Be specific. You've been wonderful since plucking me off the beach with your guns blazing like some God of water warfare, but I'm confused by your kisses and words right now. I won't survive you pushing me away again. You broke me!" she whispered. "It felt like I didn't even know you, really. You pull me in, you push me away. You're filthy, stinking rich and neither Vi nor I even knew that about you. I mean, I don't care about money, Luke, but you've had this whole life that I had no idea about, and all of a sudden you want me to forgive you? Do you know how hard it has been for me to walk away from everything I have ever known and try to live without you? After what we shared that night? You made promises that night, and then you broke my heart after surviving an attack that should have killed you. I was so relieved that you would live and then you gutted me. You shut me out!" She shook off his hands from her arms in fury.

"Of course, I know what it is like to walk away, Hazel. I did it enough that I do know. It killed me each and every time," he replied quietly.

"What are you talking about, Luke? I have never in my life pushed you away. I practically threw myself at you last fall when Violet was in trouble. It was new and exciting, and yet solid and comforting. I put myself out there and it was the right fit. It felt like everything was falling into place and then I fucking watched you practically die, Luke. I was watching those screens. I heard you whisper 'Hazelnut' before you went down. I had to sit there and pray that I'd get to tell you how I felt about you, about the future I hoped we could have. And thank God, you survived. You survived and then immediately kicked me out of your life. You survived, but my heart didn't!" she cried.

"You're right. You are absolutely right. I was a chicken shit. I have known you were it for me since the summer you turned eighteen, but I was twenty-five and deep into my service, deep into what I thought was best for me *and* best for you. And then, I just let my own fear drive me. That shit ends now. I promise you," he said.

"I don't understand what you're telling me," she said to him.

"Let me show you Hazel. Let me show you through actions, please. I will make up for what I did that night in the hospital and for telling you to leave, for the uncertainty, the pain I caused you. Please just let me try," he said.

"What does *trying* look like, Luke? We're back in danger here and I don't know what you mean by showing me. You take care of everyone all the time, anyway. What about when things are normal? How will I know? I deserve more than the dramatic and romantic rescue and then the shutout when things are going to be okay," she said.

Fuck, she was right. He'd been in charge for so long, taking care of everyone was his natural role. He was the team lead, the investor, the planner. He could never turn that part of himself off . . . but he also knew that once he committed, he was all in. He could show her, and he would.

"Let me worship you, Hazel. I will spend however much time you need to convince you, and once you can trust in my actions and words, I'll never stop worshipping you. Every single day we have, no matter what. Please."

"I'm scared, Luke. I want this, but you can't shut me out again. You can't decide something so important about *us* without me. If we do this, we have to be partners. We take care of each other, which means that I decide with you about our future," she breathed out in a whisper.

"I was scared too, Hazel. That's why I pushed you away. You had the courage that I lacked, and I hurt you. But, baby, I will make it up to you now if you let me. I know now that my decisions don't mean shit if you aren't making them with me by my side."

She studied him, holding his gaze for what could have been forever. She said nothing. His heart was pounding. She had every right to tell him to get lost. He knew it would take time to convince her, but he would make that happen no matter how long it took. She was his end game. Always had been.

He held her eyes, seeing the shift from solemn to considering. He kept his hands on her arms, waiting for whatever was going through her mind to spill out of her lips. She folded her arm behind herself and tugged on the tie holding her bikini top on. Her eyes never left his as the dark green material fell from her breasts, landing at his feet.

Her eyes shifted to playful and daring. "Worship me Luke?" she asked. "Show me Luke?"

"Okay. Show me. Worship me," she challenged.

He felt the blood drain from his head to his dick with those words, and he hadn't even broken eye contact yet. Without doing so, he reached his thumbs over to her breasts from where his hands had gone back to her biceps, her arms at her sides.

He lightly ran his thumbs along the side of her lush breasts, circling back and forth, shifting to deepen the pressure while he continued to study her. Bruises were blooming along her beautiful face from the night before, which killed him to see.

"Are you sure Hazelnut?" he asked. He would die if she said no, and very likely need Tad to airlift him to a hospital for prolonged blue balls if she changed her mind, but he wanted her to be very sure. Once they did this, once he was inside of her, he'd never let her go again. Fuck anyone and everything, she was *his*. "Is your back okay? Your head? This is what you want?" he asked again.

"Yes Luke, please," she said to him, her eyes steady on his. His thumbs circled again.

She shuddered with the ministrations to her breasts and reached up on her tip toes to kiss him. He allowed her to take the lead at first, accepting the additional consent she was giving with her body. Her tongue swept into his mouth and found his. That explosion he had felt all those months ago detonated within him again and he brought his hands up to frame her face, devouring her mouth.

She moaned into him, bringing those full, gorgeous breasts to his chest as her arms snaked around his neck. His hands swept along the back of her arms then, being careful not to touch her wounds too harshly. When he got to her ass, he palmed a cheek in each hand and lifted her off the ground, bringing her legs around his waist.

He held onto her cheeks and kissed her reverently as he eased them back to the bed and laid her out on it. Once he laid her down, he stepped back to feast his eyes on her glorious body. Her red hair was messy around her face, her ponytail loose and wavy from the sea air.

Her breasts were rising and falling with her rapid pants. Her nipples, hardened from his earlier caresses were taut and rosy pink. Her eyes were blazing at him. He reached back and pulled his shirt off one handed. His hands dropped to his shorts and slid them and his underwear off. He stood before her completely naked, very excited about what he was seeing laid out before him.

She raised up her arms to him and he gently laid down alongside her, skating his hand across her collar bone, around her breasts, down her belly until he reached the green bottoms. He pulled on the strings, baring her to his gaze and his hand. He pulled them out from where they had pooled under her hips. As he leaned over to do that, his mouth latched on the spot where her neck met her shoulder and he sucked, hard.

Her entire body jolted against his. His hand skated back to her belly, large enough that one hand covered almost all of her. He leaned more fully over her, bearing his weight on his opposite arm. He continued kissing and sucking along her neck and down to her breasts.

She whispered his name again, her voice rough with desire. He suckled one of her nipples into his mouth, his hand sweeping back up and caressing her other breast. He was leisurely in his worshipping, working his way down her body with both his hands and his mouth, rushing nothing. He knew he needed her body wet and ready for him. He would make sure this time was one that was all pleasure for her, none of the urgency of their last time together.

When he got to her hip bones, he walked his fingertips down to her wet core and dragged his fingers across her slit lightly. The barely there pressure had her arching into him, her heat seeking more. He kissed her again and then leaned back and watched his own hand as his large finger dipped fully into her. She gasped.

Fuck, she was tight. Her heat clenched around his finger. He crooked his finger and put pressure on her clit as he leaned back in, kissing along her inner thighs.

Her hips were arching into him, begging for more. He added a second finger and licked at her clit.

"Oh my God, Luke." Her hands gathered in his hair. " . . . Luke . . . so good . . . " she was mumbling incoherently. Her words made him feral with the need to mark her as his.

He stabbed his tongue against her clit as his fingers worked her into a frenzy. Her fingers had tightened in his hair, pulling. He could come himself, just like this. He willed his brain to focus on her pleasure. He stroked his tongue more deeply into her, using his lips and his fingers to make her mindless.

"Luke, I'm coming, Luke!" Her hips bucked against his mouth as she shattered against him, wetness coating his tongue. He hummed against her, "so pretty baby. So pretty coming all over my mouth like that. You're pure honey baby," she shuddered again against his mouth.

He worked his way back up her body with kisses and caresses. When he reached her mouth, she pulled his head against her own, her mouth all over his.

They kissed until he thought he would pass out from blood loss to his cock. He eased back and pulled her head to his chest, hooking his leg over hers and easing her onto her side, facing him fully. His arm skated down her side and gathered a palm full of cheek, pulling her flush to his raging erection. Her wetness was drenching him, the tip of his cock against the soft skin of her core. He could die right now and be happy.

She coasted her soft hand down his body, tracing his abdominal muscles and purring low in her throat. She continued on, dropping her fingertips down his side and then sinking them into his hips. She leaned back just enough to reach her hand between them and caress him. She wrapped her hand around his length and pumped lightly, her thumb circling across the tip and gathering the pre-cum there. She pumped back in a downward motion and opened her legs slightly before pulling him to her again, lining him up with herself. She guided him inside of herself, her wetness coating him everywhere.

They both held steady, breathing in the sensation of being together again, with nothing between them. "It's okay Luke, I have an IUD and," she gulped. "You're my only." She shyly met his eyes.

It took everything in him not to roar and plunge into her as deeply as he could get at the knowledge that she would only ever be his. He wanted her soaking him, only him, forever.

"Hazelnut, I haven't been with anyone but you since our last deployment and I'm clean," he promised her.

He rolled to his back, bringing her on top of him without ever leaving her. He gripped her hips and rolled her along his cock, slowly, impaling her but giving her the control over the depth. When she was fully seated on him, she sighed deeply and slowly began to move.

"Oh, Luke. Oh God, Luke. It's so good," she keened.

He pressed her hips down, his fingers dug deeply into her hips, and ground her against his cock, until she was sobbing in ecstasy, and he was frantic for the friction of their bodies.

Her hands had worked their way up her own body, bringing her breasts together and spreading her palms over them. Her nipples peeked through her own fingertips, and he cursed, not sure how long he could hold off.

He took one hand from her hip and guided it around her neck, gently pulling on her hair. Her eyes shot open in surprise as they met his. Her entire body was shaking, and her hands were all over her own breasts now, kneading and grasping. He bucked his hips into hers solidly and pulled down on her hair just a little harder at the same time. She came undone around him, spasming around his cock and moaning his name. Her hands collapsed down to his chest, and she licked across his neck up to his ear and lightly bit down on the sensitive lobe. Her coming around him, bare and hot, that little bite to his ear and he came. His body emptied into hers while he slowed the rolling of her hips, his own hands shaking. It had never been like that. Ever.

TWENTY-FIVE

HAZEL

LUKE ROLLED HER TO HIS SIDE, KEEPING HER CLOSE TO HIS BODY. HE wrapped one arm around her gently and used the other hand to frame her face.

"You're perfect Hazelnut, thank you." He kissed her deeply. She felt him against her core, along the sticky wetness of their lovemaking.

"Baby, I want to repeat that entire experience immediately, but I don't want you to be too sore. Stay here, I'll be right back."

He rolled from the bed and walked naked to the bathroom.

"Luke!" she cried out at him, sitting up.

"Luke Matthew Stratton, get your ass back here right now," she demanded, her bare breasts taunting him.

He'd glanced back at her over his shoulder, "what's wrong Hazel?" he asked.

She motioned for him to join her again, waving him to the side of the bed she was closest to as she sat up.

Wordlessly, she traced the tattoo that formed at the base of his spine and worked itself across the entirety of his back. The black ink outline of a hazel tree. The leaves spilling onto the backs of his arms, the little nut clusters tucked along the leaves throughout.

"You've always been with me Hazelnut. Since that day on Virginia Beach, I knew you were mine. I may have had my head up my ass about it, but I knew from that moment on we were in the *after* times. The *after* I knew you were it for me moment. I am so, so sorry for not being the man you deserve last fall but Hazel, you are everything to me," he told her.

Tears leaked from her eyes at his words. This beautiful man really did have her namesake inked across almost the entirety of his muscled back. She'd never seen anything as moving, as beautiful of a tribute, and it was for her.

"Babe, please don't cry. Yell at me for pushing you away, call me the names I deserve, just please, please don't cry," he asked her softly. He turned back to her, taking her hand in his. "I'm going to show you from here on out. I promise."

His hand came to her wet cheeks and brushed away her tears. He cupped her face and kissed her deeply. They stayed like that until the tears were dry and she eased back from his embrace.

"When?" she asked. "When did you do this? I know it wasn't here last fall," she questioned him.

"As soon as I got home from the hospital. I'm so sorry baby. I will spend as much time as you need saying that and showing you how I really feel," he promised.

"I'm starting to believe you Luke." She smiled at him. "I also know that I played in a part in us not being together. I fell apart after what happened to Vi and Max in Little Compton and then again when you and Vi both went down. I couldn't function. I couldn't think or breathe. I was on autopilot in the hospital and I never stood up for us with you. I wasn't honest, or brave. I didn't fight for what I wanted at all that day. I won't do that again. I owe it to myself, I owe it to you, I'm not going to fall apart again. You can keep wooing, and I will be right there with you."

He kissed her again. "You are brave. You've faced some crazy stuff with no training and you're holding it together. I'd be proud to have you in my corner any day of the week. Every day of the week. Forever."

He dropped another kiss on her lips and once more and then rose from the bed. "I'm in the business of wooing you now. Stay here until I come back for you."

He ran the water in the shower for her again and got the room nice and steamy before he opened the door and came back to scoop her up from the bed.

"I can walk, Luke." She laughed at him.

"I know, babe, and as much as I love watching your ass walk in front of me, I want you in my arms as much as possible," he assured her.

He sat her in the shower and lovingly washed her body. He made sure to not miss any single inch of her pale skin, paying extra attention to her core and breasts. She was relaxed and worshipped when he was done, exactly what she imagined he'd been going for. He quickly washed himself and then dried them both off before carrying her back to bed.

"I want to spend the day licking every single inch of your body Hazelnut, does that work for you?" he asked her.

"Only if I get to do the same for you, Luke-a-licious," she replied, "but shouldn't we be upstairs, trying to figure out what's happening? Should we be worried about armed attackers storming the boat any second?" she asked, concern returning to their cocoon.

"We should be watchful and on guard, which the guys are. Wills will see any threat coming with plenty of time to warn us, if a threat can see us through his wizardry. I also have a hunch that whoever these assholes are, they're running and trying to regroup right now. When things go FUBAR, that's what they have to do, and they won't hurt their best assets while they do that. I also know that the Coasties themselves, their barracudas, and NAS Key West pilots are all looking for the Perry Yacht. I promise you that we are safe. Besides, I think I can shake any information you may subconsciously have about the Perry family from that gorgeous brain of yours." He laughed and grabbed her by the ankle, pulling her to him more fully.

They spent hours kissing, licking, exploring, talking, laughing, loving. She didn't know what she did to deserve this day, yet she'd always remember it as one of the best days of her life. He was everything to her.

He told her more about his mom, his fears, his hurt and anger, then finally acceptance about his dad. He told her about the tours he'd always glossed over with her before, he told her more about the teammates they'd lost on that last mission. He asked her about Miami, her life in college, her dreams. He listened intently to her, only growling at her when she told him about her college boyfriends. He promised to wipe that memory right out of her heart and she laughed.

He asked her more about Dan. He'd been paying very close attention and had nailed it earlier, they'd dated for seventeen days exactly, to the day of the event. She couldn't believe that had only been yesterday.

"How did you guess that so accurately?" she asked.

"Please don't be mad. I can't claim to be smart about my actions regarding you up until last night. I've been having you followed. For your own safety. Are you pissed?" He rushed out the words, but not really even contrite.

"I'm not mad, Luke, although I guess I am glad I didn't sleep with Dan. I'm glad there isn't some porno footage of me out there from some surveillance camera." She shrugged her shoulders. She was completely unsurprised and really, unfazed. She knew he wanted her safe. It helped to make his case that she'd always been in the forefront of his mind, but she wasn't going to tell him that yet. She'd only mentioned sleeping with

Dan to tease him, she hadn't been ready for that with anyone but Luke.

"You're lucky you didn't sleep with him because then I'd have killed him last night," Luke growled at her.

She laughed. "Okay, Luke-a-licious., I need sustenance. I'm dehydrated from all of these shenanigans."

"Whatever my Hazelnut wants, my Hazelnut gets." He grabbed her and brought her in for a kiss before getting dressed.

She tossed on the bikini from earlier and was reaching for a sarong when he came up behind her, facing the mirror above the dresser. He reached his arms around and brought them up to cup her breasts. "I'm not sure I can handle the rest of the guys seeing you in this, Hazelnut," he growled.

"Luke, we've had sex multiple times today. I can barely walk, my neck is slightly bruised from your mouth and my thighs are covered in stubble burn, I think they'll get it," she assured him.

"Huh, when you put it like that, okay. These guys are my brothers, and I trust them. Let them see how thoroughly you've been fucked today. So far." He smiled at her, backed up and slapped her on the ass. "More of that later." He opened the door to the stateroom for her.

They walked out to the salon area to check in with the guys. There hadn't been any news and all was quiet. Their captain, a retired Navy captain Luke had hired a few years ago, had brought them to a chain of the smaller Bahamian islan they where could drop anchor if they wanted, but were in a secluded bay. Luke had a crew on board of all retired military. He was taking zero chances with their safety. He had told Hazel that he also paid these people a shit load of money to work a few weeks a year at most. They had a network to ensure the boat was staffed when it needed staffed, but mostly he wanted the excuse to be assured of safety while providing an extremely comfortable living for people who had fought for the good ole US of A. He'd told her earlier about bringing Calder in for heavy search and rescue and she tried to remember to introduce herself to him.

The fact that yet another man, one she'd never even met, had been willing to put himself on the line for her was breathtaking sometimes.

When they stepped out of the salon, she gasped at his side. The setting sun had bathed everything in that warm hue, turning the world golden again. The rest of the team, except for Tad, were outside talking, along with Calder. She noticed that they had all shucked their shirts off and were in shorts, barefoot, although there were still weapons close by. The picture these guys presented, my word. They were each gorgeous, with muscles for days. Some with intricately inked tattoos, some without. All of them could have modeled instead of serving their country. She knew their hearts too, and these guys were absolutely the best humans she could have found in her life. Her eyes stung thinking about all they had sacrificed for her, geez, even for people they'd never even met as Marines. These men and other men and women who served were willing to lay down their lives for their country and she didn't think people always gave them the kind of care and honor they had earned for that. She shivered again, thinking about how they had saved her life.

"Where is Tad?" she asked.

"He is acting command with Luke spending time making sure you're okay," Brian said. "He's on the bridge working with Cullins now."

"Ya, he'll be ready for dinner soon and then I'm taking night watch in the bridge," Sebastian added.

Heat flamed up her neck with the wicked thoughts running through her when Brian had mentioned Luke taking care of her. Luke was certainly making sure she was 'okay.'

He guided her to the hot tub and helped her in. As she sat, she hissed when the hot water hit her back. Her back was much better, particularly because Luke had put some type of salve on it earlier in the day. It just needed more time before she didn't notice every little sensation.

The other sensations she noticed were that the hot water was incredible on her very loved body, and she was glad to be surrounded in the soothing heat. Her body was running strictly on endorphins at this point, but she was sore. Being with Luke, being loved by Luke was an incredible, satiating experience, even when he was slow and gentle . . . which wasn't always the case.

He put his hand on her knee under the water, "are you okay?" he asked genuinely. His eyes were heated, but tender on hers. "I know it seems like an odd time to get in a hot tub, but I promise you we are safe right now. Wills has that tech covering us and the guys are ready. I just wanted you to have a moment." His eyes darkened with his next words, "and I assume your body needs a break."

His concern caught her in a tender spot, and she assured him, "Yes, Luke-a-licious. All good for now." She smiled at him, a sliver of ornery making its way through.

"Damn Mila and that damn nickname," he huffed, but the corner of his mouth had kicked up and the laugh lines around his gorgeous eyes were crinkled.

Sebastian's voice shook her from the hold Luke's face seemed to have on her. "Speaking of Mila, we spent the day running the guest list and haven't found anything at all. We've also been digging into each member of the Perry family and so far, nothing is too crazy. It does seem odd that they were the only ones targeted and that they knew to take Hazel," he said.

The quietest guy in the group, Nate, spoke up. "We need to follow the money more, like Luke always says, 'it's usually about the money.'" He glanced over at Luke. "We should dig into finances while we eat and see what we can find."

"Agreed." Luke nodded.

"Hazelnut, tell us how you met Dan and everything you can remember about him, no detail is too small," Luke said.

"Ya, okay, sure. I don't know how much help I'll be, but I can walk you through everything I know," she replied.

"I met Dan at a function in South Beach at the Fontainebleau.

I was there to do a write up about the new restaurant along the main pool area, overlooking the ocean. They'd recently renovated it and were after some positive press that didn't feel overly contrived, which is where I come in," she said.

"The hotel invited me to stay for a week and use the entire facility to better understand the context of the restaurant, how easy it would be to get in as a hotel guest, the entire experience. The first time I met him, he physically bumped into me as he was backing up his chair from the table behind mine. He was with another guy, and he was charming, even kind of flirty for being at a business lunch if that's what it was. It's a very vacation-y vibe at that location, and they were talking quietly, which seemed out of place. That location stands alone, between the pool and the beach, not part of the main buildings." She considered her next words carefully before continuing.

"I think that it was a business meeting because they both had suits on, but it must have wrapped up around the time his chair bumped into mine because the other man didn't stay long."

"The next time I met him, he was walking by the lounge chair I was sitting on by the pool. It was late afternoon the next day, and I'd been writing on my laptop poolside. I really wanted to nail the press kit, articles and marketing scope because it was a wonderful week of work."

"It was incredible. I read all of it and you nailed it," Luke murmured to her.

She looked over at him questioningly before rolling her eyes. "No sense in asking how you read something that isn't fully deployed yet Luke, you little cybercriminal!" she admonished.

He shrugged, unrepentant. "It was good. Also, Mila helped and relays that they need better cyber security," he said.

"Anyway, he stopped to chat that next time and asked me out for dinner that same day. I wouldn't normally have accepted, but I was . . . " she peeked over at him sheepishly at first, seemed to find some resolve and then boldly said, "I was trying to get over you, so I accepted. I had looked him on up social media before dinner and he seemed normal. He lived there in Miami and even had photographs on Insta with his mom and dad."

Luke's eyes sharpened and his hand dropped to her knee again. "I'm an asshat Hazelnut, I'm so sorry," he said.

"Yes, what he said, he's an asshat," Sebastian joined in. "How was the date?" he asked.

"It was good. He was charming enough to make me say yes when he asked if he could call me again, but not threatening enough that it felt like too much. I wasn't looking for serious, as you know. We talked about our careers, he asked about my writing, nothing too earth-shattering. First date talk. He asked lots of questions about my work for that week and the beachside restaurant write up I was doing," she said.

"In fact, we only went out a few times in the course of those two weeks," she pursed her lips at Luke. "He always asked about my work, and we were never physical past some light kissing, although he did try to go a little further after our date the night before the party. He'd also come down to Key West, and we met for dinner when he arrived. He dropped me off at the ferry back over to Sunset Key where I was staying."

Luke growled low in his throat.

"I really want to kill that guy," Luke said. Hazel rolled her eyes at him again and splashed him as she stood up to get out. She then stepped down from the deck around the hot tub and wrapped herself in one of the fluffy towels left out.

Tad came down the stairs then and sat at the round, teak table the other guys had moved to.

"The crew is going to bring out some dinner for us. While they do that, I want to talk more about what Dan's family does to be 'Miami Royalty,'" Tad said as he opened the laptop on the table that he'd brought down with him. "Our partners at the FBI are getting more concerned the more Perry holdings they examine and I think we can all assume for now that they are the targets or they would have been let go with the boats of everyone else."

"Perfect timing, man," Luke said as he got out of the hot tub and joined them. "Hazel was just telling us about how she met Fuckstick and the dates they went on."

"And you're not beating your chest like a caveman? I'm impressed," Tad deadpanned.

Tad focused on Hazel, "tell us what you know about the Perry family business," he said as an older gentleman started carrying out platters of food for the table.

The guys all jumped up to help and before long, they had a feast laid on the table and were eating and throwing out ideas about what had led to the hostage situation the night before. Hazel marveled at how in sync these guys were with each other and how smart they all were. She hadn't really stopped to think about what it took to be a special forces operator for the Marines, but she did now. She was seriously impressed. She had known Luke was smart. He'd had to be to go to Annapolis and then to get rich investing, but he also led this team of incredibly intelligent men. She gazed over at him as he sat back in his chair, thinking. She remembered something else that Dan had told her, something that she'd honestly thought was just his ego talking.

"Dan did tell me that he plans to take over the business from Ralph within the next year. They haven't talked to their board about that yet, but he was excited about it and bragged to me. I honestly thought he might be over inflating his sense of importance to get in my pants, which you all know wouldn't have worked. Anyway, he'll oversee their oil and gas interests both domestically and abroad. I think Ralph even talked about stepping aside as chair of the board. You can see why they haven't made any of that public though yet, their shares are too valuable to flood the market if that made any one board member angry. Oil is too much of a commodity to have shares move quickly. It would take a while to divest of those shares, which is why he told me it was all hush hush," Hazel said.

"I don't know if there is any truth to that though, like I said, he was bragging, and I think he only told me that to see if I'd put out. He had been drinking quite a bit. In fact, it was the date we had the night before the party when all of this came out. I wouldn't have seen him again after that because he was too pretentious for my tastes and I didn't see it going anywhere. I had decided when I got back to my cottage that night to tell him I wasn't interested in anything more after the party." She sighed.

"I wouldn't have seen him again at all of it hadn't been specifically for that party. He had begged me to go, and I'd already bought the dress. I was, stupidly I guess, kind of excited to see the Dry Tortugas all lit up and decorated for the party. I know that's typically more Vi's jam, it being an old fort and all, but it sounded incredibly romantic and gorgeous. I was already all the way down in Key West and well . . . I wanted something to take my mind off other things." She shivered and wrapped her arms around herself.

Before she knew what was happening, Luke had pulled her into his lap and wrapped another towel around her chilled arms. She felt the rumble of his chest against her back as he spoke.

"That's the key," he said, contemplating. "It has to be. They're major players in the oil and gas industry. Fuckstick is planning to take over for daddy soon and then their party is interrupted by Farsi-speaking soldiers who then take them hostage . . . the puzzle pieces are coming into view, but I can't see yet how they all fit." He went on, "We need to dig into the board members, the assets, locations, any potential buyers, you name it," he said. "Follow the money." He sent a nod to Nate.

The guys agreed and cleaned up the table. The sun had long since set, but it was a clear night and the stars were out. Tad was also asking Mila to draw up maps of all Perry holdings so they had some additional visuals to consider.

"The oil and gas market is interesting, kind of a new ball-game for me," Hazel mused to Luke as they descended the stairs to the back swim deck.

"How so?" Luke asked her, reaching his hand back to her to help her down the last step.

"I had never realized that you couldn't just sell the shares you owned until Dan talked about flooding the market," she replied.

"It's true, flooding the market with any large amount of oil and gas shares could forever alter the financial picture of the United States. Their boards are regulated tightly, way tighter than almost any other industry considering the players in the world dealing in that area. No single owner of large amounts of shares is typically allowed by their board to sell too many shares at one time, it's very controlled. That's why I think we're on the right track. The idea that Dan was telling you it was all hush hush after he had been drinking enough to loosen his tongue has me worried." Luke helped her sit on the edge of the swim deck and then sat down next to her.

"This could be big, Hazelnut. Really big. We're talking about oil and gas, market shares for the US, bad guys speaking Farsi. I need you to be safe. I'm frankly worried about you being here but I really think you are safest with me. Having said that, it needs to be your choice, we make decisions together now," Luke said. His eyes met hers, clear and worried. "We also need to loop Cullins on this idea, see if there is a there . . . well, there."

"I am safest with you, Luke. If you are all in with me, then I am all in with you. I don't want to leave you to this alone," she said, her words solemn. "It's my mess to clean up."

She leaned against him and looked up into the clear night sky, the stars sparkling again for her. She decided to be brave with him, to be honest with her heart, even though she was scared. The last time she'd felt like she came to a fork in the road with Luke, she'd quietly watched and waited while he made the decision. She shut down her own feelings and hadn't fought for herself at all, or for them. This time, she would stand her ground, be her authentic and transparent self, without fear shutting her down. She may get her heart shredded again, but she wasn't meekly going to leave the room like she had done last time. Mentally squaring her shoulders, she met his eyes with her own.

"I love you, Luke. I want to figure this out together, and then move forward together, have a life together. Travel the world together. Have kids together. Maybe start with a dog? Please? I really want a dog," she said, her voice barely above a whisper and a small smile on her face as the water moved around them.

TWENTY-SIX

LUKE

SHE WAS KILLING HIM AGAIN, THIS TIME WITH HER COURAGE. GOD, his Hazel. She was everything. Beautiful, brave, smart, sexy.

He turned toward her fully and pulled her legs up and into his lap. He wrapped his arms around her waist and met her eyes.

"Hazel, I have loved you since I sensed you outside of my makeshift bedroom door the night my dad left, right after my mom died. That first night you heard me cry myself to sleep." He saw tears gathering in her eyes and her lip quivered.

"I knew you were the only woman for me as a man, my entire heart, that day in Virginia Beach with the sun hitting your gorgeous skin and your laughter taunting me from the waves around your ankles."

"You aren't half of my heart, Hazelnut, you are not a half that makes me whole. You are half of nothing. You are everything. My whole heart, for my whole life. I love you too, baby," he said.

He gently brushed the tears off her cheeks as her smile widened. She sniffled and then laughed lightly.

"Well, now you are never getting rid of me, Luke. Not after those gorgeous words." She snuggled into his chest.

He laughed and hugged her to himself, pulling her up onto his lap. "Good. Because you are never getting rid of me now, either. Now, hold on, because I need to get dirty with you out here with the ocean and the stars caressing your naked skin . . . "

"Luke!" she whisper-yelled at him. "We're on the deck of a boat. One I am sure has cameras everywhere! And also, bad guys, remember them?"

"Oh, sweetness, I'm not even kidding," he promised darkly. "Tad cut the feeds to the cameras back here as soon as we were alone, and, babe . . . there is nothing getting to us right now. Between the tech bubble and the guys, we're okay. There is nothing that will come between me and your body after what you said to me. The loving me bit, that was my favorite bit."

He gently lifted her off his lap and laid her backward on the deck, checking with her to ensure it didn't hurt her to be on her back. Once assured she was good, he helped her slide her top off, licking her breasts as he helped. He'd discovered that she was especially sensitive to tiny little nips and licks on the underside of those gorgeous breasts of hers.

Next, he kissed a path down her stomach, dragging his lips along her bikini line, nibbling her hipbones before he untied the strings there. He licked and suckled her skin, skimming close to her aching core, but not quite right there. Her gasps and moans were low, carried to him on the salty breeze. She wiggled closer to his mouth, her hands on his shoulders, pushing him to her wetness. His girl knew what she liked and how to get it.

He settled between her thighs and licked deeply into her, murmuring words of praise against her wetness. "Baby, you are so wet for me, you are dripping," he crooned.

He worked his tongue against her clit and then added a finger, sweeping deeply inside of her and hooking his finger to press within her tightly. She was chanting his name as she exploded against his mouth.

"That's it baby, come all over me. Yes, Hazel, sweetness, come for me. Only me." His tongue caught every drop, sure and firm against her. He never stopped licking and nipping, sucking at her juices.

He had his hands dug into her ass, feasting on her for what felt like hours. When she'd come twice from his ministrations, he slowed and looked up at her. She had her eyes on him, those gorgeous green and golds hazy and unfocused on his. Her hands were on her own breasts, idly sweeping across them.

"I need you in me, Luke. Now. Please," she whispered.

He pressed another kiss against her core and sat up. He leaned back and ditched his swim trunks before standing. He reached down for her and easily picked her up, placing her on the lounger next to where she had been laying.

She sat up then, her beautiful skin almost luminescent in the moonlight shining down and reflected on the surrounding water. Her copper waves of hair tousled around her shoulders, curling around her pert breasts.

Her eyes met his and she licked her lips. "Luke, it's my turn to play." She smiled at him, pure naughtiness.

"Hazel, there is no quid pro quo here. I dream of devouring you regularly. I would do it every day if you'll let me," he said. He chuckled, but he absolutely fucking meant every word. He was harder than a rock from what he'd been doing, and he would absolutely do that every day of his life if he could.

"Oh, this isn't quid pro quo, my gorgeous man. This is me finally getting my mouth on you and worshipping." Her voice was a purr against him.

He thought then that maybe he really had died. Maybe this was heaven. His copper goddess on his *Copper Goddess*, her tongue poking out to lave his dick, the taste of her sweet juices still coating his tongue. If this was heaven, he had no intention of fucking it up.

That was his last rational thought before Hazel's mouth

wrapped around him and he almost blacked out from pleasure. Oh sweet Jesus, that mouth.

She suckled him into her throat as deeply as she could, coating him in hot wetness and then rubbing her tongue along him. She licked and sucked, played and kissed. He had his hands in her hair, guiding her when he thought he might die if he didn't get inside of her.

He couldn't take his eyes off her, his hands fisted in her hair. That gorgeous mouth wrapped around his cock. She had one dainty hand playing with herself as she sucked him in, humming around the mouthful. His sweetness, his dirty girl. God, how he loved her.

"Enough!" he growled as he pressed her back against the lounger, coming up her body and plunging into her in one smooth motion.

He saw stars reflecting in her eyes. He thought he may come from one pump. She had him so hot.

"I need you to get there fast, sweetness. I can't hold on long," he warned her darkly. He grabbed her hand and brought it down between them, rubbing her own fingers against her clit as he pounded into her.

"Hazel, baby," he groaned.

She detonated. She came around him in a firestorm. She was all he could feel, all he could see, her wetness drenching him as he emptied his cock inside of her. His hips grinding into her of their own volition.

When his body slowed and the wind swirled across their sweaty skin, he felt her giggle against his chest.

He leaned up on one of his forearms and looked down at her, love shining in his eyes. "What's so funny, baby?" he asked.

"I'm happy, Luke. You make me so happy, it just bubbles out," she said to him.

"Aw shit, Hazelnut, I'd die to make you happy. I'll kill to keep you safe," he promised her then, dropping a kiss to her lips before he stood and helped her shrug back into her cover up.

"No need for the bikini, babe. You won't need that." He laughed with her and swooped low to pick her up, closing the cover up around her as he carried her back to their room, back to their bed.

Hours later, he hated leaving her alone in their bed. She was warm and soft against him, pressed against his chest. She was in a deep sleep now, and she needed it. He had been insatiable for her. He kissed the back of her head softly and eased out from their tangle of limbs. He threw on shorts and made his way to the bridge. He couldn't help but remember the last time he'd left her in their shared bed, satiated and warm, last fall. He'd known then something awful was coming, and he had let his fear rule him.

Not this time. Never again. He felt an incredible lightness, knowing that this time was different. This time, he'd take care of whatever needed taken care of and then come back to her. He'd always come back to her. Forever.

The sun hadn't quite risen yet, and he loved this time of day on the water. He loved any time of day on the water. Maybe he should just take his money and live the life of leisure. Hazel all to himself, living on the water, traveling when they wanted, focusing on her work. Maybe the assholes of the world would be taken out by someone else.

He couldn't even finish the thought before his gut roiled. No, he was committed to their new plan. The new team. Of course, he needed to talk to Hazel about it now that she understood what it meant. She needed to know what she was attached to. He'd figure out a way. If she didn't like it, Tad could lead it and he'd help in some other manner. He was committed to her choice from here on out.

"You look happy, Luke," Tad said to him from the captain's chair. His eyes were tired, and his voice had that low quality between sleeping and awake.

"Tad, I am. Finally. Because of you brother. And Max. And Theo, and well . . . my guys. Because you all reminded me that men do not make decisions in fear. Real men do the work to rise above the fear and turmoil and take care of those they love. Thank you, brother, from the bottom of my heart, thank you," he said.

"I got you, always." Tad laughed and stood, stretching. "Just make sure you check in with Doc when you get back. Put in the work long term for both of your sakes. Elite operators need to be good in all areas of health, you know that."

"Absolutely. I won't fuck this up again Tad, count on that. Now, I'm also wondering what my Hazelnut will think about the work Titan Group is getting into," he replied.

"It's Hazel. She'll love you even more, bud." Tad smirked at him.

Tad's flippant words eased something in his chest. A knot loosened. For as short as the words had been, they'd also likely been right. He smiled at Tad, the left corner of his lips drawn upward in a way he couldn't stop.

"But seriously man, this is turning into Sex Fest and we need to get this Perry shit figured out and move on," Tad said, laughing.

Just then, Brian also came onto the bridge. "Morning guys. I wasn't sure if you'd be up, Luke, or still wrapped around Hazel, so I came to cover. Nate should be up soon, too. Good job getting your head out of your ass for that woman, bossman." He poured himself some coffee and turned back to Luke.

"I'm making up for lost time assholes. Leave us alone." Luke laughed as he took the cup of coffee from Brian's hand.

"Hey, man, get your own. You have the woman, I need the coffee," Brian protested, but Luke was already taking a big gulp of the coffee. Brian sighed and poured another cup.

"Did we learn anything good last night?" Brian asked, turning away from the coffee pot.

"Boys. Good morning. Tad, you look like shit man, go to bed," Nate said as he came onto the bridge. He'd been walking and talking so that when he got close to Brian, he took the fresh coffee cup from his hand and took a big drink before Brian could protest.

"What the fuck, man? Can no one pour their own coffee around here?" Brian grumbled. He turned for a third mug and began to pour while the guys laughed at his back.

"Is there any more coffee?" Theo's voice wandered in before his body did.

Nate, Luke and Tad were laughing as Brian held firmly to his cup. "Fuck you."

"Tough crowd, man, geez. I was just wondering if I should make a fresh pot. What happened to you, Brian?" Theo looked to his buddy.

"These assholes, as usual." He growled the response, but he had a smile on his face as the rest of the guys laughed at his expense.

"Okay, well, I can see we're in good hands here, so I'm getting rack time." Tad left the bridge for his bed. Dawn would be poking through the night soon and Luke was eager to get this figured out so he could get back to spoiling Hazel as much as possible.

"Guys, I've been thinking about this. What about how Hazel met Fuckstick? If she was at the Fontainebleau in that restaurant by the water, it would have been weird for him to be there for a business meeting, right? I've been there . . . " Theo started. "I mean, what did we learn about the Burke sisters? They have a knack for uncovering some hanky shit without even knowing it."

"When were you at the Fontainebleau?" Brian asked him, stuck on that fact.

"Errr, ummm, let's just say that I've stayed overnight there and leave it at that," Theo sheepishly replied. "Back to business though, man, focus."

"Guys, I agree with Theo and his errant dick, though," Nate said. "She specifically said that the other guy had on a suit. That's unusual for the beach-facing restaurant, right? Wouldn't you have had a business meeting in the main building, where there are plenty of places to choose from, even if you did want to have a business lunch on South Beach, which is weird in and of itself."

"Yeah, maybe our resident boy toy is on to something," Luke said as he ruffled Theo's hair. Theo ducked out of it and shrugged his shoulders.

"It seems like we could ask Hazel more specifics about that and go from there," Brian said.

"Hazel is sleeping and we're letting her get a couple more hours of rest at least, then we'll talk through this with her." Luke's tone brooked no argument.

"Sex Fest is exhausting," Theo said, straight-faced.

"Enough. I don't want her to feel embarrassed. I intend to spend the rest of my life making up to her for what an asshat I have been, so please, don't make her uncomfortable," Luke said, his voice clear and firm.

"Ten-four, boss. We love her, we love you. Glad you pulled your head out there," Theo replied.

The guys were all nodding at Luke, which made his shoulders relax. "Good, thanks boys. Now. While she rests, let's start pulling the guest registry from the Fontainebleau and any video footage of the restaurant for that time period. We should be able to figure out who Fuckstick was meeting with that day," he said.

He met Theo's eyes. "Good thinking, man. Good thinking on this," he praised Theo. Theo was their youngest and the obvious Lothario, his dimples attracting attention everywhere they went. He never wavered in his service or in his dedication to their team, though. He was solid and Luke was grateful for him.

They spent a few hours combing the guest registry and security footage after connecting with Mila and asking her to work her magic to hack into those things. Thankfully, they were able to operate outside of the direct red tape of the government and access that quickly, with Cullins's permission.

Mila was back in DC, but Wills was there with them and had

also made his way to the bridge. Luke felt badly that their work had already separated one couple, but he knew Mila and Wills were good. They'd come through the fire of their own ordeal and were so in love it was sometimes adorably annoying. They also worked seamlessly together. Those two could cover any aspect of tech that Titan Group needed-the hardware portions and the software portions. Nerds unite and all of that. He was damn grateful for both of them, and happy for them that they'd found one another.

Working together was quick work with all of them and by the time that Hazel made her way to the bridge around 8:15, they had at least grainy video footage of Fuckstick and the mystery guy to run by her. Mila had indeed worked her magic and pulled data from the Fontainebleau's back up cloud storage.

The problem was that Mystery Guy seemed adept at hiding his face and the video quality wasn't great. Not only that, but the video footage was also suspiciously missing for almost the entire property. They'd had to work hard to recover the little snippets they had, none of which showed the guy's face.

"Fuck, man, this is not good. I'm not going to sugarcoat this. Whoever we are dealing with is really good," Wills said.

"Yeah, I've gathered. That tells us something too, though," Luke said. He paused as Hazel stepped onto the bridge and made her way to him. The sun was shining brightly now and seeing her walk toward him, with the sun at her back, made his heart stutter.

"Hazelnut, good morning." He gave her a small smile and gathered her in his arms. She laid her head on his chest and squeezed him tightly.

"Morning, Luke. Looking Luke-a-licious this morning." She kissed his pectoral.

"All right, that's good guys. C'mon," Seb said as he too stepped inside. "You Burke sisters and your boy toys are always all over each other. Have mercy on the rest of us," he teased them, an ornery smile on his handsome face.

Luke laughed and kissed her again before grabbing a cup of coffee for her while she sat down on the bench seat behind the captain's chair. He handed her the cup and dropped a kiss on her waiting lips before straightening and looking at the guys again.

"We're missing something here guys, I can feel it. Hazel, tell us again about the night of the party, from the beginning. I'm talking from the time he picked you up for the date until the time I got you in that boat," Luke said.

Hazel recounted the events of the night, from the moment Dan picked her up to the moment the bullets were flying. She recounted her confusion, her anger, her fear, and then confusion again.

"Why there though? The Dry Tortugas aren't exactly the highest tech place," she asked, getting even more confused as the details zinged about in her brain. "Why not at sea?" she asked.

"And which language was that?" she asked also, turning to Luke.

"I had forgotten that detail as soon as I heard your name and learned you were there. They were speaking Farsi. At least that was what Cullins briefed us on during the initial call," Luke said.

"So, we have Farsi speaking people, focused on Dan and his family, taking over the Dry Tortugas, and one mystery meeting ahead of that, after which Dan became very focused on Hazel," Sebastian summed up, looking at Luke again, his face growing more serious.

"Iranian then?" Brian asked.

"Maybe. But let's focus on Dan too. We don't have facial recognition on the guy he was meeting at the Fontainebleau, and I think that's where this started. It just has too many oddities to not be a big piece of this puzzle," Nate said.

"Yes, let's circle back to Fuckface. He's up to his eyeballs in some shit. I can feel it. And he involved Hazel, so I'm going to kill him twice," Luke said.

Wills brought up photos up on the screens in the bridge.

Thank God they had such a great tech package available to them. There were pieces coming in fast now. This is what Luke lived for, this type of brainstorming with his guys. Having Hazel here made it that much better, although he was serious about killing Fuckface for involving her in whatever was happening.

Wills showed Hazel photo after photo while the other guys worked to rule out those who couldn't possibly have been in South Beach in recent weeks. Alibis that they didn't even realize they needed. Not that any of those guys were "clean" by any means, they just weren't the asshole of the day they were looking for. So far, they'd had zero hits on recognition.

He scanned the room. All eyes were on screens and in action but Tad's, who had come back up to join them early that afternoon.

"You okay, man?" Luke crossed the room and asked his second in command quietly as he walked back onto the bridge.

"Yeah, I'm good. But, Luke, there is something about the Dry Tortugas that keeps bothering me. Fort Jefferson was originally built to protect the deep waters of the gulf. It's the last line of defense for anyone coming in that direction, right? It's the strategic deepwater anchorage we need to consider," Tad said.

"So, is it a springboard location that a terrorist wants?" Luke asked, considering.

"Maybe," Tad replied. He looked over at the rest of the team and Hazel.

"Guys, Hazel. Help us out here, I think I have a thread to pull," Tad said.

"We have a fortified, deepwater anchorage in the Gulf of Mexico, Farsi speaking assholes, and Dan's family singled out. What do all of these things have in common?" Tad continued.

"You guys!" Hazel jumped up from where she had been sitting to look at photos of possible matches to the man she saw Dan meeting. "Oil!"

"Dan's family controls most of the oil and gas companies in

the Gulf, right? They're all along the coast." She looked around the room. "Pensacola, Mobile, Houston, New Orleans."

Luke picked up the proverbial thread from her. "If someone has a deepwater anchorage and controls those companies, they could really fuck with the American economy."

"Brother, they could fuck with the very American way of life," Theo said.

"Guys," Wills said, "Commander Cullins is calling in on the video feed."

"Men, Hazel," Cullins said as soon as his face filled the screen.

"One of the barracudas registered a small boat with a heat sig. The Coast Guard patrol closed in and has just picked up Celeste Perry floating in a lifeboat alone. She is alive and will be fine, but she is disoriented and terrified. Whoever took them has the family yacht and the rest of her family. She relayed that Dan had been separated from them once onboard," he said.

"Where was she picked up?" Luke asked.

"Roughly forty nautical miles from Key West," Cullins said, his voice hard. "I need to get the President on this, guys. Tell me you know something. Right now, Hazel is the only one cognizant enough and close enough to Dan to give us any clues whatsoever. The interviews with the other guests have given us nothing but some insider trading to chase and that doesn't feel right for this," he continued.

"I think we might have something, Commander." Luke went on to lay out their new theory and then they collectively planned to fortify those locations physically while Titan Group continued digging into Dan specifically.

Night was descending upon the boat when they ended the last call with Commander Cullins. It was good to have those oil and gas refineries covered, but they still had two hostages and didn't know who their bad guy was specifically.

Luke took Hazel downstairs to the salon area while the others took turns stretching and walking. They'd agreed to break for about an hour and then reconvene, working together as long as it took to get the breakthrough they needed. Thankfully, they were in a timeline that allowed for that quick break because Luke knew his guys, he knew himself, he knew all humans . . . with a quick step away from what you were trying to solve, the answers flowed more easily.

TWENTY-SEVEN

HAZEL

"Luke, I'm scared. I didn't care for Dan specifically, but he is a human being, and I watched those guards shoot that woman with no remorse," she said.

"I know, Hazel. This is getting more and more complicated. Thank God we got you out of whatever he had pulled you into. Let's take a break on that thinking though for thirty minutes. As counterintuitive as it may sound, the break will help us get to where we need to be on that. Slow is smooth and smooth is fast." He sat down on the couch and pulled her down onto his lap. She shifted to one leg across his lap and one folded under herself next to him so she could look at him, face to face. She had to see his eyes.

"Now, Hazel, I need to tell you about something else important. There can't be any secrets between us and I want you to know exactly what I've been working on," he said, his face solemn and his words low.

She wiggled into his lap. His face was kind of scaring her and she needed a connection to him right now. "Luke, now you're scaring me. Is everything okay?" she asked.

She wasn't sure if she could take any more surprises right now, but she trusted him. He never would have been with her again if there was something insurmountable, or if he didn't truly want to be with her.

"Hazelnut, for the last nineteen months, Tad and I have been working on creating a team for Uncle Sam, as you know. We'd been working on that when Ambassador Neil tried to kill Vi, and we've continued building that business since last fall."

"A full-time off-book team for ops? Like what you all did to save Vi? To save me?" she asked him.

"Yes, but they may not always be domestic, and it will be dangerous. Cullins intends to bring us in on smaller joint ops when stealth or diplomacy is needed most, or when things are happening and the media cannot be alerted. Titan Group is working and is ready to go on a full launch, but Hazel, I'll only continue to lead the team if you are okay with it. If you're not, I'll figure something out. Tad will understand and we'll come up with a new plan." He grasped her hands in his larger ones, his eyes boring into hers. He said quietly, conviction ringing in his tone. "I heard you on making joint decisions and I didn't want to assume that you were all in on such a potentially dangerous future. I know last fall was hard on you."

This man. He could skip away scot-free, sail around the world with his money, jet off to climb mountains, and he wanted to help people? He wanted to help people that would never know he existed, risking his life for them. And . . . he'd give it all up for her? Was there something she was missing?

"So you'd give that up if it gave me pause?" she asked, and then held up her hand before he answered her. "I think I under-stand, yet I made a promise to myself to ask questions, to know what was happening around me and not bury my head, like I did last fall, so I want to be really clear in this. It isn't that I don't trust you. I need to ask for my own need of total comprehension. Okay?" she asked, her heart thundering in her throat. "For money? To save the world, why?"

With zero hesitation he said, "Hazel, you are it for me. My everything. If you don't think we should do this, we won't do this. We'll find another way. I'm saying 'we' baby, because we are 'we' now, we are 'we' forever. There is no more I, or me, just we." His hands tightened on hers. "That is, without a doubt, the most important thing to take from this conversation. For the rest of it, well, we've all been trained for so long, we have unique skill sets, and access. Losing Alex and the others throughout our deployments taught us that more often, it was the red tape that placed us as servicemen and women in harm's way."

"Bad intel, lack of the right tech or weapons, abandoned to avoid incident, you name it. Titan Group would be how we use those skills, our access, our money, to prevent shit escalating to international levels, but only shit the President sanctions. Not vigilante, nor rank and file, yet a hybrid, and mostly on joint ops with other agencies when a deft touch is needed."

"So Captain America style?" she asked, trying not to smile at him yet.

"Only much better looking and more badass. But yes, I *am* a pilot, so that kind of tracks."

God, she loved this man. She let the smile she'd been trying not to unleash break across her face.

"Luke, I love your warrior heart. I love your planning and analytical brain. I love your protective streak. I love this entire package before me. You wouldn't be you without this and I wouldn't love you as much as I do if this wasn't who you are at your core," she promised him, her voice clear and strong, her eyes locked on his and her hands solid in his.

"If you are all in on this, I am all in on this. With you. Just us. We and us, no I or me," she continued. "I will be your partner in any way I know how to be."

She felt his deep exhale rack his entire body. He let go of her hands and brought them to her face, framing her jaw. "Thank you Hazel. I promise you that I will always do whatever is humanly possible to always come home to you," he said.

He kissed her. He devoured her lips. His hands were everywhere. He swung her around to the front of his own body, so that they were facing each other fully. She broke apart from his kisses.

"Luke, I promise to always be your safe place to come home to. Wherever we are," she vowed to him before she kissed him again. "And I can handle all the bad with the good, okay? As long as we are communicating, that's all that matters to me."

They ended up in a tangle of naked limbs, feverish kisses, guttural groans of pleasure. She sank on to him, his cock stretching her, her head dropping back. He kissed his way across her neck and breasts, the night cocooning them in the dimly lit salon. He latched onto her nipple and tugged with his teeth as she rode him, his hands on her hips, then sweeping up her back to gather her hair. His kisses scattered across her, his hot tongue tracking along her body. She unraveled around him, her arms on his shoulders. Her undoing sparking his as he came inside of her, groaning her name. It was frantic and fast, the need to be connected too intense to ignore in the safety of the salon.

Luke stood up with Hazel in his arms, kissing her softly, words of love and adoration on his lips as he carried her to their stateroom to clean up. She had never felt so light in her entire life. This incredible man was hers to love. Every part of her heart belonged to him, and she knew that every part of his heart was hers.

They climbed back upstairs to the bridge, hand in hand. They'd only been gone for the agreed upon hour break, but it felt like her entire life had shifted in that short time. She was renewed and focused, ready to take back her life and forge a new life with Luke by her side.

One of the crew had set up a large bowl of lemony pasta and fresh grilled fish and veggies, which they ate while they talked and combed through the data coming in from Mila and Wills.

"Luke, the chef you found for this boat is incredible!" Hazel exclaimed, her foodie heart rejoicing.

"He really is. I learn a new trick every time I eat his cooking," Nate said. Nate was the chef of the group, although they all knew how to cook.

"You'll have to talk to him Hazel, bounce ideas off him for your cookbook. He's an Army vet also and has traveled all over the world," Luke said.

Travel and eating was her ideal situation. That was the angle she wanted to do for her cookbook, the cultural foods from around the world that were in danger of being lost due to the drift from rural areas, war, ingredients disappearing, etc. It was a huge subject and took up some serious space in her brain. She loved researching it.

Her fork clattered to her dish. "Guys! I may have something!" She was excited, her brain racing along with possibility. All eyes were on her now, waiting for what she had to say.

"Okay, so I'm a food writer, which you all know . . . " she started.

"The best food writer ever, Hazel," Luke said, smiling at her. She laughed.

"Do you read *all of* my work?" she asked, momentarily sidetracked.

"Every single article," he confessed.

This man. She rolled her eyes. Such a little closet hacker! She refocused. She really felt like she was on to something.

"Okay, I am fascinated by this idea of lost recipes. Dishes that families eat for generations, passing the recipe or knowledge down from one to another. This idea that food connects us, through time, through cultures. We all have our cultural identities. Foods, similar to terroir for wine, depend on the soils and regions impacting where they are grown. Did you know that grains make up about 70 percent of the global diet? It's true, whether you eat them or you eat the animal that eats them. As people, we are shaped by our place and our cultural foods are a big part of that. But in recent history, those traditions are dying off as we become more homogeneous, more well-traveled, the more soil we lose to erosion, the way the tides shift, or those in power lead wars. Think of what war in Ukraine could mean for the grain supply, for example. Almost 40 percent of the EU's supply comes from Ukraine alone." She was getting rambly in her excitement, she could tell. Eyes were glazing over, but none of them interrupted her.

"Sorry, I get passionate about food. Stick with me here. I wrote an article once on pastas, and how the water and the flour used can make or break the dish. It's more popular to talk about this in relationship to pasta in Italy, or bread in France, but there are other places that this is a way of life. I've heard that even in Disney World, the Italian Pavilion imports water from Italy for their pizza crusts to be more authentic." She was gathering steam now, her voice getting more and more excited.

"Notably, in the country of Dagestan, they make khinkal, their country's traditional dish. It's made from stew meat from an animal of their mountainous flocks and pasta made from the water coming from the streams found in that small country." She paused suddenly, the fork dropping from her hand.

"Hazey?" Luke asked. "What is it?"

"Holy shit, you guys. They speak Farsi too," she rushed the last bit out. "I mean, lots of countries have Farsi speaking people, but something I heard Dan and our mystery guy talking about right when I was being seated that first day just hit me. Dan was saying something about the resources this guy would be able to access would finally offer them the show of strength they needed, and I know I heard him say 'Chechnya.'"

Every set of eyes was on her, speechless. Tad started to slowly clap. Luke picked her up and swung her around. The other guys were shouting out, "Hell yeah," and hollering her name.

"Dagestan, a region rife with uncertainty, Islamic factions, no shortage of hostile situations," Theo said. "And bloodshed among their neighboring country of Chechnya."

"Right. Maybe that's why we aren't finding an Iranian . . . what we need is a Russian. Or, more specifically, someone from Dagestan or that region who speaks Farsi, and could use oil and gas resources to cement a position of power," Luke said. He picked her up and twirled her again. "You are so fucking smart Hazelnut." He set her down and kissed her while the guys were talking through people and Wills was pulling up photos.

She felt her heart swell with affection for all of them, this new family of hers. Luke and these guys had saved her time and time again. They'd saved Violet. She and her sister both owed these men their lives. And for both women, two of these men owned their hearts. If she had one iota of insight that could help, she would be so thankful to be part of the work they did. She would be forever grateful if she could help save the Perry family from whatever was happening.

"So are we dealing with a post late '90s Islamic Jihadist movement or is this all about oil and gas resources, combined with a critical location?" Theo asked.

"Hold that thought, I'm dialing in Cullins now," Tad said. He stood up as the call connected and brought the phone to his ear. Hazel heard him relay what their discussion was, saw Tad nodding and then agreeing on a next step. It was a quick call, which she supposed was either a testament to how much Cullins trusted these guys, or how desperate the situation was, or both.

"Cullins is sending us their lists for top known threats for all Farsi speaking countries. They've had the CIA working through them since the initial call came in, but as you may have guessed, it's a long list. Lots of countries have Farsi as their Mother tongue, secondary language . . . Hell, there are countries that could be using it to throw a listener off. They were looking for a needle in the haystack," Tad said, running his hands through his hair.

"Not completely a needle in a haystack now though," Wills said from one of the screens on the display. "Hazel has seen this person, so while the video footage may be crap, she could potentially identify the man. And now, we know to start with

Dagestan and then Chechnya if we don't find anything. Hang tight . . . "

He continued, typing quickly and ringing up Mila at the same time.

"Hey, guys, what did you find?" Mila answered quickly and asked them for an update. They filled her in, and Hazel watched as Mila absorbed the details and typed on her own screens. "So we need to cross reference Farsi speakers, the watch lists, and the Eastern seaboard CCTV footage, airport footage, traffic cams, you name it," she mused. "Starting with Dagestan. No problem, give me a hot minute . . . " She trailed off, her eyes focused on her screens.

"Mila, maybe try the cameras outside of the Fontainebleau, on the boardwalk. Anyone can access the property from the beach to go to that restaurant. Maybe there are better shots of him outside of that actual property," Hazel said.

"That's right!" Theo exclaimed. "I took a . . . lady friend . . . " He cleared his throat again while the guys all groaned around him. "Okay, all right, I get it. Anyway, I took her walking on that boardwalk when I stayed there and you can access any property along that stretch you want."

"Which could be why we didn't have any hits on the guest registry. Our guy wasn't actually staying there," Luke added. "This is what knowing exactly what a place looks like matters. Proverbial boots on the ground."

"Yep. Bingo! We have a hit, guys." Mila beamed.

"Hazel, you may have just cracked this case wide open. We have Anton Magomedova on camera two hotels south of the Fontainebleau on South Beach on the day you told us you first met Dan. Hang tight . . . yep!" Mila was on a roll now.

"We also have that face on video in Key West in the Yankee Freedom office a week ago. He tried to hide from cameras all over, but a random one on the dock next to the Ferry caught a man in a Royals hat that is a 97 percent match." Mila's voice was still strong but where her face had been on the screen, they now saw a clear video shot and a prior headshot of a man.

"That's him!" Hazel exclaimed. "You guys, that's the guy. I'm 100 percent certain."

"Great work, Hazey!" Mila said. "Also, I've got programs digging into Dan and his family. Dan has been receiving major payments about every thirty days in a Bahamian account for the last four months. That doesn't necessarily mean anything bad with the assets his family moves routinely, but I did flag it just in case." She took a deep breath. "I don't see anything in the parents' accounts moving to those in the Bahamas though, so we might have a lead there." She focused on them again instead of the screen she'd been looking at.

"What next?" Mila asked.

"Stay on Fuckstick please, Mila. He seems pretty worthless to me, but if Ralph was preparing to hand the company to him, he had to have some brains," Luke said.

"I'll stay on Anton Magomedova for now Mila," Wills said. "And it sounds like Tad has Cullins on the line also to start running some of their programs and let him know who we think we are dealing with."

"Just hung up with him, he's on it," Tad responded.

"What is the Yankee Freedom office?" Nate asked.

"That's the ferry that goes from Key West down to the Dry Tortugas every day," Calder said, speaking up about his home-town. "He probably took that to check it out as a tourist. He could have been in Miami when Hazel was, or even on Sunset Key. People are back and forth between the Keys and Miami all the time, and the ferry from Key West over to Sunset Key runs all day, although you have to be staying there or eating there to board." His voice had gone hard, and she shivered, thinking about how close she could have been to this Anton guy.

"It's okay, Hazelnut. He can't hurt you now, I've got you." Luke's deep voice caressed her ear as she gazed absently out the windows of the bridge. The night was dark and the water all around her made her feel like she was floating in a bubble of safety and luxury, yet somewhere out there, maybe even among the dark waves not too far from them, danger was waiting for them.

She turned to him and wrapped her arms around him, hugging him tightly.

"I know Luke, I know you do. I hate to think about everyone who has been hurt already. I'm scared for Dan too. And Ralph," she said into his chest, her words muffled and soft.

Luke's eyes met Tad's over her head, then the rest of the guys. He saw the others nod at him.

"Guys, I am taking Hazel to bed and will be back later," he said to them.

There were murmured good nights as Luke and Hazel left the bridge to make their way to their stateroom.

Hazel sat on the side of the bed quietly while Luke brushed his teeth. She couldn't get the image of that woman out of her head now, the one who was killed at the event in the old fort. The way the blood ran through her hands, the weight of the woman's lifeless body as she laid her down. That could have been her. She could have been alone in her cottage on Sunset Key, with him right outside of her window, and she would never have known until it was too late. She never would have seen her family again, never had the courage to voice her feelings for Luke, none of it.

That's how Luke found her, teeth chattering, eyes vacant and in the throes of a terrible flashback. He reached for her, a gentle fingertip along her arm so he didn't scare her. He waited until her eyes met his. He quirked his brow in question.

"I'm scared to sleep. Every time I close my eyes right now, I see that woman going down in my arms, I feel her blood running through my fingers," she told him as she laid down, teeth chattering.

"I know baby, I'm sorry. That's a normal thing and you've

been through so much. I've got you though. You're safe here," he soothed.

He laid down next to her, and gathered her in his arms, his warm hands sweeping across her back. He kept his tone light and the strokes on her back consistent as he murmured words of love to her. How he'd always protect her, always come for her, always be there for her, no matter what.

She had long since fallen into a deep, dreamless sleep by the time he kissed her on her forehead and very carefully got back out of bed.

TWENTY-EIGHT

LUKE

"O<small>KAY GUYS, WHAT HAVE YOU FOUND</small>?" L<small>UKE ASKED AS HE MADE</small> his way back onto the bridge.

"Magomedova is definitely involved. We've got him with Dan at the restaurant on South Beach as Hazel confirmed, and we've been picking up chatter about mercenaries convening in Key West now that we know more about what to listen for. Last sighting the morning of the party," Wills said.

"Guys, remember that Hazel said there was almost confusion with the attackers when the party was first stormed?" Seb asked, a thoughtful frown marring his handsome face.

"If he'd been in the ferry office, he would have known the schedule of the ferry and thought that no one would be there that night. Maybe a few campers the ferry had dropped off, but nothing like that they found," he reasoned.

"Right, so maybe Magomedova is getting antsy and decides to take the timeline into his own hands. Maybe Dan isn't coughing up what he promised?" Theo asked.

They tossed out other options and discussed them thoroughly. They had huge pieces of the puzzle, but still some sizable gaps to understand. They just needed a few more details, but none of that was going to come that night.

"It's late guys. Cullins is working on all known associates and connections of Anton Magomedova, the FBI is combing through the board records, the others are patrolling for the Perry Yacht. We have people at the refineries physically, let's get some rack time while we can and regroup in the morning," Luke said, rubbing the back of his neck.

They divided up the watch with the crew and Luke made his way back to bed with Hazel. Even with this potential international shit show on his hands, he felt like such a lucky bastard. He had Hazel in his bed, and no secrets between them. He had a team that was covering him, and the resources to help people. He paused on the last step of the stairs before he went through the salon to his stateroom, he looked up at the cloudy sky, imagining his mom up there with her hearty laugh and dimpled smirk. He remembered how it felt to be hugged by her, her grip tight on him and his nose in her hair, how she smelled faintly of apples all the time, and he smiled. For the first time in years, a happy memory came to the forefront of his mind instead of the heartbreak of the end of her life, the end of their family. It had been years since his first thought was a happy memory and he had Hazel to thank for that. She was his light. He'd save her life every day they had left, for she had already saved his many times over.

He slid his shorts and tee shirt off and slid into bed with Hazel once he got back into their cabin, gathering her against his chest. She snuggled into his warmth as she slept, her hand curled around his stomach. He sighed deeply and closed his eyes, dropping immediately into sleep.

He was dreaming the most incredible dream of his life. Hazel's coppery curls were tickling his thighs, and her hot little tongue was lapping at his cock with little licks and wet kisses. He groaned, his hands cupping her head and gently pushing himself up into her waiting mouth. He imagined this was Utopia.

He stretched, his hands on her head and his thickness sliding between her luscious lips. The dream faded at the edges of his eyes, the very real bite of Hazel's nails gripping his hips bringing him pleasantly awake.

"Baby, this is the ideal start to the day." He chuckled darkly as he gazed down at her. She raised her eyes and smiled at him. God, that sight, her lips stretched around him, her hair wild around her face, her bare breasts ticking his thighs as her hands tightened on him.

"I'm going to come in your throat if you don't get up here." He pulled her up, popping her off him. He kissed her deeply, his tongue sweeping into her mouth, matching her hunger.

"Luke, I need you inside of me," Hazel said.

"Whatever my Hazelnut wants, my Hazelnut shall get." He laughed and flipped her over so that she was on her knees in front of him.

He gathered her hands and placed them above her, holding them firmly in place as he nipped at her.

"Don't move those until I tell you sweetness," he said.

"Luke! Stop teasing me!" she pleaded.

"Trust me babe. I've got you," he said against her. He kissed his way down her back, coasting his lips to the side of her spine, causing her to shudder wildly. Those warm hands of his smoothed back up her arms, gathered her hair and dropped it to the side of her head. He brought his hands sweeping down her back and dug his fingers into her hips, his lips nipping and licking at where her dimpled lower back met the top of ass.

His hand dropped down the side of her hip and then his fingers found her wetness. He dipped one finger in her, rubbing against her clit.

She moaned and arched back into him, her arms shaking with the effort to not move. He worked her clit while his other hand moved around her side to her breasts. He grasped her nipple and rolled it between his fingers, pinching lightly on both her nipple and her clit at the same time.

The orgasm shook her entire body, and she let out a wail of pleasure. Her wetness gushed against his fingers as he lazily stroked her through her release. His whispered words worked her up again as he lined himself up and notched inside of her.

"All of this wetness for me baby. Only me. Only ever me." He sank into her, fully seated and began to move steadily.

"Yes Luke, only ever you. Only you. Forever," she keened.

They moved in sync then, his hands everywhere, pinching and pulling. His thrusts getting faster and faster inside of her hotness.

"Baby, need you to come," he commanded. Her hands were curled into the blankets as she came around him hard, her hips moving reverently of their own volition. She was murmuring, "Yes," as she came undone around him again.

Her wetness constricted around him hotly, that perfect ass bouncing in front of him, her graceful arms stretched in front of her, while his hands gripped her hips. He shuddered with the force of his own climax, spilling inside of her. He came roughly, roaring her name. As his hips gentled against her, he leaned over her and gathered her hair again with one hand, sweeping kisses along the back of her neck and shoulders. Her back was still tender, and he kissed along her bruising and scratching softly.

"I love you, Hazel. Forever," he promised. His other hand had wrapped around her stomach, holding her upright with his large hand splayed across her lower belly. He eased them both down to the bed, never leaving her. He loved the feel of their lovemaking soaking them both. He had certainly made a mess of their bed, but God, what a way to wake up.

She turned against him and kissed his jaw, peeking up at him. Her eyes were sparkling and ornery. "Well, we could have been doing THAT much sooner!" She laughed and kissed his chest, settling back against him.

An hour and change . . . and one shower romp later, they

made their way to the salon. Most of the guys were there when they walked in, eating breakfast and talking about scenarios.

"I think we set a trap for them," Tad said. "We don't know where Magomedova is with Fuckstick and his dad and time kills deals. Let's lure them in and set a trap," he said.

"Good Lord Tad, now Luke is rubbing off on you," Seb said at his reference to the name Fuckstick instead of Dan.

Luke smiled widely. "Smart man," he winked at Tad.

"For what it's worth, I agree with Tad," Theo said.

"Me too," Brian added. Nate, Wills and Calder nodded affirmatively too.

Luke turned to Hazel, standing at his side. "Hazel, what say you? Shall we do this? Shall we wrap this fuckery up and move on? Maybe talk you into marrying me on the beach soon?" he said, the words tumbling out naturally before his brain engaged. He felt zero fear though, he knew what he wanted, and he wasn't pussyfooting around about it anymore.

Tad's eyes widened and a smile stole across his face as Hazel gasped. "Luke!" he admonished. "Fuckery? Really, bro, when you're proposing marriage?"

"Man, you used the word fuckery in your marriage proposal to the woman you have spent years pining over. You dumbass." Theo laughed at him.

The guys were all laughing but Hazel still hadn't said anything. He caught her eyes and dropped to his knee, raising his hand to her mouth and placing a kiss on her knuckles.

"Hazelnut, sweetness, marry me. I wasted too much time with my head up my ass. I know I said fuckery earlier, but my sentiment was genuine. And I know it is fast, but to me, it's slow. I've loved you for so long. I will love you forever. Please marry me," he said solemnly.

He saw the left side of her mouth tick up and his heart sped up. Her fingers tightened in his.

"Of course I'll marry you Luke." Her smile broke across her face, shining happily. Her eyes tearing up.

He jumped up and swung her into his arms as the guys clapped.

"You two nuts are made for each other," Theo said.

"These Burke sisters and their boy toys, I tell you . . . " Seb started. He'd also seen so much of Vi and Max falling for one another, he knew the drill.

Luke's throat constricted. This incredible woman had forgiven him. She loved him. She was going to marry him. He crushed her to his chest and whispered into her ear.

"Wherever we are Hazelnut, you're my life," he said.

"Well guys, I hate to break up the happy moment. A happy moment that will go down in history for its sheer romanticism. But alas, there is still fuckery afoot," Tad said.

Luke lowered Hazel to the ground and kissed her quickly on the lips.

"Tad's right, as usual," he said against her lips. She laughed happily, caught up in him.

"Our best chance at a safe exfil for Fuckstick and his dad are to control the timing and atmosphere, so let's get started on what that could look like," Brian said.

Luke saw Hazel's happy bubble pop. Worry streaked across her face, and she turned her eyes back to his. She bit her lower lip in consternation, "I feel terrible. I'm the happiest I've ever been and yet Dan is in danger. I don't know him well, and I wasn't going to go out with him again, yet I'm still scared for him and his sweet dad." Her eyes held guilt.

"It's okay, Hazel. You're allowed these glimmers of happiness. God knows I haven't always known that myself, but you get to have this. You've had a rough go through this and it's okay that you are now safe and happy," Sebastian's soft voice floated to them.

She turned for Seb and thanked him, reaching over to him and giving him a quick hug.

"We're going to do what we do best Hazel, kick some ass," Theo said, all bravado.

That broke the tension that had filled the salon, and they all eased into seats to plan their next step. Luke sat next to his fiancé, his hands finding their way to her as often as possible. He'd completely bungled proposing to her, but she'd said yes, which was all that mattered. Fuck, he hadn't even had a ring for her.

He'd make that up to her later too, they just needed to get this Anton Magomedova situation figured out. Then, he'd marry her as fast as possible and fully launch Titan Group.

TWENTY-NINE

HAZEL

SHE TRIED DILIGENTLY TO TRACK THE CONVERSATION AROUND HER and participate, but she couldn't focus to save her life. Hells bells, was she really engaged to Luke Stratton? Did he really just ask her to spend the rest of her life with him? She couldn't stop smiling, and that also kind of made her feel like an ass, considering what they were talking about.

"Luke, I need to talk to Vi. Can you make that happen?" she asked him quietly.

"Absolutely. Let's head to the bridge and you can video chat. We need to pull the entire team together to plan anyway so let's do that after you and Vi catch up," he replied, standing and holding his hand out to help her stand.

"Guys, we're heading back to the bridge to talk to Vi and then we should all start mapping out our strategy to wrap this up. I have a goddess to marry now, so I feel urgency," Luke said and laughed.

The guys chuckled, varying responses of agreement to connect on the bridge sounding throughout the salon.

Luke and Hazel made their way up to the bridge, seeing the

captain inside. Seeing Luke enter, he let them know that he was going to take a quick break and then he'd rejoin them shortly. Luke dialed Vi and Max on the secure video technology they had and then turned to her while they waited for an answer. He grabbed her around the waist and brought her to him swiftly, his lips finding hers immediately. What he intended to be a quick peck turned hot quickly though, and before he knew it, Max was heckling him through the video feed.

"Is this a new live action pay-per-view situation?" Max asked, laughing at them.

"Hazey! Um, hey, Sis. What's going on there?" Vi added, laughing at Max's comment. They quickly broke apart and turned to face the monitors.

"Vi! Max! We're engaged!" Hazel was smiling broadly, her joy radiating. He pulled her back to his front and wrapped his arms around her again. Feeling his own smile splitting his face, he added, "I pulled my head out of my own ass and begged Hazel to make an honest man out of me."

"Oh my goodness guys, finally! I'm so happy for you!" Vi cried. She had tears streaming down her face, which set Hazel off too. Before too long, both women were blubbering through their happy tears and smiles.

"Ladies, I love you both, but please stop crying," Luke said, as he dropped a kiss to Hazel's lips, wiping her cheeks dry with his thumb.

"My baby mama can cry whenever she wants Luke," Max said, laughing.

The ladies caught up on how Vi was doing with her pregnancy, the preparations for Baby Alex they'd been making in the Dupont Circle property and then, long before they were ready, Luke broached the subject of Anton, Dan, Ralph and the tangle of puzzle pieces. He caught them up while they waited for the rest of the team to join them on the bridge.

Once everyone was there, Tad also dialed in Mila. They'd decided to come up with a plan and then connect in Commander

Cullins. Tad had been communicating almost real time with him, and he was up to speed.

The group tossed around ideas, Mila and Wills adding background details about what they were seeing in the business records. None of their planning was working out theoretically unless they knew where the other yacht with the hostages physically was. They couldn't lure if they couldn't communicate and up to that point, there had been zero activity at the refineries. Cullins had those covered, but they needed the head of the snake. They needed Anton Magomedova.

"What about the Marquesas? Maybe even tucked into one of those uninhabited islands in the Key West National Wildlife Refuge? There are over 1700 islands making up the Keys down here, tons of places to hide a boat of any size. It isn't all the Duval crawl down here," Calder added. No one knew the Keys like he did. His family had been in the area for generations, and it was where he had gone home to once his service in the Coasties was over. He was an avid fisherman and often chartered out his own boat for sport fishing.

"Wasn't Hemingway a big fan of fishing the Gulf Stream and docking in the Marquesas? I think I read he was even stranded with his 'mob' on Garden Key once because of a storm," Hazel added.

"That's right. They fished during the day traditionally, and they would dock in the Marquesas at night," Calder agreed. "And you're right, on the last big fishing expedition, the group hit bad weather and had to shelter in Fort Jefferson on Garden Key for seventeen days. They had provisioned well and caught fish close to the end to eat, but that's where they were stranded," he said. "If a storm was on the water, I'd rather take refuge in a brick fort than the uninhabited atoll of the Marquesas."

"Why not go back to Fort Jefferson if you're Anton?" Seb asked. "If that was a target for the deepwater anchorage, they probably haven't abandoned it completely. If it were us, we'd wait to ensure whoever grabbed Hazel was gone and then we'd go back. They wanted the property for a reason, and they've already taken care of the National Park unit there for security. If Hemingway and his group, who knew the islands extremely well, chose to ride out storms at the fort, why wouldn't our guys use what they know? It's a literal fort to his point, why not use the assets they have?" he said.

"I agree. The last place most people check is the original 'scene of the crime.' Plus, Celeste Perry was picked up between there and Key West, so they weren't too far away. That's what . . . " Luke looked to Calder. "Fifty miles?" he asked.

"It's seventy miles from Key West to Fort Jefferson on Garden Key, with the Marquesas and the wildlife refuge along the route in the Gulf Stream. My money is that they're back at the fort," Calder confirmed, having mulled over what Seb was saying.

"Right, so if we send in the recon drones again, we'll be able to tell quickly if they are there. We had trouble accessing satellite images last time, but those drones will tell us where people are in the fort. Then, we use the same framework of planning that we did to grab Hazel, only neutralizing Anton and his men this time," Tad said.

"Yes, exactly. We neutralize and then remove Dan and his dad Ralph, getting them clear of whatever is happening so we can get this Anton guy," Sebastian added.

"Are we sure we don't want to leave Fuckstick there?" Luke asked, mostly joking. Hazel lightly slapped his arm at that comment.

"Wills, how is the cloak of invisibility holding up? Will we be able to get close again and keep this boat safe?" Luke went on.

"Yes, we're good. I'd stay behind to manage our tech. I assume Mila can work it from another angle to see if we can get anything from them and the Perry yacht if we get close enough. Mila, how does that sound to you?" He asked the screen with Mila's face.

"Yes, I can do that. I'll have your back." She nodded. "These assholes are messing with my bestie which obviously pisses me off. Also, I need my boy toy back at home." Some of the sunshine had returned to her face and voice now that Hazel was safe, and they knew what was going on to more of a degree. She laughed lightly after she mentioned her boy toy and Wills blew her a kiss.

"Thatta girl!" Theo chimed in. Mila blushed on the screen.

Hazel saw Luke meet Tad's eyes and then nod. She watched him nervously as he turned to her and put his hands on her arms. He was stroking her arms, his tone soothing as he said, "Hazelnut, you'll need to stay on the boat. But baby, I'm staying with you. I can't risk your safety." His eyes were pleading with hers now.

"I understand, Luke, but I think you should go onto the island with your team. You are the team leader, right?" she asked him.

"Yes, but Tad is second in command and we do things our own way now baby. No more Uncle Sam telling us exactly how we have to do every single thing," he replied.

"Yes, but *baby*, that works for you all. That's your MO and so far, it has worked mostly well for you. I think you need to stick with it. Wills will have us covered here on the boat, anyway. Right, Wills?" she said, looking over to where Wills was sitting, watching the byplay between the two of them like the others were.

"Um." He coughed. "Yes, yes, that's true. But Hazel, it is new tech so Luke is right on the planning," Wills said.

"Oh, right, okay. We're doing the primary, alternate, contingency and emergency again, I gotcha. I love this comms tool guys, and the planning that goes into it. It makes my journalist heart happy," Hazel replied. "And guys, I understand what you are all saying, I never want to be a weakness for this team. You guys are amazing, and I don't want to hold anyone back. I trust you all to do your jobs and do them well." She gazed back into Luke's eyes, this time it was her turn to stroke her hands down his arms. "I can't be why you don't operate Luke. This is part of who you are, it is part of why I love you. This is your life."

Luke gathered her in his arms then, kissing the top of her head.

"Any one of these guys would die to protect you Hazel. Any one of them would kill to protect you, you are part of us now too. But Hazelnut, I will still be operating, just from here. Tad's got this. I need to hold down this fort as part of the plan. I love that you are strong enough and trust us enough to do our jobs, that's part of what makes you so incredible. You get me," Luke said, his voice carrying throughout the bridge. "And just to be clear babe, *you* are my life." He smiled at her then, that cocky smirk that she loved so much.

She saw their heads nodding, and she heard Vi and Max talking to each other on the screen.

"It's settled. Tad is taking point, Seb is second and the guys will cover them on site. Wills and I here, Mila covering. Captain, sounds like we are heading back to the Dry Tortugas," Luke said.

They spent the rest of the day planning and going through their levels of plans. With their yacht, they could be back around Garden Key by nightfall if they needed to be. They decided to get close, hover out of range again, trusting that their tech would hold, send up the drones with heat sig technology and then if Magomedova and his men were there with Dan and his dad, they'd know right away. After that, they'd approach it much the same way they had when they extracted Hazel earlier. The largest difference was that Tad was leading this and instead of breaching immediately, they'd wait until the wee hours. They'd hit the fort at the witching hour, at 3:00 a.m.

THIRTY

LUKE

HAZEL HAD REFUSED TO GO TO BED IN THEIR STATEROOM EARLIER when he'd begged her to go get some rest, but she was asleep on the couch in the bridge now. The low murmurs of his team filled the room and the darkness around them acted as a cocoon. He loved this phase of his work. The planning, the preparation, the team coming together to think about how it could go FUBAR and then planning for it to indeed go FUBAR. In their work, if you didn't plan for that, you didn't last long.

It would be time for the others to go before too long. They'd confirmed that Magomedova, his men, Fuckstick and his dad, were all there based on heat sigs and positioning on the yacht. They had indeed gone back to the fort. They had some additional measurement data from the tech Wills had created, indicating that it was likely they'd found Magomedova, and the Perry men specifically.

They also had additional heat signatures that they had to assume were mercenaries helping Magomedova. There appeared to be nine men on the yacht anchored at Garden Key, most of whom were sleeping, leaving two awake to keep watch from what they could tell. They'd also counted seven patrolling the fort.

The first item of business when they breached was to take the lighthouse. They needed Nate positioned as high up on the island as possible for effective overwatch. Fortunately, the light-house had recently been restored, and they'd been able to easily access the internal schematics via the cloud, thanks to the project manager sharing phase updates with her colleagues via email.

Luke was studying those again now, as he had when they'd prepared to exfil Hazel. He looked over at her sleeping. He wanted nothing more than to let her sleep through this mission, but the safest plan was to have her awake and alert. He set the lighthouse plans down and made his way over to her.

"Hazelnut, baby, it's almost time. I need you to wake up." He dropped his hand to her shoulder and gently squeezed. She stirred, opening her eyes at him and blinking rapidly to clear the sleep lingering there.

"Sweetness, rise and shine." He leaned over and kissed her quickly as her hands snaked around his neck and held him to herself.

She was quiet sitting up and stretching, watching the surrounding activity.

"You guys are a well-oiled machine," she said through a yawn.

"If you want something done Hazel, send a Marine," Theo said as he walked past her, winking. She laughed at his cheekiness, but also vehemently agreed with him. She'd heard Luke say that very thing practically her whole life. It had been the memory of that very sentiment that spurred her to call Luke last fall, when Vi was in trouble and she didn't know what else to do.

The guys were loaded up and heading for Fort Jefferson thirty minutes later. Wills had outfitted the guys with more new tech that he'd been working on, some pieces that Hazel had seen in action before when the guys had helped Violet. Each guy had clear little patches on them that acted as mini cameras, which would help if their helmets and typical cameras were knocked off. They weren't trying to blend into a party tonight, but having the little patches might give them more data and the more you knew going into a situation like this, the better. She shivered at the memory of watching Luke go down via one of those little patches last fall, of hearing him say her name as he went down over the comms, thanks all to that tech Wills had created. She pushed down a lump of fear and déjà vu and refocused on what they were doing. They had on Kevlar under their neoprene suits, helmets and their weapons were ready to roll.

Hazel and Luke watched from their comms as Nate breached the lighthouse undetected. Their boat was quiet around them, all eyes on the screens in the bridge.

Moments later, Nate signaled back that he was in position for overwatch. Tad gave the follow up signal and before their eyes on the screen, three of the seven mercenaries patrolling were picked off via the sniper.

If Luke didn't know where the guys would rise out of the water from, he wouldn't have seen them, they were that good. He pointed to different screens in front of them to show Hazel how they were progressing. Less than five minutes since breach, all seven of the mercenaries patrolling were dead.

Luke let out a deep sigh, but something in his gut was bugging him. They were the best, they were well trained, and they had the most cutting-edge tech available on the planet . . . but when things went too smoothly, it made you leery.

He forced his breathing to slow down, as if he was with his guys. He rolled his shoulders down from where they'd bunched up closer to his ears and rolled them back. The screens were reflected on Hazel's face as he turned to her, quietly watching.

"Hazel, this is the hard part. You know what to do if we get separated right?" He squeezed her hand.

"Yes, but that won't happen, Luke." She squeezed his hand and met his eyes. "Don't let that happen and we'll be fine."

The faith she had in him was staggering and yet he knew to

plan for the worst, just to be safe. He quickly hugged her and then they refocused on the screens with Wills.

Max, Violet, Mila and the Commander were on the comms from their respective homes and offices in DC as well. There was a low murmur from Wills as he communicated real time with Commander Cullins. Max, Vi and Mila were silent, watching and in Mila's case, monitoring.

"Onboard starboard side," Tad whispered into the comms.

"Onboard portside . . . " Theo started before cutting off to silence the guard who was right in front of him. They heard a grunting and saw the man go down on comms, Theo setting his body gently on the deck to remain as quiet as possible.

"Onboard stern," Brian checked in.

They knew there was one more guard awake and on patrol from their reconnaissance. Eyes were glued to the screens as the guys swept the boat for the other guard. Nate was still on over-watch from the lighthouse and would stay there as their "fail safe," in case any of them got away. Commander Cullins had the Coast Guard en route from their earlier position higher up in the Keys. The goal was to handle this as quietly as possible and try for containment.

The guys were sweeping in a pattern and preparing to enter the salon of the Perry yacht when all hell broke loose.

Wills typed faster and switched feeds. No sooner had he said, "Heat sigs on the move," than the boat lit up like mid-day, sending a flare over the comms and onto the screens. Shots rang out on the deck and shouting in both English and in Farsi sounded across the waves. Men had swarmed out of the bridge and the salon on the Perry boat.

"Luke! What do we do?" She was worried, he could hear the fear in her tone. She watched as her friends were caught in hand-to-hand combat.

"We hold the line, Hazel. Stay put," he said. Watching his men fight off these assholes from this distance was brutal, but this was the safest plan. The more layers of Marines between them and Hazel, the better.

"They're still okay, Hazel, their feeds are still on and active, see?" He pointed out different angles to her.

Wills had a larger UAV in the air. The larger drone had a payload for weapons, and they'd fitted it with smaller bombs and flares. He dropped a flash bang above the stern, starboard side. That sound and light startled the mercenaries, giving Theo and Brian both a chance to take out their attackers.

"Taking one now," Nate's steady voice rang out as they watched one more of the mercenaries drop on the main deck. "Again," Nate said as another mercenary went down.

Tad was still fighting guys but had taken out two of them already. Wills dropped another flash bang as Nate dropped three more mercenaries in rapid succession, the light and noise discombobulating them.

There was grunting across the comms as the men grappled for position. Luke saw a flash of a knife as he shouted into the comms.

"Theo, eight o'clock!" he barked just in time. Theo twisted out of the way and rolled, his momentum giving him the advantage to take the guy out. He'd barely turned back from that man as another charged him. Nate's calm voice sounded over the comms . . .

"Down, Theo," he said. Theo dropped to the ground and Nate shot the attacker, one more down.

Brian and Tad were fighting back-to-back with attackers and winning when they started to lose comms again.

"Fuck!" Wills slammed his hands down on the screen. "Something is happening, we're losing the connections."

They were losing connections, the screens getting fuzzier and fuzzier, the sound coming and going.

"There!" Hazel shouted, pointing at one of the screens as the connection got fuzzier and fuzzier. "That's Dan!"

Luke saw Dan, his father Ralph and Magomedova coming

out of the salon, surrounded by the last of the mercenaries right when they completely lost the feeds.

Wills was shouting now, trying to regain contact. Mila's voice was in the background too, and Cullins was barking orders in his office.

Through the cacophony of voices around them, Luke took Hazel's hand again, this time giving her a knife and a gun.

"Hide the knife in your clothes and hold the gun Hazel. I need to be ready to fight anyone who makes their way on this boat that shouldn't. If anyone comes close to you, shoot them. If you can't . . . babe, you let them get close and then you gut them. You got it?"

Her eyes had been on his the entire time but she hadn't said a word. He swept his hands up the outside of her arms. "Hazelnut, do you hear me? Are you okay?"

She shook herself and then nodded her head. "I'm with you Luke. I got it. Shoot and stab, got it." Her hand shook slightly as she reached out for the weapons, but she took them as he kissed her on the head. She was ready.

"And, Hazelnut, I love you. I'll be right here with you, I just need you to be able to defend yourself if the worst happens," he said.

She looked up at him again, her namesake-colored eyes clear and wide. "I love you too Luke, so much. We're going to have forever, I know it. Wherever we are, it will be together." She popped up on her tip toes and kissed him on the lips.

"Now, let's do this," she said, easing back down to her normal height.

He smirked at her then, his little warrior princess, his copper goddess.

THIRTY-ONE

HAZEL

She was terrified, but she refused to show it. She knew these guys were the best. She had to have faith in them.

The bridge was a hive of activity and still no comms. Wills had sent another UAV in the air, and they still had active heat signatures. They just didn't know who those belonged to at that moment.

"Incoming!" Wills yelled, racing out of the bridge and looking into the water. "One of our boats—looks like Theo, Dan and his dad," he said, relief resounding in his voice. He raced back onto the bridge and relayed to the team not physically there, "We've got one back with the hostages."

He went to work was trying to reconnect with the guys on the Perry yacht from the bridge.

"Oorah!" Luke shouted out, grabbing Hazel's hand. She launched herself around him, jubilant to know her guys were okay. Together, they made their way down the stairs to the back swim deck to help Theo and the Perry men on to the boat.

"Theo! I'm so happy you're okay!" she exclaimed as she practically launched herself at him on the swim deck.

Laughing, he hugged her tight and then set her back down. Luke had clapped him on the back and she was just stepping around Theo to say hello to the Perrys when she heard the distinct cocking of a gun.

She spun to Luke as fast as she could, but it was too late. Dan had stepped around Theo faster than a snake and grabbed her by the hair. He held the gun to her head, inching toward the edge of the yacht.

"Dan!" Ralph, his dad, shouted as Theo and Luke pulled their own guns. Both men had theirs ready, but not pointed at Dan. They couldn't. Dan was using Hazel as a human shield and the gun in his hand was tight to her temple.

"One move my way and she dies," he snarled. "She has been fucking up my play since I met her on South Beach. I should have killed her there while I had the chance, but shit, I thought it'd be easiest to push her overboard when we came back from the party. Fuck! You are all fucking up my play!" Spittle flew from his mouth as he raged. His eyes were wide and unfocused, but his hand holding the gun to Hazel had never wavered.

The barrel of the gun was digging into her skin. She felt his wiry strength clutching her to his front, ready to kill her or Luke, or Theo.

"Dan!" Ralph shouted. "Son, what is this all about? They saved us. We're okay!"

"Fuck you, Dad. We're not okay. You are not okay. Magomedova isn't the brains here, I am." His lethal words falling on all of them, stunning them.

"I don't understand, Dan. What did I do?" Hazel pleaded. She felt like such a fool. She had been filled with bravado thinking about Luke and his team, but here she was, the weak link.

"Don't hurt her man, whatever this is, we can figure it out," Luke had said. His eyes were steady on Dan, his voice sure and strong. "Please, let her go and I'll help you figure this out," he tried to rationalize with the man.

Theo was watching intently, his pose as relaxed as possible to not appear threatening to Dan. He kept his gun pointed at Ralph, in case Dan wasn't the only traitor.

"There is nothing to figure out. She could have blown up my entire deal, everything I've been working on for years. Magomedova is my buyer, you dumbasses. I set this up. Only she had to see us together, then hear us together. I wasn't sure if she heard any of our conversation or not, but I knew she was the one writer who could connect me to a Russian. I couldn't leave the loose end. I even tried to get her to talk about it by bringing up taking over the company from my dad, but she never budged. I can't risk it. I can't take over everything and then sell it off to Magomedova without worrying she'll talk. She's a fucking writer. They are bloodhounds," he raged more.

"So what?" Luke asked, trying to draw more of Dan's attention to himself instead of Hazel. "How is that worth murdering Hazel for? Anyone could have seen you in South Beach, anyone could have questioned why you sold your company to a guy from Dagestan," he continued.

The gun was still painfully digging into her temple, and her heart racing in her throat. The arm he was using to hold her as his shield tightened, cutting off more of her air. She had to keep him talking, hoping the others would come to see what was taking them so long. She knew there were cameras everywhere, and she knew Wills would have had them on.

"I don't even pay attention to oil and gas, Dan! I don't know what you think I could have done. I promise there is a way out of this," she tried to reason with him.

"Please, put the gun down and we can talk about this. You can sell your company to anyone you want to. Let her go and I'll help you, man. You can sell to whoever you want to. I'll buy it. Name a price and it's yours. Just let her go," Luke tried again.

"No, he can't." Ralph poked. "It's my company and if he sold any shares he inherited to Magomedova, he'd have given control of the company away to Magomedova's foreign interests. The majority of US oil production would have been in the hands of Russians." Ralph lowered his head then, defeated. "He had my proxy votes for whatever he needed while we worked through the transition, and he had his own. It would have been enough for the board to not have a say in ownership until it was too late."

"Son, why?" he asked, looking back up at his only son. He knew he was beaten at that moment. A once powerful patriarch now felled by his own son.

"Magomedova didn't want anyone to know, did he?" Hazel asked. She was done standing there quietly while a crazy asshole was holding a gun to her head.

Dan laughed. "Bingo. Told you writers were fucking bloodhounds. I couldn't risk anyone on the board connecting us until it was too late, couldn't have dear old dad realizing his proxy votes were never coming back to him." He laughed again, derision laced in his words. "And he couldn't let anyone know what he was up to, either. He thought he was getting access and resources, but he couldn't have his enemies scoop him. He legitimately wanted the business."

Theo caught her attention subtlety and flicked his eyes quickly to the stairs behind her. She understood. Someone must have come down from the bridge.

"Dad, you know what this is about. You raised me to love it. Money. why else?" Dan continued, thankfully unaware he was being surrounded.

"Selling makes me the richest man in America, one of the richest in the world. Do you even understand the power that gives me? I can take over whatever I want once I have that money, and then I'll just take my company back. I'd have a home field advantage," Dan droned on. He was shockingly laissez-faire about a potential war of his own making on American soil. He bragged about his entire sordid plan, setting up Magomedova, his plans to murder her and his parents, everything.

Hazel had been watching Luke during Dan's tirade. She saw the moment his gaze had flicked from Dan's hand to her own eyes. She knew what to do. In the excitement of seeing Theo returning with the Perry men earlier, she still had the knife in the sleeve of her long-sleeved t-shirt. The angle was going to be tough, but she could do this. She just had to sidetrack Dan a bit first.

"So the party was all a set up to clean house, basically? Was that you or Magomedova? Were you really planning to kill your own parents?" she asked. She was incredulous, but she also wanted to keep him talking until she was ready.

"You're smarter than I thought you were, Hazel. Yes, the hostage situation was my idea. I talked Magomedova into thinking that he would be the one who saved us, and that would be all it took for the board to look favorably on him. He bought that shit hook, line and sinker. I just had to act scared." Dan laughed again.

"We can help you get your money. Just let her go. We can talk about this. That is the easiest way out of this. There is no other exit here now that you're on this ship. We're all here, seeing this shit." Theo tried a different tactic to keep Dan's focus drifting. "You just told us all everything."

Dan laughed maniacally, "and it's all her fucking fault! Magomedova transferred the money today so I have enough I can change the plan for now. I don't need to buy the company back, and he will never get board approval, if he even survived your takedown back there. I just need her to die for fucking this up for me. Once we're clear of here, she can take that fucking midnight swim she should have taken after the party. With a bullet hole in her head. I can disappear. With the resources I have now, you'll never find me." He shuffled backward toward the motorboat.

The vehemence of his words when he spoke caused a flash of terror throughout Hazel. He really had lost it. And shit! She couldn't get on that boat with him. He'd get away, and she'd be dead. She squeezed her eyes shut, envisioning Luke as he'd held her this morning, the soft light coming over the horizon, sparkling across the blue waters. She thought about Vi and Max, and Baby Alex. Her heart clenched painfully. She wanted to live. She wanted to see her family grow and she wanted one of her own, with Luke. Luke, who would never forgive himself if something happened to her, especially right in front of him, on his own boat. He'd waste his life on vengeance, and every single person she had come to love within Titan Group would suffer. She couldn't let that happen to them, to Luke. She would not allow herself to be part of making his biggest fears come true. Dan clearly didn't know who he was dealing with. He'd be hunted relentlessly the moment he left this boat.

She was being dragged backward to the motorboat. They were almost at the edge again, but she wasn't going down without a fight.

"Follow us and you'll watch her die!" Dan yelled. He only had one more step to go. It was now or never.

She kept her eyes on Luke's while she intentionally slowed her breathing. He deserved a woman who could handle herself in this situation, and he'd trained her well. She was going to do what she could to save herself. She knew she could do it. She took another shallow breath and focused on Dan's words, blocking out the feel of his arm banded around her waist and the barrel of the gun jammed into her temple.

As soon as he finished yelling that last threat, she made herself dead weight in his arm, dropping downward. As she crashed down, she turned herself and slashed out with the knife, hitting him in the side as they both went over the edge of the swim platform and into the dark waves. He grabbed a handful of her hair and her scalp screamed in protest as the waves knocked her apart from him.

Dan's screams and curses sliced through the rough waves as he pointed his gun at her and fired, as water began to claim him.

She had kicked free of him, leaving a clump of her hair in his fist, but he was thrashing in the waves, and one shot hit right by her. She sank under the water to escape him, going deeper and deeper until the shots stopped.

The water was so much colder out here in the open ocean, and it was terrifyingly dark. Fear was hammering her heart against her ribs and her chest pinched tightly for air. She tried kicking upward and outward from where she had last seen him and the direction the shots had come from. Darkness closing in, her lungs burning. She was getting disoriented down here, in her own death spiral. She was in a crushing mass of deep sapphire and her eyes were burning in the salty sea water. She needed to breathe and soon. That underwater numbness was taking over again, and she refused to let it. This time, she'd fight through that fear. She kicked her legs again, hoping she was swimming in the right direction.

Two strong kicks later, she slammed into a hard chest. Arms banded around her and lips descended to hers, breathing into her mouth while strong legs kicked them both upward. He'd come for her, of course he had. Her Poseidon.

They broke through the waves together, entwined. Her muscles were freezing up, but Luke had her. He must have hit the water almost immediately after she went in, and she was so glad he had. He shielded her from the shots she heard hit the water, and then there was blissful silence.

Theo had finally made contact with Dan, his bullet striking the man in the head, his arm still reaching out to fire again at Luke and Hazel. Wills had indeed seen that they needed help and came in the nick of time. While he took care of Dan, Calder had also dove in after her and Luke. She hadn't even seen them make it back from the fort and yet there he was, hauling them back to the safety of the *Copper Goddess*.

It had all happened in a moment. One second, she was being clutched to the front of a madman, his gun digging into her temple and the next, Luke was helping her back onto the deck of the boat and gathering her in his arms before the dark abyss could claim her too. He sat back and crushed her to his own chest, wrapping his arms around her and kissing her face. He was saying something, but she couldn't hear him. Her ears were ringing, and she was shaking violently. Her throat and eyes burned, and she gulped fresh air in as fast as possible. She wrapped her arms around him without even realizing she had done so.

"It's okay, Hazelnut. I've got you. You're safe now," he spoke low, murmuring words of love to her as she shivered against him. Wills and Theo had moved to Ralph, helping the older man sit down and turning him away from where his son's body had gone under.

The crew had descended with warm blankets and there was noise everywhere, but still Hazel couldn't quite make out the words. She was bone cold and crushingly tired. Another giant shiver racked her body, leaving her shuddering against Luke.

"We need to get her warm!" Luke had picked her up and was carrying her to their stateroom, practically running.

"Wills, Theo!" Luke shouted again.

"On it, Luke, we've got you," Wills answered.

Hazel's limbs acted as if she was still under water. Even though she knew she was okay, she couldn't get her lips to work, or her arms, for that matter. She was numb, but she was fighting to keep her eyes open.

Seconds after thinking that, Luke had her in the shower, with warm, steamy water cascading down all over her. He got her under the spray and then removed both of their clothes. He pulled her against his naked chest, his muscles rippling against her hands, but she couldn't feel him.

"Hazel, you're in shock, sweetheart. Stick with me. I need to get you warm, okay?" He was sweeping his hands all over her, back and forth, rubbing life back into her limbs.

Her shivers were slowing down, and she was starting to feel

again. It was as if needles were stinging her all over her entire body, the sharpness taking her breath away.

"Love you," she mumbled to him, her lips still numb. "Not going anywhere."

"Oh, Hazelnut, I love you too, babe. You were so brave. I'm proud of you. But shit, Hazelnut, please don't ever do anything like that again. I can't lose you." He moved his hands to her face, stroking the wet hair away from her eyes. He bent down and kissed her. He kissed her gently, until the warm water had penetrated her frozen skin, until her lips could feel his again.

Once he had her warm, he turned off the water and got them both out. He wrapped her up in a fluffy towel and then wrapped her hair in another fluffy towel for her. She heard a faint knock at the door and moments later, he was back with a cup of hot coffee for her.

"Compliments of the chef, Hazelnut." Luke smiled at her and got dressed quickly. He got out some sweats and a sweatshirt for her also while she took some tentative drinks, keeping her hands wrapped around the warm mug.

"I need to get back to the bridge and assess. Do you feel up to it, or should I wrap you up in bed and make everyone come down here? I can't leave you right now Hazelnut, so you tell me your preference," he said.

"I'll be okay, Luke, because you came in the water after me. I was terrified I'd die down there. I had no idea the water would feel like diving into a million little knives. And that shot, he could have killed you, Luke!" she cried.

"Babe, he almost killed you. I'll see you going over the side of this boat in my nightmares until my dying day," he replied.

"And yet again, you saved me. My knight in shining armor rides again. Wait, I mean, swims again," she said.

"Hazelnut, you saved yourself before I saved you. And if we are keeping score, you saved me the moment you forgave my stupidity. Your love has woken my dumb ass up, and I'll love you forever." He gave her a goofy grin then, something she hadn't seen him wearing for years.

Her heart was light in that moment. He was ready, and he loved her. They were going to have a family. Wherever they were, they were going to be together.

She leaned up to kiss him on the lips. "Then I guess you better marry me soon," she whispered.

THIRTY-TWO
TWO DAYS LATER

HAZEL

THEY'D ARRIVED BACK IN KEY WEST TWO DAYS AGO, ON THE HEELS of a helicopter that had picked up Anton Magomedova from Garden Key. He was currently cooling his heels on NAS Key West, facing multiple rounds of questioning.

They'd docked, yet were still using their yacht as their home base. She found herself sitting on the back deck again, the sunset celebration on Mallory Square in full swing as the sun set on the horizon over Sunset Key. She was by herself for the first time since Luke fished her out of the water, after finally assuring him that she was okay. Of course, he wasn't far, just on the bridge talking with the guys about wrapping up this incident.

She dropped her chin to her knees, which she pulled up to wrap her arms around. Dan had fooled them all, that asshole. He had seemed like the quintessential nice guy on the surface, but once the layers were revealed, the worst kind of asshole. He'd brought Russian interests to the States to take over the Perry oil and gas empire, all for the money and power he perceived it would bring him. He'd been willing to bring war to America's shores in service of himself, all for money.

Hazel couldn't believe she'd been duped by this man. She was intelligent, a journalist, someone who saw things others didn't, but she hadn't seen the evil lurking within Dan. She could never have guessed how rotten he had been to the core.

Dan hadn't just bumped into her at the pool that next day, the day he and Magomedova had met for the final details of their deal. After he had left the restaurant, he'd looked her up just to be safe. That one story about Dagestan and the cultural food had popped up, and he'd been worried he'd been found by a secret agent. His paranoia launched his own undoing. He simply couldn't be sure she hadn't heard anything important, and the payout was too large to risk.

As their exchanges had increased, he had believed she was toying with him and really, she was only a food writer who happened to be in the wrong place at the wrong time, and who had written one story about Dagestan. The article, the location, and the fact that she was from DC had been enough to convince a madman that she was a threat. He had it set up to appear as if Magomedova had taken over the party and then killed her and Dan's family once they were on the yacht. In reality, Dan was the killer. He'd planned to kill his own parents and then her, and then he'd finalize the deal with Magomedova before being "released" back in Key West. As he'd bragged that night on very swim deck she was sitting on watching the sun set, Magomedova believed a completely different story about rescuing Dan and Ralph. He thought it was supposed to look as if he'd saved them to the board so the sale would easily go through. In return, he would get oil and gas resources all along the Gulf and had a foothold in American business to build his family's company.

She sighed and stretched her legs out. In the morning, Tad and Seb would go back to further questioning with Magomedova, while the others stayed with her and helped the authorities deal with Ralph Perry and any loose ends that may come from those questions in real time. So far, they'd learned that Anton Magomedova wasn't entirely a bad guy or a good guy.

He'd had enough evidence to give Cullins a clear picture of what had happened. He was only too happy to share as much information as possible, as he himself had been working to legitimatize his own family's business interests. To take them from the darker side of their work to the legitimate aspects of their business. His crew had been turned against him by Dan, and he'd been as much a hostage as Ralph Perry had. Tad worked in the higher echelons of the alphabet agencies to broker a deal for Anton and he was likely to be allowed to return to his home across the globe, grateful to Tad and the men and women of Titan Group. As long as the further questioning didn't turn anything new up. Who knows, maybe someday, having an ally in Dagestan would prove critical to Titan Group. Someday, Titan Group would need those allies.

And poor Ralph and Celeste. Her heart broke for them. They were beside themselves. They might not have been typical parents as she knew parents to be, but they were inherently good people who had been completely oblivious to what their son had become. She supposed the rest of their lives would be spent wondering how they missed the signs, and she hoped that they were able to find some measure of peace.

only let his own mom go because Hazel had been taken by then and he didn't know who was helping her, so he needed bait. He'd used his own mom as bait. Hazel still couldn't believe it all.

Tad, Brian, Seb, Calder and Nate had the remaining men on the Perry yacht secured and were all okay, and in discussion with them earlier that day, they realized that it had indeed been Dan's idea for them to go back to the others with only Theo. They had returned to the boat just in time to see Hazel, and then Luke, go over the side of the enormous yacht. With Calder's training, he was the ideal guy to go after them . . . thankfully.

Dan would have killed Theo on the way to the *Copper Goddess*, but the damn security system Wills had in place was too good. He couldn't have found it without Theo guiding their tender in, which was the straw that broke the proverbial camel's back of Dan's sanity. Every time he thought he had a plan, Titan Group had foiled it somehow. Knowing he had the money in his account from Anton, he was willing to skip part of his original plan, just as long as Hazel died for setting in motion the changes to that plan, even if he had done that to himself.

She knew that was how a narcissist behaved, she got that, knew it wouldn't make complete sense to others. As she sat there, on such a gorgeous yacht, anchored in one of the most beautiful places, watching the people celebrating the sunset, she realized that what had happened may never make complete sense to her. She was a rational, normal person, not hellbent on money, or vengeance, so maybe it was okay that she didn't understand how Dan's brain had worked. He was clearly sick, and figuring out what drives that sickness or why people like that kill others would never make sense to her.

She was going to be okay with that knowledge, or rather she would be, because she'd do the work to be okay with it. She was resolute now. She had learned about herself that she was indeed strong enough to stand at Luke's side. He'd never doubted her, yet she had needed to know it for herself.

She'd put herself out there, left all she had known in DC, and made a life for herself in Florida. She'd walked right into danger, but she hadn't just laid down to die when everything was stacked against her. Not like last fall. She had done her part to save herself and she had needed to do that, to know that she could do that. She loved Luke with all of herself, and now she felt strong enough to stand beside him in all aspects of life, and not ever sit on the sidelines watching it all happen again. What she and Luke would build would be worth any hard work and courage she had to muster.

She smiled to herself then, thinking that perhaps Dan's biggest miscalculation, other than targeting her when he hadn't needed to, was in underestimating her. She would make damn sure no one did that again.

She felt Luke before she saw him. The energy changed on the back of the boat and moments later, he eased himself down on the swim deck next to her.

"Gorgeous sunset with my gorgeous girl," he said, shifting against her, wrapping his arm around her and pulling her into his chest, her back to his front. She snuggled into him, his lips coasting down her ear, then the column of her neck.

She felt his lips at her collarbone, his nose trailing the sensitive skin there. She looked back out toward Sunset Key, the fiery oranges and red of the sunset streaking across the ocean. Soon, it would settle into those deep purples and sapphires she loved, her favorite time of day. She wanted to stay down here forever, in the Keys, on the water, on this boat, but she knew they'd have to head back to DC soon to wrap up a few things. That was good with her. She needed to hug Vi and Baby Alex would be there soon. She wanted to be there for her sister, and the baby snuggles that would follow.

"You gonna make an honest man out of me, Hazelnut?" She felt his words vibrate against her ear before they registered in her brain, before she felt his fingers working something cold up her ring finger. She gasped as she saw what he'd done. A stupidly large marquis cut diamond was resting on her left hand ring finger, glittering in the setting sun.

A smile split her face, tears prickling at the corner of her eyes. "Are you asking me something, Luke-a-licious?" she asked as she turned in her arms. "Is there fuckery afoot?"

"I'll ask you to be mine every single day we have left on this earth if that's what it takes, Hazel. I promise you, not a single day will ever go by when I don't prove to you that you were meant for me forever." He dropped his forehead to hers. "I was trying to do it right this time."

"The answer won't ever change, no matter how you ask it. Yes, of course I'll marry you, you silly man." She smiled back up at him.

"Good, now turn around. You're missing your favorite part." He laughed against her.

"No, Luke, you're my favorite part of every day," she said, turning more fully into him and throwing her leg over his, bringing her body flush to his, eyes locked on his. "My very favorite part."

He growled at her and stood with her in his arms, throwing her over his shoulder and heading for their stateroom while her laughter rang out.

Up on the bridge, Tad sighed while watching the camera feed. He'd forgotten to turn them off and then the guys were all too invested to do so.

"Personally, I liked the fuckery version of the proposal. This one was pretty cheesy," he said.

"Well, thank God she said yes. The last handful of months with him were rough," Theo said, laughing.

"No shit, thank God. Or Tad, because I am pretty sure Tad is the one who finally got him to wake up and start processing after she left his ass in that hospital bed," Seb replied.

"Nah, nothing I wouldn't do for any of you," Tad said.

"Oh shit, man, are you going to cry? You big softie!" Theo crowed.

"Fuck you, Theo. Someday you'll be in the same boat and you'll wish for me to play cupid's little assistant for you too." Tad laughed with the rest of the guys.

And actually, Theo would indeed need Tad's help. He didn't know it at the time, but his days as a playboy were numbered.

THE END

EPILOGUE

FOUR MONTHS LATER

LUKE

"HAZELNUT! OHHHH, HAZELNUT, COME DOWN HERE!" HE YELLED up the stairs.

"Just a minute, babe. Be down soon," he heard back from the direction of her office.

He snuggled the sleeping puppy in his arms into his chest and dropped a kiss on her head. Hazel was going to flip out and he couldn't wait.

"Mommy is going to lose her shit to meet you, little muffin. Let's go into the library to hide."

He felt a wide smile stretching across his face. He seriously could not wait to surprise his Hazelnut with this tiny cotton ball of slobber. He'd lit a fire in the fireplace earlier as fall was coming in fast to DC and the weather had turned downright cold in the last few days. He laid the sleepy puppy down behind the leather couch on the little bed he'd bought for her and then jumped over the back of the couch, settling himself with a book to act as nonchalant as possible. This part was a tough sell. He seriously had no chill. Thankfully, he heard Hazel's footsteps coming down the hall. It was go time.

"Hey, babe. What's up?" she asked, walking in the room and over to him.

"I just want to make out with my fiancée, is that too much to ask?" He smiled up at her from the couch.

"Oh, well, why didn't you say that to begin with?" She laughed and gracefully sank down on his legs, straddling him. She leaned in to kiss him, settling herself against his chest.

He let himself get lost in her, the feel of her against him, her mouth. He loved this woman with everything he had. Every day with her was better than the last, even though their lives were busier than ever lately.

When she eased back to kiss along his jaw, he shifted slightly, gently pulling her back. "There is one important thing to discuss, Hazelnut. I wanted to congratulate you on finishing your first cookbook." He framed her face with his hands and dropped another quick kiss to her lips.

"Thank you, Luke. I can't believe I'm finished, and the publisher accepted it. It was like once I finally sat down to put all the recipes and stories together in my head, it all happened fast. I can't believe it'll be in print soon!" She had that dopey smile on her face again.

"I don't know why you are surprised. You're amazing. Of course you did what you set out to do," he said.

She laughed again and tried to snuggle back into his chest. When he didn't immediately return her affection, she sat back and studied him questioningly.

"Babe, what's wrong? Has something happened?" she asked.

He opened his mouth to reply when he heard her shriek, scrambling off his lap so fast she almost fell off the couch on her ass. If he didn't have finally honed reflexes, she'd have been on the floor.

"Something cold and wet just touched my ankle . . . " she started, drawing her legs up around her on the couch. Luke was laughing so hard he was doubled over next to her.

"Luke!" She peered over the edge of the large Chesterfield sofa as Luke leaned down and swooped back up with the wriggling ball of fur in his arms. He held the pup against his chest with one arm and pulled her back to him with the other.

"Sorry, babe. I thought she was still asleep," he said between his laughter.

"Oh my goodness, Luke!" Hazel held out her arms for the puppy and quickly brought her to her own chest. She snuggled the pup's downy head into her neck and was laughing then too.

"Congrats, Hazelnut. I'm so proud of you for finishing your first cookbook," Luke said.

"Oh, Luke, thank you! This is seriously the best gift ever. What should we name her?" Hazel pulled the puppy away from her own body slightly and stared into the puppy's sweet face.

"You pick. I'm sure I'll love whatever you decide." Luke settled both Hazel and the puppy back into his chest then.

"Marlin. I think she should be named Marlin, so I can always think of the Keys when I say her name," Hazel said. She looked up at him then, so much love shining in her eyes. "Thank you, Luke. I love you."

"Marlin it is, sweet Hazelnut," he replied. "But, Hazey, I also bought us a house in the Keys, and we can spend as much time on the boat as you want. You know that, right?" he asked her.

"Seriously?! How do you expect me to ever get any work done if I am always on vacation?" she asked.

"Every day feels like vacation with you anyway babe, might as well be on the water as often as possible. Besides, we can work from anywhere. Why not the boat? I have it on good authority that your boss." He smirked at her, as he was her "boss" for some of the Titan Group cases they'd taken on in recent months. "I have it on good authority that you can work from wherever you want, whenever you want."

"Ohhh, sleeping with the boss does have its perks. People were so right!" She laughed at him and continued, "that's a good point though. Now that Baby Alex is sleeping through the night and they've settled in, maybe we should spend some time out on the water, give them some privacy around here?" she mused. "I want to snuggle him all the time, but I also know they need time to be a family."

"Why don't we make some of our own to snuggle?" Luke asked, his face serious.

"Really?" she asked.

"Hazel, I want to get you pregnant as soon as possible. I'm ready. If you aren't, then I am happy to practice. As often and as frequently as possible, really. But babe, I'm ready when you are. I wasted enough of my life denying myself living in your light, living in fear. We have the team around us. Titan Group will be fine, and we will continue to kick ass. If you're ready, I can't think of anything better than decamping to the boat and indulging in Sex Fest with the end goal of making mini-Hazels," he said.

Her smile was soft on her face, her eyes a little teary. "Sex Fest it is, Luke-a-licious. Let's go re-live more swim deck moments. Maybe I'll come home with a mini-Luke." She laughed at him, watching as he picked up his phone.

> LUKE: Tad, hey. Hazey and I are heading for the Keys and our boat. Give us a few days and then we'll be back online.

> TAD: Copy. I take it the dog went over well. Tell Hazey congrats again. Be safe, you two. Please use the cloak of invisibility for the boat so no one has to see your naked ass anchored somewhere.

Luke tossed his phone onto the couch next to them. "Tad says happy Sex Fest, we should go make mini versions of ourselves," he said as he pulled her more tightly to himself.

Hazel just laughed at him. She'd read Tad's text over Luke's shoulder. She knew what he said. The puppy licked Hazel's neck then, causing another fit of giggles to break out, exciting the puppy. Luke looked down at the laughing woman in his arms and the wriggling puppy kissing her. He sent a silent prayer of thanks up, loving his life.

———

If you liked this book, please consider leaving a review on Amazon and Goodreads!

ACKNOWLEDGMENTS

Thank you to all the actual badasses and their incredible families who serve our country.

I want to acknowledge my family for living through a monster of a transition so that I can write romance books. My love of smut books only pales in comparison to my love for you. Thanks guys.

A tremendous thank you to:

Margy Poer Hogarty for her beta reading, editing work and encouragement.

My cousins, Kim Clements and Melissa Liby, for beta reading and editing work, all unpaid labor, of course.

My incredible bestie Melanie Owings for beta reading, offering support in a million ways and for always being a great cheerleader.

Sarah Payne for listening to me lament about content on socials and in turn, engaging with everything I post to help my tiny algorithm.

More cousins! Burke Clements, for endless work on all aspects of my author career, Canyon Liby, Sydney Clements and Aspen Liby for all of their (also unpaid) work.

My Aunt Sandy and my mom Nancy, who share my social content talking about my books. I need all the help I can get.

Leah Blanchard for also always engaging with my social media, her messages always bring a smile to my face!

The team at Red Fern Booksellers. I don't even know where to
start in listing all the ways they help this author.
Jamie and Shane for launching amycolebooks.com, you are
seriously the best!
The team at Greys Promo, for all of their guidance and patience
with my endless questions.

Let's connect!
Consider signing up for the newsletter!
amy@amycolebooks.com

ABOUT THE AUTHOR

Hi friends! I'm Amy. I'm an 80's baby who picked up my first romance book putzing around an antique store when I was 11 and I've been reading them ever since. Behind every romance writer lurks a devout reader. . .and that's me.

I married my high school sweetheart after dating for 10 years. We have two sons and two black labs. We live back in the Midwest, and in the middle of our hometowns so that we can raise our kids around our families. We live where we swore we'd never move back to and regret nothing about breaking that vow.

I'm a small-town girl who was fortunate enough to travel domestically and internationally for years for work (and for fun). I love to be outside, and give me a campfire at the lake, a ski run down the face of a mountain or a beach sunset any day. I love them all. Equally, please ask me where to eat or what to do in cities across the U.S. and France and I will immediately produce a 10-page itinerary. I love food and I love people watching. There is a story behind everyone, and the journalism kid in me wants to learn them all. Don't worry, I'll make up some details to add an element of romance or mystery to every story.

I love my family, my friends, dogs, books, love stories, traveling, Murder She Wrote re-runs, sports, history, trivia and food. I'm kind of a smart ass, which I like to say is better than a dumb ass.

You want me on your trivia team and if you read my books, I'll happily be your friend forever.

Photo credit to the lovely and talented Suni Michaelsen.

instagram.com/amycolebooks
pinterest.com/amycolebooks
facebook.com/61562893197128

ALSO BY AMY COLE

Read Max and Violet's story:
In Every Lifetime

Read Wills and Mila's short story:
Every Day Kind of Love